The Jade Frog

The Jade Frog

The Second Mystery in the Chilcotin Trilogy

Bruce Fraser

GRANVILLE ISLAND
PUBLISHING

Editor: David Stephens
Copy Editor: Kyle Hawke
Cover and Text Designer: Jamie Fischer
Cover Art: "The Jade Frog" Malcolm MacDougal
Chilcotin Map: Jamie Fischer
Author Photographer: David Hay

Library and Archives Canada Cataloguing in Publication

Fraser, Bruce, 1937-, author
The jade frog : the second mystery in the Chilcotin trilogy / Bruce Fraser.

(A Chilcotin mystery ; 2)
Issued in print and electronic formats.
ISBN 978-1-926991-54-2 (pbk.).
ISBN 978-1-92661-63-4 (epub)

I. Title.
PS8611.R366J33 2014   C813'.6   C2014-907554-5
                                        C2014-907555-3

First printing 2015
19 18 17 16 15   5 4 3 2 1
Printed in Canada

Granville Island Publishing   Granville Island Publishing
212 – 1656 Duranleau   1855 Pipeline Road
Vancouver, BC, Canada V6H 3S4   Blaine, WA, USA 98230-9746
Toll free: 1-877-688-0320   Toll free: 1-877-688-0320
Tel: (604) 688-0320   Tel: (604) 688-0320

www.GranvilleIslandPublishing.com

For Becca, Carol, Julia,

Megan & Nancy

Chilcotin

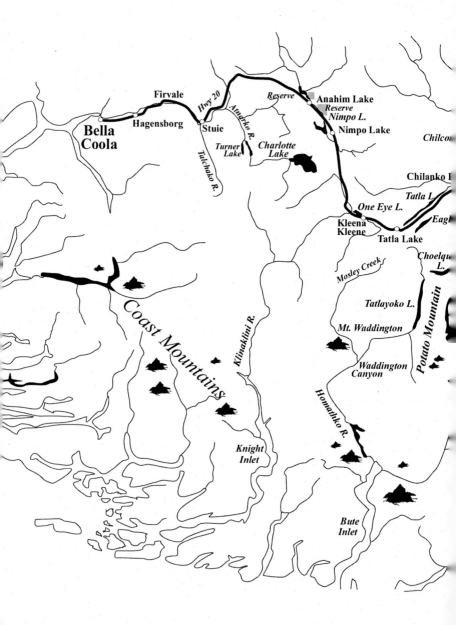

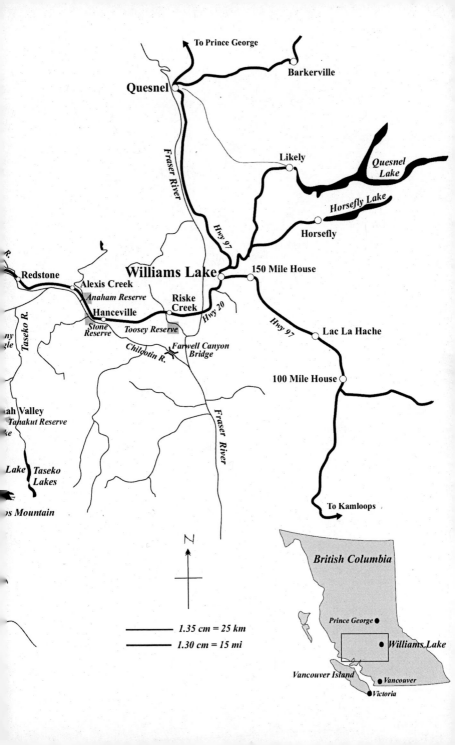

Acknowledgements:

I thank my constant readers, Angela Ammann, Sarah McAlpine, Andrea Horth, Adam Garfunkel and D.K. Fraser.

I am also indebted to Father A. G. Morice for his book on *The History of the Northern People of British Columbia,* published in 1978 by Interior Stationery (1970) Ltd. and to Livingston Farrand, author of *The Traditions of the Chilcotin Indians.*

Prologue

In the heart of the Chilcotin on a crisp October morning, Old Antoine lay dying in his lean-to on the shores of Tatlayoko Lake. At first light, Antoine's granddaughter, Justine, stood by his bed adjusting his covers.

"I'll be back in a few hours, Granddad. Noah and Stan will keep you company."

She indicated her husband, Noah, and their friend, Stan Hewitt. Antoine smiled at his granddaughter as she left the room.

The men settled down to a quiet watch when Antoine became talkative, going back to the days of the war chief Klatsassine, to a murder trial in Williams Lake, and to the death of Bordy Hanlon. Noah, at the foot of the bed, and Stan, sitting by the old *deyen*, listened intently to his every word.

During a pause, Stan's lawyer instincts prompted him to ask a question.

"My friend, who killed Bordy?"

"The spirit of the Chilcotin," Antoine answered.

Noah had a revelation about Antoine's meaning—*there is a shadow line between spirituality and reality*. He was drawn to the head of the bed and knelt on the floor. He grasped Antoine's hand.

"I understand the connection between the land and our people," he said to his *deyen*, "between *Ts'il?os* the mountain and Lendix'tcux the transformer, and between Ta Chi and nature."

Old Antoine smiled, not least at the mention of Noah's birth mother. He nodded his head and with his last breath, he faintly squeezed Noah's hand. By virtue of that touch, Noah became in name the new *deyen* of Clan Raven.

Stan Hewitt was the only witness to the exchange between Antoine and Noah. They hadn't had time to summon the others to say their final goodbyes.

It was as if Antoine, having done all that he had to do in his life, had consciously ended his tenure on Earth by simultaneously indicating his successor and surrendering his spirit to his Creator. The two men remained in Antoine's lean-to, unable to move until the stillness of that morning in 1959 was disturbed by the familiar background sounds of cattle stirring in the corrals of Empire Ranch. It was then that they summoned the others.

Wawant'x was the name his Chilcotin birth mother had given him. He was baptized and given the Christian name 'Noah' by the priest and raised on the ranch by his white adoptive parents, Bordy and Belle Hanlon. He had studied painting and had managed Bordy's ranch, but he had no sense of who he was until he fell in love with Justine Paul and was rescued from a life as an outlaw by Ta Chi. Together, Justine and Noah had gone through their trials of fire and water in the world of the 1950's. It was on Potato Mountain where he discovered what he was and who he was meant to be.

Before Antoine's death, Antoine and Ta Chi had prepared Noah for a greater role amongst the Stoneys, the people of the mountainous west Chilcotin. He was shown the mysteries of the plateau by Ta Chi as she guided him through the trails, lakes, rivers and streams. It was there in that vast classroom he was taught to be at one with *Ts'il?os*, their sacred mountain overlooking their world. He had learned from Antoine the myths, ceremonies and prayers that bound the Chilcotins to their lands and waters. Antoine's first teachings were the telling of the Chilcotin creation stories.

Later that night in the quiet of the ranch house, Noah told Justine of Antoine's last hours; even that Antoine had admitted to trickery in the handling of evidence in a murder trial. She listened intently to Noah's words and after each new revelation uttered an exclamation.

"My grandfather," she smiled when he was done, "was a wise man. I'm glad that he shared his last words with you."

"Antoine was a wise man, he was the *deyen*. I've been given a sacred trust by your grandfather, Antoine, to be the next *deyen* of Clan Raven."

Justine sat upright in bed.

"Noah," she exclaimed, "what a great honour!"

"It is, but I'm not worthy of it."

"You are, and with my help you will be," Justine assured, her quick mind seizing on Noah's strength. "You're an artist. You've painted a mural of the Chilcotin: mountain, water and sky. Now that you are *deyen*, you'll paint our Creation story."

They buried Old Antoine at the ranch, in the Hanlon graveyard fenced by white pickets next to his grandson Peter who, had he lived, would have been the *deyen*.

It would take years of fasts, prayers, painting and ceremonial smudges for Noah to try to fulfill the role that Antoine thrust on him, to discover his generation's shadow line while struggling to overcome the inevitable setbacks and missteps in life.

FROG

1

Johanna Barton met Malcolm Kent in April of 1959 at the annual fraternity-sorority songfest. She was completing her final year in English Honours and he was the older brother of one of the singers. The after-party had been at a home in the university district, and Johanna had gone into the den alone to catch her breath from the crush of the singing, dancing crowd. She was admiring an Emily Carr painting when he came into the room.

"I see you appreciate art," he said.

"Yes, my aunt gave me a small sketch of hers," she answered, pointing to the painting, not taking her eyes off it. "She also gave me a Vivien Cowan painting. You know, Vivien is influenced by A.Y. Jackson."

"No, I didn't know."

She had turned to see an elegant man, black hair parted and combed flat, dressed in a dark three-piece suit. Their eyes met and she felt that she was Elizabeth Bennett looking into the eyes of D'Arcy in *Pride and Prejudice*.

"Oh," she said, with a hint of surprise. "I'm sorry. I tend to babble on about art. It must be the teacher in me."

"Don't be sorry. I'm a good listener. Do you teach art?"

"No, I *collect* art. I intend to teach English. Who are you?"

"I'm Malcolm Kent, Barry's big brother."

"That explains it."

"Explains what?"

"You don't look like a student. I thought you might be a *professor.*"

"No," he laughed. "I'm a lawyer."

They spent the rest of the evening sparring with each other and exchanging knowing glances. He had driven her home.

Johanna's prior experience with men had been limited to a high school crush, her eccentric classmate Vladimir, and necking with fraternity boys in the back seats of cars. Malcolm was significantly different; a city of Vancouver prosecutor and twelve years her senior. She was amused and enthralled by his courtship. It hadn't escaped her that he had conducted his seduction as if she was the most important case he had ever argued. To have a successful, cultured man give her his full attention proved irresistible to Johanna. They married the following April when she was taking her practicum for her qualification as a high-school teacher. They honeymooned at Qualicum Beach, on Vancouver Island for a week of strolling on the sand, eating oysters and sleeping in. Malcolm hardly ever consulted the file he had brought with him for a trial starting the following week.

Not long before the wedding, they had attended a student art showing at the Emily Carr Gallery, and Johanna had been enthralled by the work. When she opened her wedding present from Malcolm, she gasped. In her hands was the painting of a salmon jumping over a weir she had taken a particular liking to. Touched by her husband's gesture, she raved to all in attendance about the artist.

Malcolm took this as a cue and, at the first opportunity, invited the artist and his wife to have dinner with them.

The artist, Noah Hanlon, was Chilcotin, as was his wife, Justine. Johanna was delighted to discover that Justine was born on a ranch at Tatlayoko, as she had spent a summer working at a guest ranch at Nimpo Lake. The two young women found common ground on the high plateau. Realizing they'd barely discussed Noah's art, Johanna recounted the story of showing the painting at the wedding and talked of having seen his gallery showing earlier. The Hanlons invited the Kents to their home to see more of Noah's art.

The Hanlons lived in Acadia Camp, a cluster of army huts left over from the Second World War on the grounds of Johanna's alma mater. She and Malcolm parked outside the compound and wandered amongst the drab rows of grey huts, one indistinguishable from the other, looking for the Hanlons' place.

Johanna recognized the Farwell Canyon Bridge spanning the Chilcotin River painted on the front door and excitedly cried out to Malcolm.

"This is it!"

They were greeted at the door by Noah, Justine and their baby Elizabeth, held in her mother's arms. Johanna held out her arms to Justine. With Elizabeth cradled between them, she looked down at the baby,

"She's adorable," she gasped. "May I hold her?"

"Sure," Justine laughed. "But come in first!"

Johanna stepped over the threshold and took Elizabeth in her arms. The baby immediately cooed and nestled into her shoulder.

"She likes you!" Noah exclaimed.

Johanna's attention was already elsewhere. Baby held tight to her, she slowly scanned the walls. These had been transformed by surreal sketches and paintings-in-progress of what Justine described as the Chilcotin creation legend. Johanna walked around the room, looking at the mythical monsters transformed into birds, fish and animals by *Lendix'tcux*, the half-dog, half-man transformer.

"Noah, this is amazing! I'd like to take one of these walls and mount it in our living room."

"I'm still learning. Justine lets me practice on the walls. One day I'll do a huge mural on the Chilcotin creation story."

"There's more in the other two rooms," Justine offered.

She led Johanna through a quick circuit of the bedrooms before rejoining the men in the living room. When they re-emerged, Elizabeth, with her back to her mother's shoulder, was looking shyly at Johanna. Johanna didn't notice. Seeing the room from the new angle, she brushed past the men to study a portrait of a frog on the edge of a pond. Malcolm looked at Noah and shrugged apologetically. Noah simply smiled.

"Isn't the frog a Haida symbol?" Johanna asked.

"We have our own myth of how frog was made."

"Could you tell us the story?"

"Not now, Johanna," Malcolm chided. "I've brought some expensive wine that demands to be drunk and commented on."

After dinner, when their hunger and thirst had been satisfied, and Elizabeth had been put to bed with her own story, Justine looked at Noah. She lit a candle and dimmed the room lights. Recognizing the cue, he nodded.

"Wawant'x, of the house of Raven," she announced, "will tell you about how Frog was made."

Noah and Justine sat cross-legged on the floor. Johanna immediately followed their lead. Malcolm very stiffly copied his wife, forming a circle around the candle. Their shadows danced in the flickering light, interacting with the painted figures on the walls.

They settled and the room became quiet except for the sound of breathing. Justine produced an eagle's feather, which she passed to Noah. He took some time to compose himself before speaking.

"The making of Frog by our transformer *Lendix'tcux* is a part of our creation myth. I will tell it to you as it was told to me by Old Antoine, my *deyen*, who was our shaman. Antoine died last year and I'm trying to fulfill his trust in me."

Noah breathed slowly and his voice took on a different cadence, a slow drumbeat. His melodic baritone now ceremonial, reverential, reverberated through the room. He cupped his hands before him.

"This was before my time . . .

> *"So they started out, Lendix'tcux and his three sons—Qontse'rken, Qonta'in and Qunsu'l. Before very long, they came to a river where there was a ford which allowed for crossing. A great moose stood in the river just below the ford. Lendix'tcux wished to go over at once, but Qontse'rken said that his mother had warned him about the moose and told him it killed every one who tried to cross.*
>
> *However, Lendix'tcux insisted. He tied boughs in his hair so his sons could watch him, then started into the water while his three boys sat on the bank and waited. When he came to the middle of the ford, the water swept him off his feet and carried him downstream to the moose, which opened its mouth and swallowed him."*

Noah spread out his arms, his hands open to the ceiling illustrating the moose swallowing the transformer.

> *"For a while the moose stood still. Then, suddenly, it began to sway from side to side and started for the shore with long*

*jumps. It reached the shore with its last jump, then fell down
dead. Immediately, the boys skinned it. Opening the chest, they
found their father sitting there alive and well. Lendix'tcux had
cut out the heart, built a fire, and cooked and eaten it, and that
was what had killed the moose."*

"This is very Old Testament," Malcolm interrupted,
"instead of a whale, you have a moose."

"Yes, the old religions have learned from us," Noah
smiled. "But would you like to hear about Frog?"

"Ignore Malcolm and go on, Noah," Johanna insisted.

*"So they cut the carcass up into small pieces, and from the pieces
they made all sorts of animals and started on their journey again.
Soon, though, they remembered that they had made nothing out
of the brain.*

*"They went back. They tried again and again to make some
animal from the brain, failing each time. At last they succeeded
in making Frog, but he was so ugly that they threw him into the
water and told him he must live there and not on land."*

Noah flung down his outstretched arm and open hand in
a tender careful movement. Justine had beamed through
Noah's telling of the myth and brought her hands together
in a silent clap at the finish.

Seeing Malcolm about to make a comment, Johanna held
up her hand. He gritted his teeth,

"Thank you for sharing your sacred story with us, Noah,"
she said. "I'll think of Frog differently now. But I don't think
Frog is ugly."

By June, the two couples were becoming close friends.
Malcolm confided in Noah that living on a prosecutor's
salary in Vancouver was too constraining. He was thinking

of setting up a law practice on his own in the Cariboo administrative centre, Prince George. Noah introduced Malcolm to his stepfather, Stan Hewitt, of the law firm of Hewitt and Bates in Williams Lake, a two-hour drive south of Prince George, where he was offered a partnership. He liked the idea of being a partner in an established law firm. The letterhead of "Hewitt, Bates & Kent, Barristers & Solicitors" was impressive.

It wasn't until he had the offer in hand that Malcolm approached Johanna with his plan for their future. He took her out to dinner at Bishop's on 4th Avenue in Kits. Over cocktails, he broke the news.

"Darling, we have just been made an offer from a prestigious law firm. One I believe we cannot resist."

"You mean," she said coyly, "you're going to practice law in Paris while I study comparative literature and take French cooking lessons?"

"Not quite. You *are* partly right, though. The offer does entail a move from Vancouver. Perhaps not to a metropolitan centre, but nevertheless the centre of the Cariboo-Chilcotin."

Seeing the surprise in his wife's face on hearing his news, followed by her draining her martini glass, he, without waiting for a response, signalled the waiter for more drinks.

When the waiter came over, Malcolm ordered the specialty of the day, steak Diane for two, accompanied by a bottle of Châteauneuf-du-Pape. Johanna didn't speak until a second martini was secured in her hand.

"Does this centre of the Cariboo-Chilcotin have a name?"
Of course. Williams Lake."

During the course of the meal, Malcolm convinced Johanna that they would be happy in the country and that Johanna would be able to teach high school in Williams Lake. She did welcome moving to a part of the province painted with nature's colours as by Noah Hanlon—the land of lakes and ponds. The decision was soon made to move to Williams Lake. Malcolm would practice law and Johanna would teach high-school English.

In August of that year, they drove to their adoptive land. That was the way Johanna saw it: the Cariboo-Chilcotin was adopting them. The Trans Canada Highway from Vancouver to Cache Creek stretched eastward along the flat farmland of the Fraser River delta, stretching for a hundred miles to Hope, where the great river spills out of the Coast Mountains. Johanna grew nostalgic on leaving the delta.

"I'll miss the moodiness of the coast, the moist corn-growing weather and sea air."

"For heavens sake Johanna, it's less than an hour's plane ride away from Williams Lake."

"I know, but climate has an effect on me. I'm not comparing. I find the Chilcotin is different, it's crisper. The air is sharper and the sky is larger."

Malcolm's response was to roll his eyes.

At Yale, the highway follows the Cariboo Gold Rush Trail through the Fraser River Gorge to Lytton. It was lunchtime when they drove into hot, dusty Lytton on the water's edge, where the Thompson River joins the Fraser. They ate lunch watching the swirling blue waters of the Thompson being swallowed by the brown muddy waters of the Fraser, inhaling the dry semi-desert smell of sagebrush.

Leaving the Gold Rush Trail to wend its way up the Fraser, they drove on to Cache Creek, skirting the rushing waters of the Thompson. As they approached a massive boulder in the middle of the river, Johanna looked at their travel guide and identified it as Frog Rock. She almost screamed.

"Malcolm, pull over here! I want you to take a photograph of me and Frog Rock."

"Oh, all right," he said in a petulant tone. "I hope Noah's story about the Frog isn't becoming an obsession."

"Frogs play a significant role in culture and literature," she answered in the measured tone of a teacher.

Malcolm took the picture and they drove on to Cache Creek in silence. Malcolm's mind was on his future law practice, while Johanna felt rebuked for her enthusiasm. From there, they headed north on Highway 97 into the Cariboo-Chilcotin through the Bonaparte Valley. The sight of the lush green irrigated hayfields and the yellow and rust-coloured hills moved Malcolm.

"Now *there*," he announced, "is a good photo opportunity."

"Yes, let me take your picture with the hills as a backdrop."

They joined the Gold Rush Trail again at Clinton, north of Cache Creek. The plateau's grasslands unfolded through 100 Mile House, past Lac La Hache, through the San Juan Valley to 150 Mile, and on to the lake. During the eight-hour drive, Johanna could hear the Chilcotin calling.

Welcome home, Frog. Welcome home.

2

Two years later, the Hanlons returned to their ranch on Tatlayoko Lake, Noah to paint and ranch and Justine to nurse at Tatla Lake. His paintings hadn't attained any commercial success, but Noah was only concerned with interpreting his feelings for the land and the traditions of his people.

Johanna started buying his work, and she urged him to join A. Y. Jackson along with local artists Vivien Cowan, Sonia Cornwall, Vivien's daughter, Enid Wright, and others who had formed the Cariboo Arts Society. They were showing and selling their art at the Cowboy Museum in Williams Lake. Noah soon had a local following, which kept him in paint.

In the autumn of '63, Johanna had taken one of Noah's paintings to a small Vancouver gallery, Joseph Steins on South Granville. Joseph had liked it and offered to hold an exhibition of Noah's paintings in the spring. If Noah accepted the offer, he would have half a year to create a dozen paintings.

Johanna approached Noah with Stein's offer. Noah was wary of the opportunity. He had made some thumbnail paintings and sketches to be completed in his studio during the winter for a Williams Lake showing. He didn't know if he was ready to accept this new challenge, and the Chilcotin in him resisted meeting a deadline.

"Just think what it will mean for your work to be shown to the outside world," Justine urged.

"I *hate* deadlines."

"Johanna has gone to the trouble of arranging this. You need to make up your mind."

"I'll have to consult Raven to see if this is what the Chilcotin wishes."

He went to where Antoine had gone to speak to the spirit: a cave overlooking the Homathko River that runs west through the coastal mountains to the sea. After Noah had fasted for a week, Raven gave him his answer. He agreed to the exhibition.

* * *

In the spring of '64, Noah travelled to Vancouver with Johanna and his stepfather, Stan.

Justine couldn't find a replacement at the nurses' station at Tatla Lake, so stayed behind. Johanna went because she had made the initial contact and she was en route to Victoria to visit Malcolm who, having made a name for himself as a prosecutor at the Cariboo Assizes, had that winter signed a five-year contract with the Ministry of the Attorney General as assistant deputy in charge of criminal prosecutions. She would join him at the end of the school year.

The show at the Stein gallery on South Granville over the Easter holidays was preceded by a showing for the critics and the media. The major papers' art critics were in general agreement. The *Vancouver Sun* proclaimed, "These paintings—the artist calls them portraits—of the Chilcotin landscape show the glory of the Interior through the lens of West Coast Native art. Strength and beauty shine through." The *Province* trumpeted, "The indigenous peoples of the Chilcotin were warriors, traders, and middlemen between the Coastal Natives to the west and the Shuswap to the east. The various tribes' stories and mythology is shared and adapted and Hanlon's art, following that tradition, borrows from the Coastal forms of the ovoid, inner ovoid, U-form and S-form, and adapts these to his own vision of the magnificent Chilcotin plateau. We have a vibrant artist in our midst."

Before the show opened, Stein persuaded Noah to increase his asking prices to three times what he charged in Williams Lake. Stein reasoned that the critics' praise warranted the price.

"A stockbroker, banker, or big-firm lawyer would think they were being cheated if they didn't pay a four-digit figure for a painting," he said. "When one of your paintings is hung by the owner on a prominent wall in her house and her guests are drawn to it by its art, the owner will impress them even more by telling them how much she paid for it."

The public crowded into the gallery for the Saturday night opening. Amidst laughter over white wine and nibbles, the loud talk was all about the discovery of a bold new artistic talent.

The night was intoxicating. Red sale stickers were affixed to all the paintings within the first hour. Stan left the gallery early and returned to their hotel room while Noah continued to party.

Stein coaxed the last of the guests and hangers-on out the door at about midnight and invited Johanna and Noah for dinner at their hotel's restaurant.

"I just wish Justine was here," Noah kept saying as the evening wore on.

They didn't finish dinner until two. Stein said his goodbyes. Noah and Johanna went up the elevator to their adjoining rooms.

It's true that late dinners, good talk and the flow of wine could cut through fences. That shouldn't be an excuse, Noah thought, but despite his misgivings at the door to Johanna's room he invited himself in for a nightcap. She looked delicious to him at that moment, and he wanted to prolong it. Johanna didn't encourage him, but she didn't say no. She sat cross-legged on the bed. He went to the liquor cabinet.

"What would you like to drink?" he asked.

"I've had enough to drink."

She was watching him. It wasn't like Noah to help himself. Flush with his success, he poured himself a double scotch and drank it neat.

"You know, Noah, someone should write your story."

"Oh? What would the title be?"

"I'd call it *The Aboriginal Painter and Deyen from the Land of Ts'il?os Conquers the Vancouver Art Community*," Johanna said in a mocking tone.

"You should write the story," he said, sitting down beside her on the bed.

"No, you should. You could praise yourself in writing as well as painting."

He laughed and placed his hand on her thigh.

3

Noah quietly opened the door to his room. Stan was awake and reading in bed, but didn't say anything. Noah went directly to the bathroom and showered. When he came back into the room in his pyjamas, Stan put down his book.

"I stayed up 'til you came back so I could tell you something I should have told you some time ago. I put it in a letter I wrote the day Antoine died and named you *deyen*. Antoine told us who had killed Bordy and who your real father was. The letter I wrote was going to be given to you when I died, but since I seem to be taking my time about that, I'm now going to tell you what I heard."

Stan paused, a judgmental look in his eye, Noah thought. Or maybe it was just his guilt.

"I noticed that you and Johanna were very close this evening," Stan continued, "and that's understandable. She's a good friend to you and Justine. When Antoine breathed his last, you interpreted his words to mean that your father was part of the fabric of the land. The artist and the mystic in you created a *Ts'il?os* myth, that you were sired by the Chilcotin. That wasn't what the old shaman was telling you. He left no doubt in my mind that Bordy, your adoptive father, was also your biological father. He had many good qualities, Bordy did, but he was governed by his hot blood and couldn't resist a skirt. I thought I would tell you this now before your natural urges get the better of you and you ruin your friendship and maybe your marriage."

Noah listened to his stepfather's advice. He turned off the light and spoke to the darkness.

"I was on fire tonight. Success measured in money is an aphrodisiac. I've sobered up. Justine is my only love. "

Neither Stan nor the darkness said a word in response.

Sleep did not come on swift wings. The excitement of his exhibition and sale, the wine and whiskey, the seduction, the guilt, all swam through Noah's mind. Stan was sleeping on his back in the other bed, his deep breaths broken by occasional grunts. It seemed hours went by in this suspended state before he found a calm dark spot where he sheltered.

After a time, he looked about him and saw a small woman sitting by a small fire chanting and whispering to herself. He wanted to stay in the shadows, yet he was drawn toward the woman, a Chilcotin, to hear what she was saying. He hesitated at the edge of the fire and the woman looked up. It was Ta Chi, his birth mother, who fixed him with her burning eyes reflecting the fire.

"Wawant'x," she said clearly, "you have betrayed me once as did your father before you. You, born of *Ts'il?os* and man, swear to me you will be faithful.

"Mother," he shouted, "I swear by the great spirit that I will be faithful."

And he reached out, and in reaching out to touch his mother, he fell.

Noah's shouts woke Stan. He switched on the light and saw Noah on the floor sobbing.

"I will be faithful," he repeated.

In the morning, Stan, Noah and Johanna met for breakfast. They each acted as if nothing had happened between the two young people. Nor was there any mention of Noah's dream. They gave Stan a breakdown of the events of the evening at the gallery and read the reports in the newspaper of his success.

Not long after breakfast, Johanna checked out and was off to Victoria. Stan and Noah returned via Williams Lake to Tatlayoko Lake, where Justine was waiting. Full of remorse, Noah was determined to bare his soul and tell Justine he had been unfaithful. There she was, waving to him from the ranch house, as ready to congratulate him on his success as when he left her waving goodbye. She was like the Chilcotin, a constant inspiration in his life. While he, instead of arriving as a proud artist, appeared a contrite and humble man. He wrapped his arms around her in an iron embrace for a full minute without saying a word.

"I'm preparing a dinner celebration," she said excitedly, pulling back from him a little. "I've invited all the neighbours and our friends to hear all about your showing, the critics' remarks, the sales . . ."

"Come with me, Justine," he interrupted gently. "I have something important to tell you."

It was early afternoon. He took her to the barn by the hand as young lovers would do, and sat her down on a hay bale. He sat there, holding her hand, staring at the lake and surrounding mountains as if he were seeing them for the first time. He smiled at her. She returned his smile, waiting for him to tell her what was so important that he would lead her back to the place where they had first realized they were in love.

He spoke softly, sure of his feelings for Justine, but unsure of how to express them.

"I've been so caught up in my art and in myself that I haven't told you how much you mean to me. That without you, nothing is possible."

"You don't have to say that to me. You tell me of your love every day in the way you look at me and act toward me."

"We haven't made love in a while because of my obsession with this show in Vancouver."

"I understand," she spoke into the silence of the spring day. "But Noah, you didn't bring me here just to say you love me."

His intention had been to confess to Justine that he had slept with another woman, Justine's best friend, and ask for her forgiveness. Now, seeing how vulnerable and lovely she was, sitting there trusting him, he convinced himself of how selfish that would be.

"I love you. And I've been neglecting you."

She smiled, speaking slowly in words he would never forget.

"It was here that we first knew of our love. We comforted each other on the death of my brother. He also left the Chilcotin for the city, but he never returned. You have returned to say that you love me. That's enough."

They stood and he took her in his arms and they kissed. They walked back to the house arm-in-arm.

Pulling him closer, Justine said, "I've prepared dinner for my hero."

4

Malcolm had not wanted children until they were more financially secure. This had been a source of contention between them.

Now, with a five-year government contract, he was, with Johanna's urging, satisfied that they could afford and educate a child. Although Johanna had wanted more children, Malcolm was content with their daughter Mary, who was born in 1964 and named in honour of Johanna's Italian mother.

It was in May of '69 when the Kents returned to Williams Lake. Malcolm rejoined his old firm while Johanna, who had obtained her master's degree in English from the University of Victoria, had on her return to Williams Lake resumed her teaching position at Anne Stevenson High School. She also secured a position starting in the fall teaching summer school English at Cariboo College.

Justine phoned Johanna within days of the Kents' arrival in town.

"Why don't you and Malcolm and Mary come to the cattle branding at the ranch this weekend? It will be fun for the children and we can get caught up over dinner. We have plenty of room here and you can stay overnight."

"Thank you so much, Justine. Elizabeth will be quite the lady now and Mary wants to meet your two youngsters, Brent and Liam."

Malcolm was not as enthusiastic about the invitation as his wife. He was working on a brief, but agreed to go on the understanding that he could spend most of the time preparing for the hearing the following Monday.

They arrived at the ranch in time for a picnic lunch served under a tarp beside the field where the herd were milling about in organized confusion. The cowhands were taking a break from the branding for a hotdog, coffee and cow talk.

Elizabeth now had the field to herself and when she saw the Kents drive up, she took advantage by galloping her horse amongst the cows and scattering them.

"You get in here for lunch," Noah shouted. "And stop showing off!"

She galloped her horse right up to her father and reined up in front of him. She jumped off the horse, throwing the reins to him as if he was her groom. The Kents walked up beside Noah as she landed.

"Well, Noah," Johanna remarked, "I see you have a rodeo rider in your family."

"Hello, Johanna. It's good to see you. Elizabeth is a handful. Is that Mary I see peeking from behind your skirt?"

Justine stepped up and greeted Malcolm. While they were getting reacquainted, the Hanlon boys, at Noah's urging, ran up to Mary and asked her to play. Johanna and Noah shared a quick smile—not the wistful sort that drew them back to shared memory, but a knowing one which spoke of small things showing that their friendship with healing time had survived their transgression. With many greetings and details to be shared amongst old friends, it was a while before Johanna and Justine had a quiet moment together.

"Justine," Johanna smiled slyly, "you didn't tell me you were pregnant."

"You can tell," Justine smirked.

"You're glowing!" Johanna burst.

"Yes, I'm so happy."

They hugged as old friends. Johanna put her hand on Justine's belly.

"We're expecting the child in September. How about you? Do you intend to have more children?"

Johanna sighed, not trying to hide her disappointment from her friend.

"No. We're fortunate to have had Mary."

* * *

Joel was born on September 11th, 1969.

On the strength of his successful exhibition in Vancouver, Noah had become a recognized and collected artist. From his studio in the barn overlooking Tatlayoko Lake, he was recreating his surroundings with his paintbrush. His philosophy and approach to his art was to strip the Chilcotin landscape to its essentials and paint it as if it was a nude with a sense of eroticism. The public approved and he was able to support their growing family, for there was no fat in a small ranch.

* * *

Back in Williams Lake, Johanna devoted herself to raising Mary while Malcolm applied himself to the law. The law rewarded Malcolm's application. He was elected a bencher of the Law Society, was made a Queen's Counsel, and in his late fifties decided that the judiciary was the next logical step in his career. Johanna had done her part for Malcolm's career by balancing his reserve with her verve. By any measure, Johanna was an asset to Malcolm, an asset which Malcolm was aware of, but took for granted. When judicial appointments were made, government decision-makers looked not just at the lawyer, but also at his or her spouse. That assumption was the reason he hadn't confided his judicial ambitions to his wife; that and avoiding the embarrassment if he didn't get the appointment.

Early in her marriage, Johanna had recognized her husband's growing inattentiveness, and lately absentmindedness, in matters not connected with the law. But when he forgot their silver wedding anniversary on the excuse that he was in Ottawa arguing a case at the Supreme Court of Canada, she was upset. Soon after, he followed this oversight with an insensitive response to her invitation to accompany her to her thirtieth high-school reunion in 1985.

"Johanna," he said impatiently, "I can't think of anything more boring than making nice to a roomful of strangers frantically trying to recapture the promise of their youth— which most of whom have failed miserably to realize."

He had overlooked that his wife was one of those frantic people. This, she resented.

"Malcolm is right," she thought later, turning it over in her mind. "I haven't captured the promise of my youth."

5

By his late forties, Vladimir Volk had exceeded his high-school promise. The invitation to the upcoming thirtieth anniversary of the class's reunion had escaped his attention. He was at his desk in the city, thinking of financing a gold mine in Chile, when he picked up an envelope marked 'Confidential' and opened it. An old classmate, Larry Feller, was asking him to attend the reunion. There was a reminder of the good times they'd had making homebrew in Larry's parents' basement. A postscript read: *Johanna Barton will be coming.*

Vladimir hadn't thought about high school since he'd left, although he had thought of Johanna Barton. On his return to Vancouver from London years ago, he had hoped to renew their adolescent love. He'd made enquiries only to find that she had married and moved out of town. Larry's letter awakened a flood of memories.

When Vlad had his first stirrings for the opposite sex, he took an interest in Johanna, who had been the youngest member of their class. In those years, he was a loner known for his intellect rather than his social skills, and therefore mostly shunned by his peers. For that same reason, Johanna noticed him and accepted his invitation to go fishing. They were not alone; Arlene, Vlad's mother joined them as a chaperone. As Vlad fished, Arlene watched the two young people argue about literature: the relative merits of Tolstoy, Dostoyevsky, Jane Austen and George Eliot.

The last time Vlad saw Johanna was to say goodbye on her doorstep before he left for Dalhousie University. He kissed her once then, a chaste kiss. For years after that, while acquiring some much-needed social skills and enjoying an uninhibited sex life, Vlad included Johanna in his sexual fantasies.

In the yearbook from Vlad's graduating class at Lord Stanley High School, the written summaries of his class's ambitions matched the pictures of each of the eager young grad faces. All were full of glowing adventure in the golden innocence of their youth. Vlad, who was on the editorial board of the yearbook, had arranged to have two side-by-side deadpan pictures of himself — one facing the camera and the other in profile with the caption: *Born to be free*, under his name, VLADIMIR BLACK. In Johanna's copy of the yearbook, he had written, *To live a life of crime*. Everyone thought that the inscription was so clever, but they had underestimated Vlad, for it was one of the last truths about himself that he allowed the world to see—until the reunion.

* * *

It was a warm evening in September when the class of 1955 gathered at the Royal Vancouver Yacht Club to celebrate their thirtieth reunion. Vlad was a member of the club. He arrived, dressed in white flannels and shoes, blue blazer and club tie, topped with an admiral's cap. He was alone and purposely late so that his class standing on the balcony overlooking the moorage would see and hear him throttling down the twin inboard engines of his mahogany-trimmed speedboat. He had arranged for the wharfkeeper to be at the slip in front of the clubhouse and tie up his boat, as a groom would for a horseman's spirited thoroughbred, so as not to interrupt his steady progress toward his gawking classmates.

His entrance went as he had planned. He noticed Johanna immediately. She was dazzling in a sequined jade-green gown with a modest neckline, set off by a string of pearls. She was seated, talking with some of her old friends. After dealing with the crush of male classmates, most of whose names he had forgotten except Larry, with whom he exchanged only a few words, he stood in front of her table. Removing his cap with a flourish and tucking it under his arm, his eyes settled on one of Johanna's friends. He flashed a smile meant for the whole table.

"So good to see you, Jane. You look as beautiful as ever."

Jane was not beautiful and probably knew it, but she didn't seem to mind his insincerity.

"Vladimir, you look as honest as ever," she smiled back.

He laughed at this, sharing his laughter with the table and, in this way, catching Johanna's eye.

"Johanna. It's been a very long time."

"Hello, Charlie."

Surprised, he smiled remembering that she had been the only one who'd ever called him by his middle name.

"Is your husband about? I'd like to meet him."

"He's a very busy trial lawyer. He couldn't make it."

"What a pity."

She eyed his nametag.

"I see you've changed your name to *Volk?*"

"Yes, that's my father's surname. He's Russian, and Volk is wolf in Russian. I see your table is full. After dinner, would you save a dance for me?"

Vlad joined Larry's table and listened, without showing his irritation, to Larry outline a business venture which only needed one hundred thousand dollars of seed money to get off the ground. After dinner and speeches, he re-approached Johanna, who was still protected by a flock of her female classmates.

"I believe, madam, that you have pencilled my name in your dance card."

"I have, sir," she laughed. "Shall we dance?"

They had a number of dances, and she proved to still be the precious, polished emerald he had dreamed of and wanted for so long. By the end of the evening, he knew all about her daughter Mary, her job teaching English, and her home. He asked nothing more about her husband. The fact that she was an English teacher fascinated him somehow, and he listened to her get excited about her students. She talked with animation of the Chilcotin, and how the heavens seemed to conspire to encircle it—certainly in the paintings of the artist Noah Hanlon, of whom she spoke almost rapturously.

For one of the few times in his adult life, Vlad's feelings for another person were awakened and he didn't know how to act. He used every strategy he knew to be pleasant and win Johanna over. It had always been successful in his business dealings. It was always the chase that had given him the most excitement, and the chase usually ended in victory and his defeats were invaluable lessons. This was different. He felt a need to share his life with this woman, not possess her.

Johanna's descriptions of the bench lands along the Chilcotin River reminded him of the Russian steppes. Her story of how she adopted the Chilcotin frog symbol enchanted him. Here was a challenge for him—a chance to control a whole territory as part of his financial empire, and to be closer to Johanna. He knew even less than most Vancouverites about the mysteries of British Columbia's Interior, which until now had seemed dull compared with the lustre of the coast's ocean, mountains and money. Still, he was immediately confident that he could exploit the Chilcotin as he had other places.

"I have a client in Williams Lake," he said. "Lars Larson. He and I are planning a joint venture, so you may see me up there in the next while."

"Lars and his wife Gertrude are good friends of ours."

Vlad knew Henry 'Lars' Larson from the annual Truck Loggers conventions and their after-parties, where he had observed Lars drunk out of his mind. Lars owned a small logging and sawmill business, and Vlad's only dealings with him had been when he was able to supply Vlad's orders for cedar when the larger companies couldn't. Vlad knew he would get to know and use Lars a lot better in the coming months.

Near the end of the evening, they were sitting at a table looking at the city skyline pointing up at the lights on Cypress and Grouse Mountains. Vlad was still questioning Johanna for information when she raised her hand.

"Enough about me," she laughed. "All I know about you is that you're a bachelor, a financier and a wolf. Where is your lair?"

"On an island in the Indian Arm of Burrard Inlet," he answered. He thought, *Thank heavens she still has a sense of humour.*

"How exotic! I was born and raised in Vancouver, but I've never sailed up Indian Arm."

"It's a long, deep fjord. Wigwam Inn is a lodge at the head of the fjord. The Yacht Club bought it last June as an outstation. It has an interesting history."

"I'd like to hear about that," she said, her eyes sparkling.

"It was built before the First World War by a German count, who had invested successfully in the Vancouver real estate market," he said in a low voice, as if confiding a secret. "Of course, good timing and luck are the investor's best friends, but in the count's case, both were against him. When war broke out with Germany, he became an enemy alien and his assets were seized."

"Surely those elements are not limited to investing."

It seemed to Vlad that thirty years had just been erased from his memory and he was back sparring with Johanna on their fishing excursions.

"Of course, but do you want to hear the story or not?"

"Proceed, sir."

"The lodge was hardly used between the wars. Finally, in the early sixties, a young enterprising lawyer, Rocky Meyers, thought that this would be the ideal place for a gambling club. His patrons would come by boat, play cards, drink illegal booze in the large reception rooms and Rocky would grow rich. Again, bad timing and poor luck came into the play. At first, because of its remote location and Rocky's select clientele, he made money—and a reputation as a man who thumbed his nose at convention and paid the police to look the other way. In July 1962, thirty officers in two boats raided the inn and ended Rocky's dreams."

"Poor Rocky," she mocked.

Vlad noticed the party was winding down and decided he was having such a good time, he didn't want it to end. He suggested that he take her back in his speedboat to her hotel downtown, across English Bay from the yacht club. To his delight, she accepted.

In Johanna's eyes, Vladimir Black had made a lie of Malcolm's cynicism, and she was going to enjoy Vlad's company as he was obviously enjoying hers. He helped her into his speedboat, took off his jacket and gave it to her to protect her against the sea wind.

The engines started with an angry growl. He manoeuvred the boat out of the Jericho moorage to the open waters of English Bay and opened the throttle. Johanna responded with excitement to the wind whipping her hair, to the city spread out in front of her, and to the sense of freedom. He cruised around Stanley Park, past Siwash Rock, under the Lions Gate Bridge and into Coal Harbour. He docked the boat at the wharf at the foot of Cardero Street.

He walked her to her hotel, the Bayshore. She was surprised when he didn't try to make a move on her, even at this point in the night. She had no idea of how she would have responded. He took her hand in the lobby of the hotel. As she'd thought, she didn't know what to say or do.

"Would you," he asked, "join me for breakfast tomorrow—say about nine o'clock?"

"Yes, I would like that," she smiled hesitantly, uncertain if she was showing too much interest in him. "I'm catching the noon flight to Williams Lake."

She squeezed his hand in what she considered to be a friendly gesture. As she entered the elevator, she turned and waved goodbye. She couldn't quite make out the expression in his parting smile, but she suspected that he had interpreted the pressure of her hand as more than friendly. She might be able to identify his feeling the next morning, she thought, realizing she was anxious to know.

At breakfast, they sat at a table overlooking the harbour. The sun shone on the North Shore Mountains, making the top of Grouse Mountain sparkle with a fresh dusting of snow. Johanna talked about Mary.

"That's her," she beamed, showing him a photo from her wallet. "Isn't she beautiful? She's very bright. She's in first-year law at the University of Victoria."

"She's almost as beautiful as her mother."

Johanna blushed with the compliment. He placed a small blue box on the breakfast table in front of her.

"You were talking about frogs last night."

"I don't eat them. I hope it isn't alive."

He smiled. She opened the box to find a necklace and a jade and gold frog pendant. The frog had abalone shell eyes.

"Do you like it?"

"Yes! It's beautiful."

She held it up to admire. As she unclasped the necklace, he stood. He took it back from her and moved around behind her chair to fasten it around her neck, brushing her exposed shoulder as he did. She froze for a second, thinking, *I wonder if Frog is a symbol for sex.* The gold necklace was short, positioning the frog pendant just below the hollow of Johanna's throat, so that it could be seen when she was wearing a blouse or V-necked sweater.

"Thank you, Charlie," she gushed. "It's very elegant. And so wise with its big abalone eyes."

"It suits you beautifully. I collect Native art work and the frog caught my eye. As do you. You two are a good match."

She hadn't had so much attention from an attractive man in years. But surely he had another woman in his life to shower gifts upon? Something didn't seem right about the situation, but she was enjoying the moment too much to think about it any further.

He drove her to the airport and saw her to the check-in.

"You'll be seeing more of me in the next year," he promised.

He took both her hands and kissed her briefly on the lips. She didn't turn away.

"Thank you for the green frog with the big eyes," she grinned, now turning to walk through security.

On the flight back to Williams Lake, Johanna was overcome with the feeling that she had met a charming, dashing, unattached, attractive man who had the same interests as she did. *It was just an innocent flirtation, but now I have to get back to my country and my lesson plans.* Whenever her feelings overcame her, she remembered the balm of the Chilcotin—her refuge, her counsellor—coming ever closer as the plane broke through the clouds on its descent to Williams Lake.

6

On the Monday after the reunion, Vlad was in his Roberto Cavalli dressing gown at breakfast, reading the *New York Times*, delivered every morning to his island by water taxi. Frida, his mistress, sat across from him, at work on a spreadsheet.

Without preamble, he said, "Frida, I'm buying a ranch in the Chilcotin."

"Oh? Where is that?"

"In the middle of the province."

"Why would you?" she said covering a yawn with her hand.

"I've flown over it, and it reminds me a bit on a smaller scale of the steppes of Russia. Besides, I like the idea of owning land and the hunting rights."

"It's up to you."

"I thought I would tell you as I intend to spend half my time up there."

"You don't expect me to come with you?"

"Of course not."

Vlad had met Frida, in Mexico City where she ran a bordello. She had followed him to Vancouver along with her brother Jorge where she doubled as his hostess. The arrangement had suited them both. For him, there were no romantic entanglements. She was able to manage her family's drug-growing and smuggling business under the cover of his outward respectability, posing as a legitimate entrepreneur, and she provided him with financing through money which he laundered into his investments.

* * *

Vlad had come to his decision to buy a ranch in the Chilcotin on the Sunday, the day he said goodbye to Johanna at the airport. He had piloted his floatplane from the airport to his island home and spent Sunday in his den, reflecting on his life as a bastard, rejected by his father and doted on by his mother. He was four years old when his mother, Arlene, told him about his absent father, Boris Volk, a Russian business-man. When Vlad was a year old, Boris had suddenly returned to Moscow, assuring her that he would send for her and little Vlad. He never did.

Later, when Vlad was asking questions, she told him that she had met Boris in Ottawa when she was a secretary at the Canadian External Affairs Department. She, a proper Pres-byterian, had insisted that they marry before Vladimir was born. She discovered later that Boris was already married and that her marriage to him was a nullity. She also learned that Boris's business was a cover. He was, in fact, an industrial spy attached to the Russian Embassy who had used Arlene to give himself credibility. He was recalled when his cover was blown.

When Vlad was six, they moved to Vancouver, where her brother lived, and she had Vladimir's surname changed to Black, her family name. She worked for the provincial government and poured all her suppressed love into her son while heaping scorn on his father. Vlad benefited from the maternal love, which placed him as the male head of the household, but he rejected his mother's hatred of his father, whom he looked upon as a god, or at least a demi-god.

Boris acknowledged his son during Vlad's early years by sending him birthday and Christmas cards, all of which Vlad kept in a locked box under his bed. They were now in a file in the safe with all the other personal papers of his life. He went to his safe, took out the file and placed it on his desk as gingerly as he would a baby. He was about to open it when there was a knock on the door.

Frieda came in.

"It's five o'clock. Time for your scotch on the rocks."

"Not tonight, Frieda. I'm busy."

"You promised me a good time tonight."

"I think it was the other way around. You will have to amuse yourself."

She left in a huff and he opened the thick file. It was arranged chronologically. Under the years 1945 to 1950 were the colourful cards addressed to 'my dear son'. He had known then that if they were found lying about, his mother would have destroyed them, and those cards were evidence of Boris's obligation to him.

In his teens, Vlad had reinforced his father's paternal feelings by sending him flattering letters. There in the file were the copies, under the years 1950 to 1955.

Boris had two children in Moscow—Ivestia, who was three years older than Vlad, and Parita, who was two years younger. When Vlad turned sixteen, Boris, who had risen in the Russian foreign service, sent him a letter which he pulled from his file.

Dear Son,

You know that I would like to visit you, but I am not welcome in Canada. Enclosed is a money order to cover the cost of taking Russian language lessons. When you have a grasp of our language, I will pay your way to St. Petersburg where we can travel throughout the Motherland and you can get to know me and your sisters.

A year later, having mastered conversational Russian, he took advantage of his father's offer. When he travelled with Boris, he felt an immediate connection to the grassland steppes of the Volga. The pictures of Boris, himself and his two half-sisters posed in the Hermitage, and on the steppes spoke of times past.

On his return to Vancouver, Vlad's fantasies about his father, which were encouraged by Boris, had Boris in the higher echelons of the Kremlin, despite their ancestors having been counts under the Tsar. Vlad was well-read in the novels of Tolstoy and Dostoevsky, which fed these illusions, and he felt a deep attachment to the character of Dmitri Karamazov in *The Brothers Karamazov.*

Vlad's newly-acquired pride, cultivated charm and predatory instincts were more than enough to win him respect and women at Dalhousie, in his fourth year of university. When his father was posted to the Russian Embassy in London, all of Vlad's dreams about using his father to advance his future were realized.

Vlad graduated with honours in economics, and he prevailed upon Boris to finance his education at the London School of Economics for his graduate studies. He returned the favour by reclaiming his father's surname, Volk. But in his last year in London he dishonoured his father's name by sleeping with his half-sister, Ivestia. When Boris learned of this, he disowned his son and cut off his funding before his last year at LSE. Vlad found himself without a degree, the penniless son of a Russian count—a god who had thrown his son out of Heaven.

Vlad returned to British Columbia to the welcoming arms of his mother, whose support for him was unwavering as was her hate for his father. He found a job in the forestry industry as a lumber broker, where he soon understood the shortcut to success in the coastal rainforests of BC—where the trees were felled, skidded to the sea, and rafted into booms the size of small towns—was to buy directly from the log salvagers known as beachcombers, some of whom could be described as modern-day pirates.

By law, salvagers were allowed to pick up stray logs that broke free from the booms, and since each log was stamped, it could be identified and returned to the owner for payment of a salvage fee. Those were the rules, but on the longest-treed coastline in North America, where there were more grizzly bears than people, the booms could as easily be broken by humans as by storms, and timber stamps could be changed.

With these modest fraudulent beginnings, over the next decade, Vlad turned his growing brokerage fortune into an investment-banking house. He didn't exhibit his wealth. He didn't buy a mansion in Vancouver's rich enclave of Shaughnessy or build a show house on the Golden Mile of Point Grey Road. He bought this island on Indian Arm and built a modest house, blasted out of rock with a tunnel leading from the dock to the house. It had the advantage of privacy— access was limited to seaplane or boat—yet it was but ten miles from Vancouver's city centre.

He remained a bachelor. His idea of feminine beauty had been shaped by Johanna, and he'd never found a match. His real interest was in using the power of cool reason to control others. He was goal-oriented, and the success of a plan meticulously conceived and executed was his greatest reward. His growing fortune seemed to reinforce his concept of mind over feeling. If one stopped to analyze his predatory conduct, which Vlad hadn't, it could have been traced to his belief that he came from Russian aristocracy and the rest of the world's inhabitants were but serfs. He regaled his friends with stories of Indian Arm, and one of his favourites was the one he told Johanna about Rocky Myers. At the end of the story, when Rocky is sent to jail, Vlad usually added, "I wouldn't have made that mistake."

His friends, taken in by his charm and wealth, believed that the mistake he was talking about was breaking the law, but in truth he was referring to getting caught.

* * *

Frida located the Chilcotin on a map and discovered from her brother that they did not do business in the Cariboo-Chilcotin. She knew of Vlad's obsession with his Russian heritage and smiled at his boyish dream of a *dacha* in the wilds of British Columbia. Had Frida known that it was his love of Johanna that had prompted Vlad to make that decision, she wouldn't have cared, but she also wouldn't have believed it, for this was the one emotion that she had never seen in Vlad. It had set him apart from the other men in her life.

7

The Stampede meant family time in Williams Lake. The July 1st long weekend in 1986 brought the Cariboo and Chilcotin together, town and country, Natives and whites, clerks and cowboys alike. The annual outdoor roundup of parades, pipe bands, colourful floats and games with Native drumming and dancing was something no one could miss. On the stampede grounds, there were tests of cowboy skill in roping and riding and the chance to bet on a horse race. At night, the busiest place in town was Squaw Hall, with its music and mayhem. The Natives from the ranches and reserves brought their old and young, and the whites left their worries for a few days to spend precious hours with their children. The Kents and the Hanlons sat in the bleachers, accompanied by Lars and his wife Gertrude. They were watching the women's calf-roping competition when the last contestant was announced.

Johanna cut Lars off in mid-sentence by raising her hand palm up.

"Mary's riding now."

Mary's Stetson was jammed on her head to her bent ears. She was riding Radium, a high-strung quarter horse fidgeting under a tight rein. Her draw was a whiteface bull calf, rangy and quick. Out of the gate, it seemed to know its fate and used its every instinct to avoid it. Radium tracked down the animal, and the cowgirl was about to throw her lasso when the calf tacked hard. Radium veered in pursuit. Regaining their balance, horse and rider bore down on their prey. The lasso snaked out and caught the calf's back hoof. Radium backed up to keep tension on the rope as Mary leapt off. She flipped the calf on its back and wrapped the loose rope around its hoofs. She raised her arms to the cheers of the crowd, the loudest coming from her mother.

"Mary Kent's time, forty-five seconds." the announcer said in a monotone.

It was one second more than Elizabeth Hanlon, riding Faraway. It earned Mary the white ribbon, with the blue going to Elizabeth.

With the excitement over, the crowd quieted down. Taking advantage of the break, Johanna turned to Lars.

"Lars," she said, "I would like to use your cabin for the next week. I need some thinking and reading time alone."

Her request caused a disinterested Malcolm to pay attention. It also surprised Lars' wife, Gertrude, who had planned to use their cabin herself over the next few weeks, but she had no chance to say anything before Lars responded.

"Of course you can, Johanna," he said grandly. "You just go up there and enjoy yourself in the wilderness. I'll drive you out there and see you settled in."

In that deft, apparently innocent, request, Johanna had let her husband know her intentions.

Gertrude tried, but couldn't think of a quick excuse to reclaim the week of her cabin which Lars had just given to their friend. In the awkward silence that followed, everyone turned to the arena, watching intently as the ground was cleared for the next competition.

"Hey, the winners are up here!"

Elizabeth leaned in to her parents, who stood and hugged her, beaming. Beside her, Mary put one arm around Malcolm's shoulders, which he responded to with a tight smile and a nod. Joel stood behind the girls waiting, if a bit impatiently.

"Well done!" Noah exclaimed to Elizabeth.

"If you had a better draw, you'd have won," Johanna smiled wryly at Mary before embracing her.

Justine turned at this, but Mary caught her eye before she said anything.

"Elizabeth deserved the win, Mum. She's a damn good rider." Looking at Justine, she added, "With a damn good teacher."

"So are you, Mary," Malcolm stiffly offered.

Looking to break the tension, Noah reached back to put his hand on Joel's arm.

"Good luck on your ride, son," he said.

"You're kidding, right, Dad?" Joel smirked. "You don't need luck if you're good as I am."

Elizabeth elbowed him in the ribs and he shouted in mock pain.

"Let's get you ready, cowboy," she said, turning to leave with a wave. "See you all later."

The adults settled back into their seats as the children left. They talked about the girls' performance, but the awkwardness had returned and, in no time, they were again staring at the grounds, waiting for something else to focus on.

Even when the bronc riding began, Johanna found herself lacking any interest. Perhaps when Joel's turn came around she'd have a reason to watch, but in the meantime, she found herself scanning the crowd.

She noticed Mary talking to Robin Redford, a former student of hers who had left before graduating to sing country music in Calgary. She and Mary had been good friends at school. Johanna wondered what she was doing in town. The curiosity was idle but nagged at her the rest of the day.

Driving home from the stampede grounds, Malcolm said to Johanna offhandedly, "I didn't know you were planning a retreat."

"I'm reading Margaret Laurence's *The Diviners*. I need to reconnect with nature to get her full meaning."

He didn't follow up nor did she expand on her explanation. The next kilometre of road was met with silence.

"Well as it turns out," Malcolm suddenly volunteered, "I couldn't take the time off to join you with that trial starting Tuesday. I'll be working late every night."

It seemed Malcolm worked late every night, trial or not. With silence and a tight-lipped smile, Johanna tried to convey sorrow that Malcolm had shown so little interest in her retreat, rather than the annoyance she actually felt.

"I'm expecting a call from the Deputy Minister of Justice," Malcolm said, finally breaking the silence.

"Oh? What's that about?"

"I'm in the running for an appointment to the Supreme Court sitting in Williams Lake."

"That's nice," she said in a bland voice.

They drove into the driveway of their house on the lake. She had grown used to Malcolm's pronouncements and found that nothing he said or did surprised her any more. It seemed to her that the distance between them was growing. Margaret Laurence wasn't the only reason she wanted this time alone; she was thinking ahead to the surprise she was planning in the next week at Larson Lake.

8

She was named Robin by her father on account of her first cry, an on-key warble. She was thankful that she hadn't sounded like a loon or a goose. The Laboucher family name fitted her father, whose greatest gift was talking, but it didn't have the right grandeur for the stage, so she took the stage name 'Redford' when she wrote and recorded her first single, "Memories of a Wasted Youth".

That was five years ago, while she was still living with her parents in a cabin on Horsefly Road, fifteen miles northeast of Williams Lake. Passing the old store at Crosina's 153 Mile House, she recalled the first time she had seen their cabin in the spring of '80. It was a bit depressing then, but she had lived in these rundown cabins wherever they had landed. It wasn't long before her mother, Mert, had tidied up the place, and her father, Paul, had planted a garden, alternating one row of corn with another of weed. Her father was an itinerant log builder who built the old-fashioned way, laying log on log with bold white chinking in between rather than scoring the logs, and then chainsawing them along the score line, hiding the insulation.

"My way is the way God and the Hudson's Bay Company intended," he told prospective customers. "I don't know about God, but the Bay's trading posts are still standing."

When he fast-talked a stranger into having him build a cabin, he would order a truckload of pine logs, and he and Mert would camp on the site until the building was complete.

Paul had other skills and occupations. He played the fiddle and wherever they went, he joined up with other musicians and played at square dances. Through Robin's childhood, she and her mother always tagged along. By the time Robin was six, he had her performing, singing a few songs and strumming a guitar between sets.

The familiar sights brought back good memories of how she first met Johanna and Mary. Her parents' nomadic lifestyle meant that she had to change schools every few years, which never seemed to be a consideration for them. At the time, it bothered her a whole lot, but it turned out to be a blessing as she had a lifetime of hardship to write and sing about.

She remembered the schoolbus had picked her up at seven a.m. in front of the cabin on a Monday morning in May. There were a few other children in the bus who giggled when she got on. Jerry, the driver, who wore a coat over her pyjamas, was friendly. *How else could she be in that get-up?* Robin had wondered. The bus dropped her off at Ann Stevenson High School. On the bus home that afternoon there was no giggling. She had used her father's rich vocabulary laced with profanity to reduce her fellow bus riders to silence. She waved a cheery goodbye to Jerry, the bus driver, who now wore pants and a sweater. As she leaped off the bus, she shouted over her shoulder.

"I liked your outfit this morning. It had that lived-in look."

Mert had greeted her at the door, one eye on her daughter and the other on the NASCAR races on TV.

"Why the big smile, girl?"

"I met someone I liked," Robin answered, unable to contain

her joy. "In English class, Ms. Kent was reading *Animal Farm*, and the whole story came alive with all the animals sounding off and her explaining that it was all an allegory. After class, I met Mary, Ms. Kent's daughter, and we sort of connected."

"Sounds kind of weird to me," Mert said.

"Yeah, well, I told her I play the guitar, and she said that was cool. We're going to get together on the weekend."

"I meant the animal part."

Paul, who had come up from his garden and had overheard the last of the conversation, chimed in.

"Why didn't you tell your Ms. Kent the tall story you told me, like about how you and Jake Lamonte got lost in the backwoods for a whole night and walked the night away yelling out to scare the bear and the lion?"

"I don't tell stories anymore," she interrupted smartly. "I sing sad cowgirl songs of longing and rejection."

She had learned the trick of steering her father's conversation like a helmsman would a four-master. He responded to the change of course.

"I'm playing at a dance at the Lac La Hache community centre on Saturday night," he offered. "You can try out your new rejection song after singing the Dolly Parton and Patsy Cline numbers."

He would have said more, but she carried on into the house past her mother's critical eye and mouth.

"What about this girl you met?"

"I don't know. She's interesting is all, different from the rest, sort of holds herself back. But when you talk to her, she listens. She's more into classical music, but jazz, country and bluegrass is fine with her. I'll bring her along to Lac La Hache."

Robin was brought back to the present when Paul came to the door smoking a joint and yelling into the wind.

"Look who's here, Momma. It's our darlin' daughter."

"Hi, Pops. Why aren't you in jail for possession?"

"Hell, the cops are waiting to bust me for something bigger than that."

She could hear her mother shouting at the TV from inside the house.

"For God's sake, Junior! You should've made a pit stop afore now."

She was pleased to see that the folks hadn't changed any. Soon, they were sitting on the porch facing the road while Robin brought them up to date on the last two years. There was some traffic and most cars slowed down and honked as they passed the house. Some cars seemed to Robin about to turn in but they all veered away and carried on except for a red Mustang. It pulled in, stopping well short of the house. Paul walked over and spoke to the driver. The sun was in her eyes so Robin couldn't make out who he was, but the car was familiar. Paul passed a package to the driver, who did a quick turn, and the car raised some dust as it gained the highway and headed south towards Williams Lake.

"I see business is good," she said as Paul returned.

"Yep, the corn crop is good this year," he said with a sly smile. "I hear you're going to tour the Cariboo and you'll be playing at the Halverson's barn end of August."

"Yeah, I hope you all come."

"Wouldn't miss it for the world, girl. All hell breaks loose at that party."

9

Lars picked up Johanna early on Tuesday morning. She had intended to speak to Mary that evening, but Mary had gone to the dance at Squaw Hall and was late. She left a note, which she tucked in Mary's bedroom door asking her daughter to visit her at Larson's cabin on Friday for lunch.

Johanna was fond of Lars, a big shambling man with Nordic blue eyes set in a florid face. A good-natured lumberman, he appeared to her to be quite successful despite his lack of a formal education. She liked that he tried to improve himself by taking her evening adult education English literature courses at Cariboo College. He tried to discuss the books that he was reading, clearly valuing her opinion. She tried, in turn, to take an interest in his lumber company, but dollars and board feet measures fogged her brain.

They drove west on Highway 20 into the Chilcotin, then turned south off the highway on a private gravel road to Larson Lake. Calling it a lake was a bit of vanity—on a bluff overlooking the Chilcotin River; it was a pond which Larson had dammed, raising the water level and tripling its area. It didn't matter to Johanna, a weak swimmer who preferred to wade in and splash about near the shore—all she was seeking was solitude.

Lars unloaded her supplies from his yellow pick-up, then showed her around the cabin. It was a neat clapboard structure with a large porch and separated from the lake by thirty feet of lawn. He insisted on cutting the lawn and then doing some other chores—Johanna was hoping he would go. Mid-morning, he made a pot of coffee and they sat down on the porch with a cinnamon bun, which she had brought in with her supplies.

"I will look in on you from time to time," Lars promised, his usual good humour particularly strong that day.

"Thank you, Lars, but that's not necessary."

"I'm happy to do it. It will give me some peace of mind to know that you're safe."

"Why wouldn't I be safe in this beautiful place?"

"Well, it has been peaceful. But Vladimir Volk, my new neighbour, bought the ranch over that ridge. He's building a house, and he can be a bit troublesome."

Caught by surprise on hearing that Vladimir owned the adjoining ranch, she nervously fingered the frog pendant she was wearing. The partly-treed rocky ridge rose above the lake to the west looked unmenacing.

"Don't worry," she said. "I'll send Charlie packing if he comes my way."

That wiped the smile off Lars' face.

"Charlie? Are we talking about the same person? My neighbour's name is Vlad."

"I knew him in high school. His middle name is Charles. I called him Charlie."

Lars' voice lost its bounce and he nodded knowingly.

"I see."

10

The airfield northeast of Williams Lake was cut from the pine and fir forests. An Air Cariboo DC-3 circled it lazily.

Carter Gordon, sitting at the back of the plane, looked down on this town peacefully laid out below him in a neat geometric pattern next to a small lake—what he hoped would be his town. From the air, the forests dominated the rolling plateau, excepting large blocks cleared of trees, harvested like a rancher's hayfield. Grass, the fuel of the cattle industry, has a yearly cycle; lodgepole pine eighty years and Douglas fir longer. The logging scars would last at least a lifetime.

The twin-engine plane descended, lurching from side to side and landing with a bump on the runway. Its high front wheels touched first, the engines throttled back and it settled on its low back wheel, nose up, slowly taxiing to the terminal.

Carter walked up the sloped aisle to the exit, the last passenger off. He had planned it that way so that Stan Hewitt, the octogenarian lawyer who said he would meet him at the airport, could watch him cross the tarmac to the terminal and be impressed with his assured and confident manner.

This was his best asset for his job interview, his last chance for a foothold at becoming a lawyer.

Most of the articling jobs in the large Vancouver law firms were reserved for the top third of his law class, and the law school hadn't granted him that honour. The rest of the Lower Mainland, Vancouver Island and what Vancouver lawyers called upcountry law firms picked over the rest. He had been a law school underachiever. Had law firms been looking for a good bridge player or a goalie voted player of the year by his varsity hockey team, he would have had no trouble getting articles. He shared the plane with a noisy group of young men with scraggly beards and long hair. He had talked them up, learning they were a band on a summer tour of Northern British Columbia featuring their vocalist, hometown girl, Robin Redford.

Later, on his own, the scenery—even seen from above—reminded him of his last trip this way.

Last summer, he had made the journey to Williams Lake on the BC Rail dayliner from North Vancouver. The train had hugged the shoreline of Howe Sound up to Squamish, and from Squamish rode up the river valley to the mountain resort of Whistler. Then he was in the middle of the Coastal Mountain range, surrounded by ski lifts and glaciers. The train gained altitude through the Pemberton Valley to D'Arcy and passed the aquamarine Anderson and Seton Lakes to Lillooet and the Fraser River, arriving in the Cariboo. From there, climbing, always climbing, the train stopped at Clinton, Lone Butte and the high plateau country. The pioneer ranches flashed by on the open grasslands—Bridge Lake, The Club, Overlook, Faraway, Enterprise, Onward, The Mission.

He had worked at a Larson Forest Products mill near Puntzi Lake in the Chilcotin. His first day on the job had been hell, followed by four months of galley-slave effort pulling heavy slabs of freshly-cut lumber off a moving chain. The overwhelming smell of pine resin had hit him full-on when he showed up for work and remained with him throughout that summer.

"Oscar Kreutziger to the front office. The new employee, Carter Gordon, is here," the receptionist had called on the intercom, echoing back with a slight delay on the loudspeaker.

His foreman entered the room, surprised at the sight of Carter.

"Oh. You're white," he said. "I was expecting a Native. You'll be working on the green chain."

They crossed the yard towards the screech of a gang saw slicing through a pine log. Reaching the sorting deck, they climbed up and passed the edger. From there, they watched three Natives pulling green lumber off the chain and sorting it in stacks for the forklift to pick up.

"It's pretty simple," Oscar yelled above the saw noise. "We sort according to dimension. You'll team up with John over there on the far side."

The short-staffed workers were running hard under the eye of the foreman to keep up with the steady flow of lumber. Missed pieces fell off the end of the chain. They would have to be picked up by hand and sorted later. Carter got down to work.

At 10, a whistle blew, the machines stopped and the crew gathered in the shade to drink coffee. He joined them.

"Hi. I'm Carter."

They looked at him. The youngest, who had been working with him on one side of the chain, nodded; the other two looked away.

"What should I call you . . . Johnny or John?" Carter asked.

"Johnny."

"Been working here long?"

"'Bout a month."

The other two looked at the surrounding mostly-forested hills, caught up in their own thoughts.

"I see some cedar going through the saws. Where does it come from?"

"I dunno."

Carter turned to the others.

"Do you know where the cedar comes from?"

The younger one, handsome with his front teeth knocked out, motioned to the north.

"Yeah, up near Barkerville."

The older man ignored him.

Carter could hear the forklift operating over by the planer mill. He was curious. *Why work through the break?* After two hours on the green chain, every muscle in his body was screaming at his brain to stop. The forklift rounded a pile of stacked lumber and headed for the green chain. All he could see of the driver was a shirtless man wearing a yellow baseball cap and sunglasses. The vehicle kicked up dust as it approached with speed, and then braked hard in front of where the crew were sitting. The dust rolled on, engulfing them.

"Got dem," the older Native coughed.

The driver dismounted and sauntered toward them. Approaching Carter, he accosted him.

"What the hell we got here? A white working on the green chain?" he smiled. "I'm Cowboy Cam and that there," he pointed to the forklift, "is my horse Charity."

"Yeah, well, I'm King Carter and these here men are the Knights of the Flat Table."

Johnny told him later that Cam Larson was the owner's son. Carter got to know a bit more about Cam during that summer. He didn't seek Cam's company, but Cam joined him for a beer after work from time to time. It seemed that the only thing on Cam's mind that summer was bedding a girl from Williams Lake named Mary Kent, who he thought read too many books. In order to impress her, he pretended to be fascinated with the written word. Later, while drinking beer in the Alexis Creek Arms, he had sought out Carter as an instructor.

"Mary says that *The Catcher in the Rye* was one of the books that liberated teenagers from oppressive parents. Of course I agreed, but what the hell was she talking about?"

"Have you read the book?"

"I don't have time for that. I'm too busy learning the lumber business."

Carter then gave him a synopsis of the novel.

"What should I say about it.?"

"Tell her that Holden Caulfield, the main character was a mixed-up rich kid who cried out for parental attention."

On Monday, Cam reported back to Carter.

"God, what you told me about Holden worked like a damn. After I said that, she was all over me."

Towards the end of the summer, on the morning of Carter's last day at the mill, Cam had announced his victory by shouting to Carter before the green chain started moving.

"Larson takes a brilliant pass from Gordon . . . he shoots . . . he scores!"

His reverie was interrupted by the plane hitting the tarmac.

The band preceded Carter into the terminal and were milling around a blonde girl while waiting for their instruments. Carter assumed this must be the singer they'd talked about.

Robin Redford was animated and loud and he could make out her end of the conversation from where he stood staring at her, ten feet away.

"You'll meet my Dad, Paul . . . You can't miss him . . . His cherry-red pickup has an 'I LOVE THE RCMP' sticker on the right back bumper and . . ."

She stopped, seeing Carter staring. He winked and turned away.

". . . and I SUPPORT NATIVE ARTS AND CRAFTS on the left," she continued.

He heard and smiled, but had his own affairs to tend to. He looked around for the old man whom he hoped would be his principal. But Stan Hewitt wasn't there.

11

Exhausted from the dance, Mary had slept in.

She remembered, barely in time, that she had to go to the airport to pick up a law student Stan Hewitt was thinking of hiring. She looked at herself in the mirror and saw the after-effects of a hard day's night at Squaw Hall. She had a quick shower and congratulated herself for having her hair in a ponytail for the summer. She dressed and rushed out of her room. A note fluttered from the door jamb and she glanced at her mother's precise writing asking her to visit at Larson Lake. With no time to think about her mother, she stuffed the note into her purse, ran through the kitchen without stopping for a bite and drove to the office to pick up a brief that she had worked on for a trial that morning.

The stream of cars she met coming down the road from the airport told her that the plane had already landed. The small terminal came into view and she braked hard in front of the exit door of what appeared to be an empty passengers lounge.

Mary ran into the building and saw, to her relief, an athletic young man dressed in suit and tie. She walked up to him, the only person left in the terminal, and offered her hand.

"Hi, you must be Carter. I'm from Mr. Hewitt's office. He's not feeling well. We'll talk in the car."

He shook her hand and nodded.

In the confusion and rush, he didn't get her name if she gave it. Carter was already taken off-balance by Hewitt's no-show. Being met by this no-nonsense, all business, olive-skinned energetic woman, with her hair swept back off her forehead and tied at the back in a ponytail, threw him even more. She was dressed in a black skirt, white blouse, a tight-fitting tailored black jacket and sensible shoes. She picked up Carter's bag, and he followed her out.

As they pulled out of the airport, she handed him a file.

"This is for you."

"What's this?"

"There's a custody hearing at the courthouse in an hour. It's a twenty-minute drive. Read the file. Then you'll have just enough time to meet with your clients before you go into court."

"Whoa, I don't have any clients. I don't know if I've got a job."

"They're Mr. Hewitt's clients. I would guess you *may* have a job depending how you handle this case. The clients are trying to get their nine-month-old daughter back from Child Welfare. They live on the Redstone Reserve. He works for Larson Forest Products, but is presently laid off."

"Why was the child apprehended?"

"She was left unattended outside a beer parlour."

He opened the brief. There was the motion filed by Children's Services applying for permanent custody of Jewel Eagle and a countersuit for an order to return Jewel to her parents. There were the statements of the social worker, an RCMP officer and the defence statements of the parents, John and Celia Eagle. He skimmed the statements, mumbling to himself. When he came to Johnny's statement, he looked up.

"Hey, I know Johnny Eagle. Last summer, we pulled lumber together on the green chain."

"Well, I hope you parted on good terms," was the girl Friday's terse reply.

He finished looking over the file as the car pulled up in front of the courthouse.

"Why didn't Mr. Hewitt ask me to apply for an adjournment? That's something I could do."

"The parents want their baby back today. They're leaving town tomorrow."

"Then he should have got another lawyer to handle the case."

"They're all busy," she said, as she drove into the parking lot. "There they are. We don't have a minute to lose."

Carter had a close look at his clients. He was the same Johnny who had pulled lumber off the green chain with him for four months last summer. He hadn't met his wife before, who was noticeably pregnant and appeared very agitated.

Mary opened the car door and waved frantically.

"Johnny, Celia," she shouted, "come over here and meet your lawyer."

"Hell, Carter," Johnny said, "I knew you was going to be a lawyer, but I figured you'd be in the big city. This here's my wife, Celia."

"Hello, Celia. Johnny, Celia, look, we haven't got much time. Do you want to go ahead with me as your lawyer?"

"If you're good enough for Mr. Hewitt, then you'll do," Celia said. "I want my baby back. The government's not her mother, I am."

"Why did you leave her outside the beer parlour?" Carter asked.

"Everyone knows she's my baby; no one's going to take her. The police stole her."

"Are you working now?" Carter asked Johnny.

"Nah, I got laid off a while ago. I'm on unemployment insurance."

"Can you look after the baby, Celia?"

"Of course. I'm eighteen years old." She then added in validation, "And I'm expecting another child."

"We've got to go," Mary said. "It wouldn't be a good idea to be late."

She steered them into the building.

Judge Morrison was entering the courtroom as the four of them came through the main doors into the public seating area. The judge appeared to Carter as the height of judicial stern-ness—not the provincial court judge, who raised pheasants as a hobby and looked condescendingly on law students.

The judge ran up the few stairs to the raised bench and perched on his chair as if he was going to conduct the case for both prosecution and defence. That and his pencil-thin moustache gave the impression that he would not tolerate any sloppiness on counsel's part.

The clerk called the court to order. A number of lawyers were seeking various orders and the judge dealt with them quickly. He had read their material and counsel had only to introduce themselves before he announced "Take your order."

The one exception was a young lawyer whom he put through his paces. He was seeking a similar order to that which the judge had given to an older lawyer in the preceding application.

"No, no, Mr. Rumple, that won't do. You'll have to come back tomorrow with a further affidavit in support."

Carter leaned over to Mary.

"Why not give him the order?" he whispered.

"This is the second time Rumple has made the same application and the second time the judge has turned him down," she whispered back. "Judge Morrison is from the old school. He is training Rumple to be more precise and professional."

Rumple dejectedly gathered his papers and walked slowly from the room. This left only Carter and his clients sitting in the public section and a woman lawyer at the counsel table whom Carter assumed was acting for Child Welfare.

"The Child Welfare and Eagle," called the clerk.

"Jane Bell for Child Welfare, your honour. I don't see Stan Hewitt, counsel for the Eagles in the courtroom."

Carter rose hesitantly to his feet.

"Your honour, my name is Carter Gordon. I am appearing on behalf of Stan Hewitt, who is not well. I graduated from UBC Law School this May, and Mr. Hewitt has expressed an interest in hiring me as his articling student."

"Would you mind coming forward to the counsel table, Mr. Gordon?"

The judge's request had the honeyed tone that a fox would use to a gopher. Carter did as he was told.

"There, I can see and hear you so much better now," Judge Morrison said sweetly. Then, suddenly in a severe tone, he warned, "If you intend to be a lawyer, sir, the first thing you must remember is to be seen and the second is to be heard. What are your instructions, Mr. Gordon?"

"My instructions, your honour, are to proceed with the trial with myself as counsel for the Eagles."

"What do you have to say about that?"

The judge looked at Ms. Bell, who was watching with an air of amused detachment.

"Your honour, my instructions are to proceed today. The witnesses are here and the case should be over by lunch."

"Mr. Gordon, are you prepared to conduct this case? If I allow it, you may only act pro bono. You are not a lawyer, and you cannot charge a fee."

Carter swallowed hard. The Eagles, Stan Hewitt and his girl Friday had expressed faith in his taking on the case.

"Yes, your honour."

"All right, I will allow it. You couldn't be any worse than some of the lawyers in this county."

Jane Bell called her first witness, Constable Albert Smith, who intoned in a monotone voice while glancing at his notebook.

"At seventeen-hundred hours, I was dispatched to Victoria and Third, to the Cariboo Arms Hotel and Beer Parlour. I arrived in my cruiser and detected a shopping cart on the sidewalk outside the door of said beer parlour. The cart was from the local grocery store with four wheels and . . ."

"Please, constable," the judge sighed, "direct your mind and memory to the contents of the shopping cart and not the number of wheels it had. I can take judicial notice of that. For all I know, it contained nothing but diapers and potatoes."

"Yes, your honour," the young constable blushed. "A baby girl and groceries occupied the cart. I would guess her age to be about nine months. I apprehended the baby by picking her up and placing her in the arms of Ms. Stark, a social worker who had just arrived on the scene. As I did this, a woman emerged from the beer parlour and screamed . . ."

He glanced down at his notes.

"'What the fuck are you doing with my baby?' The woman then ran to the social worker and, had I not restrained her, she would have taken the baby from Ms. Stark. I informed the woman—who I now recognize as Celia Eagle, who is seated behind defence counsel—that the social worker was taking the baby into care. There was a lot of yelling and a man came out of the beer parlour. He stumbled and there was beer on his breath. I see that man, John Eagle, seated beside his wife. I repeated to him that the baby was being taken into custody by the social worker, and that the baby would be well-cared for. Ms. Stark then drove away in her car with the baby while I restrained the parents."

"Thank you, constable."

Ms. Bell sat down.

"Now, Mr. Gordon," the judge looked down from his perch, "this is where you get to ask questions of the police officer. We call it 'cross-examination'."

As a goalie, Carter had learned to turn aside slapshots, so he ignored the sarcasm and started his first cross-examination, not knowing where it would lead.

"Constable, who contacted the detachment about Jewel Eagle?"

"The call came from Miss Ella Mae, who owns the shop next to the hotel."

"What did she say?"

"Mr. Gordon," the judge interrupted, "that is hearsay, but I will allow it. Ms. Bell can call Ms. Mae if necessary."

The constable looked at his notes again.

"She said, 'I saw a Native woman leave a baby on the sidewalk and go into the beer parlour.'"

Carter looked at his notes.

"So you contacted social services, asked them to send a social worker to that address and drove to the site in about five minutes?"

"Yes, your honour," the constable replied addressing the court as he had been trained, rather than Carter.

"That's all my questions. Oh, just a minute, constable. Was the baby crying when you first saw her?"

"No, your honour, she started to cry when I picked her up."

Mary was now busily scribbling notes in the back of the room. *This guy is not doing too badly,* she thought. She moved from the public area to the counsel table and whispered to Carter. He nodded and looked up at the constable.

"Did the baby look well-nourished?"

"Your honour, the baby was plump."

"Thank you, constable. You're excused," Carter concluded.

The constable got up and took a seat in the courtroom.

"Your honour," Carter addressed the judge, "may my assistant sit at the counsel table?"

"I believe your assistant has a name, Mr. Gordon. Shall we call her Mary Kent? And, yes, she may sit at the counsel table. I think that she will be an asset to you."

Carter's whole attention had been focussed on the trial, his only chance to impress his principal. He previously hadn't caught the name of Hewitt's assistant. He turned and watched Mary approach the counsel table. He recognized the name the instant he heard it—she was Cam's last-summer romance. He also recognized that she was smart and the judge knew her. He hung his head to compose himself until she sat at the table.

"Thank you, Mary," he whispered in a flustered voice. "I need all the help I can get."

Ms. Bell called the social worker to the stand to confirm the constable's testimony about apprehending Jewel. Ms. Stark, clearly more familiar with the process than Carter, went on to say after questioning that the baby was in a foster home in the city and was adjusted and well-cared for.

In cross-examination, Carter started with the home.

"How many children are in the foster home?"

"There are five."

"What are their ages?"

"They range in age from nine months to six years. But this is temporary. We will be finding a permanent foster home for Jewel."

"When you picked up the baby, was she well-nourished?"

"Yes."

Mary shoved a scribbled note in front of Carter. He read it and asked.

"Ms. Stark was the baby clean and did she appear well-cared for?"

"Well, she had soiled her diapers."

"Apart from that, how was the baby?"

"Yes, she appeared to be well-cared for," Ms. Stark reluctantly replied.

"Those are all my questions."

Ms. Bell rose to her feet.

"That is the case for Child Welfare, your honour."

"So Mr. Gordon, are you presenting any evidence, calling any witnesses? I suggest you do."

"Yes, your honour. I call Celia Eagle."

Celia stood at the witness stand and was sworn to tell the truth. She gave her testimony in a halting manner with her eyes downcast. Surrounded by the formality and the trappings of the courtroom, she seemed to have lost her feistiness. Carter hoped she would find it again before he finished her examination.

"Now, Celia, you and your husband had come to town from your home on the Redstone Reserve to attend the stampede and to shop?"

"Yeah."

"You may lead this witness, Mr. Gordon," the judge volunteered, wishing to shorten the process.

"Johnny went to the lumberyard, and you took Jewel with you while you shopped, and you and your husband arranged to meet at the Cariboo Arms Hotel?"

"Yeah."

"Now, you went to the hotel at about three p.m. to meet Johnny. Tell the judge in your own words what happened."

"Jewel was sleeping in the grocery cart."

"Where were the groceries?"

"The groceries were in the cart too. I went inside the beer parlour to get Johnny."

"Why didn't you bring the baby with you?"

"I don't bring Jewel into a beer parlour."

"How was Jewel when you left her?"

"Jewel was fine. She was asleep."

"How long were you in the beer parlour?"

"'Bout ten minutes."

"Why so long?"

"Johnny was finishing his beer."

"Did you have any beer?"

"Yeah, I had a sip of Johnny's beer. I told Johnny to come, and I went outside."

"Then what happened?"

"I . . .," she raised her eyes and her voice. "I saw that RCMP man take my baby from the cart and hand her to a woman and I ran screaming at them to leave my Jewel, and give her back to me. But they wouldn't, and the woman drove away."

"Were you worried about leaving your baby outside the beer parlour?"

"No. Everyone knows my baby."

Then, out of the blue, a question came to Carter's mind, a question that broke the advocate's rule of knowing what the answer to a question would be before asking it.

"Did you see anyone on the street that you knew?"

"Yeah, Wheelchair."

"Who is Wheelchair?"

"Gilbert Sorrel. He gets about in a wheelchair. That's what he's called."

"Where was Gilbert?"

"He was across the street in his chair. He saw me leave the baby. I waved at him."

"Those are my questions, your honour."

Ms. Bell began her cross-examination.

"You were in the beer parlour more than ten minutes."

"Maybe."

"You were in there at least a half-hour."

"Don't think so."

"You had a couple of beers, didn't you?"

"I had a sip."

"Your baby could have been stolen while you were in the beer parlour."

"No."

"How do you know that? You weren't there. You left her alone on a public street."

"'Cause Gilbert was there."

"You mean Gilbert Sorrel, who was run over by a truck and whose brains are all shook up?"

"Yeah."

Ms. Bell sat down with a satisfied look on her face. Celia's face was a study of smouldering anger.

Carter called Johnny Eagle.

"You had a beer at the Cariboo Hotel beer parlour?"

Johnny thought a bit before answering.

"Yeah, I had two."

"How long were you there?"

Again, Johnny turned this over slowly in his mind before answering.

Carter watched as Johnny again weighed his answer. He knew that this would continue, that Johnny would ponder each answer, unaware of how the court would read his silences.

"'Bout an hour."

"Did you see Celia?"

Carter waited, aware the judge's eyes were on him during the pause.

"Yeah, she come and got me. I was just finishing my second beer and Len Crooks was telling a story. She had a sip and she left."

"Did she say anything to you?"

"Yeah, she said we had to go."

No pause. Carter tried to pick up the pace.

"What happened next?"

"I hear a ruckus outside. Celia is screaming."

"What did you do?"

"I ran outside and a lady has Jewel and a cop is holding Celia."

"Thank you, Mr. Eagle. Ms. Bell will have questions now."

Ms. Bell rose from her chair with the assurance of a hunter in a blind looking at a sky full of low-flying geese.

"Come now, Mr. Eagle, you had more than two beers, didn't you?"

"Were you there?"

"I ask the questions, sir. You had three or four beers and you were drunk."

"No," Johnny barked out his answer.

"You stumbled out of the beer parlour."

"I tripped, coming out of the dark into the light."

"Celia was in the beer parlour for a half-hour?"

"Don't think it was that long."

"She drank several beers, didn't she?"

"Like I say, she had a sip."

Ms. Bell sat down, satisfied.

"Is that your case, Mr. Gordon?"

Mary whispered to him. Carter stood and pulled his jacket straight.

"May I ask for an adjournment over the lunch hour to get instructions, your honour?"

The judge leaned over his bench.

"I don't find your witnesses to be too convincing. I look forward to this afternoon."

He rose and left the courtroom.

Jane Bell walked over and shook Carter's hand while Mary escorted the Eagles outside.

"I hope this experience won't sour you on the law. Judge Morrison is on loan from Vancouver until we get a new Provincial Court judge appointment and, as you can see, he's a hands-on adjudicator. He seldom changes his mind, and he doesn't believe your clients."

Outside the courtroom, Carter huddled with Mary and his clients to discuss their next move.

"When do I pick up my baby?" Celia asked.

"We won't know that until after lunch," Carter replied. "Right now, we need to find Gilbert."

He looked at Mary, who was shaking her head as if to say perhaps that wasn't a good idea.

The four of them got into Mary's car and trolled the streets of Williams Lake. In an alley behind the community centre, they spotted Gilbert sitting in his wheelchair with a group of young people around him.

"Hiya, Celia," he called out, waving.

"Hi, Gilbert, these are friends of mine. They want to ask you about Jewel."

"I like that name—Jewel."

"Gilbert, when did you last see Jewel?" Carter asked.

"In town a while ago."

"Do you remember seeing the police take her from a grocery cart in front of the Cariboo Arms Hotel?"

"Yeah, Celia was mad."

"Can we buy you lunch?"

"Sure."

* * *

Approaching noon at the cabin, Lars slowly got up from the table to leave. Johanna went with him to his truck to see him off. He sat in the driver's seat with the window down.

"How will you keep yourself busy out here on your own?" he asked.

"I've got a lot of reading and thinking to do."

"What are you reading?"

"*The Diviners*. Margaret Laurence," she said, distracted. "Oh, and thank you, Lars. That was very kind of you to drive me out here."

"You know I would do anything for you, Johanna."

She laughed at that and waved goodbye. He drove off.

As the sound of the truck faded away, she removed her shoes and danced on the lawn, singing out loud from the score of *The Sound of Music*. The mallards feeding in the shallows honked and flapped away. Exhausted, she flung herself on to the grass and turned to the sky.

"Free at last, free at last," she shouted. "Thank the Lord almighty, I'm free at last."

On his way to the mill that afternoon, Lars stopped by the library and signed out one of its two copies of *The Diviners*. The blurb on the cover read, "*In 'The Diviners', as in all her works, everyday incidents lead to the emotions that shape life.*"

12

They were back in the courtroom before two p.m. Carter took Ms. Bell aside.

"I'm calling Gilbert," he whispered.

"You're kidding. He's the town simpleton."

They all rose when Judge Morrison entered the room.

"Your honour," Carter said. "I'm calling another witness. Mr. Gilbert Sorrel."

Gilbert manoeuvred his chair to the front of the courtroom, his head bobbing and his eyes rolling.

"Do you swear to tell the truth the whole truth and nothing but the truth, so help you God?" the clerk asked, administering the oath.

"Do you swear to tell the truth, so help you God?" Gilbert slowly repeated.

"Mr. Sorrel," the judge intervened, "that was a question the clerk put to you. Do you understand the question?"

"Yeah."

"What's your answer?"

"Okay."

The door at the back of the courtroom opened. An old gentleman with long white hair entered and sat with the Eagles. He was dressed in a black suit, vest and string tie.

The judge acknowledged his presence with a nod, then turned to Carter.

"All right, counsel, you may proceed with this witness."

"Mr. Sorrel, you know Celia Eagle?"

"Yeah, she's pretty."

"Did you see her in town a few weeks ago with her baby, Jewel?"

"Yeah, pretty baby."

"You must not lead here, Mr. Gordon."

"Where did you see Celia and the baby?"

"I seen her by Cariboo Arms."

"What did you see?"

"I seen pretty baby in grocery cart."

"Where was Celia?"

"She go into beer parlour."

"What did you do then?"

"I crossed street to see baby when police car come. Policeman take pretty baby."

"Did you see Celia again?"

"Yeah, she comes outta beer parlour shouting."

Carter sat down, not wanting to chance another question. Ms. Bell began her cross-examination.

"Do you remember the weather that day?"

Gilbert scratched his head.

"Was it sunny?"

"Can you describe the baby?"

"Pretty." He paused. "Small."

"How much did you have to drink that day?"

"I don't drink anymore."

She sat down with a shrug.

"I take it that is your case, Mr. Gordon? I will hear argument now, counsel."

Carter was arranging his papers, thinking about how he

could win the argument. Then, it occurred to him that there was an outline of the law and an argument in the brief that Mary had handed him. He pulled it out.

The judge seemed impatient.

"Since Mr. Hewitt has joined us," he said, "perhaps he would like to argue the case."

Carter turned and stared at the old man. This was his future principal—assuming that Hewitt was prepared to sign his articles, which he might not do if his clients didn't get their baby back.

"No, your honour," Hewitt's baritone boomed from the back of the courtroom. "My student is up to the task."

Hewitt's stature had diminished with age, but not his voice. The endorsement by Hewitt only made Carter more nervous.

"I . . ." he composed himself, "have an outline of the law for the court and a copy for my friend."

"Ms. Bell is not your friend yet, Mr. Gordon. If you are called to the bar, then she will be your *learned* friend."

"Thank you, your honour. If your honour accepts the evidence that baby Jewel was healthy and well-cared for, which is undisputed, the only issue is whether she was neglected for that brief span of time. The explanation by the Eagles is reasonable. Celia Eagle left the sleeping infant to fetch her husband. She knew that Gilbert Sorrel was keeping an eye on the baby. I submit that Child Welfare has not shown neglect on the part of the Eagles."

"Thank you, Mr. Gordon. If all counsel were as succinct in their arguments, justice would not be as delayed."

Ms. Bell stood up and ruffled some papers.

"Perhaps you need not hear from me, your honour."

"Not on the law, Ms. Bell, but what have you to say on credibility?"

"Time by the clock means nothing to the Eagles. They both could have been drinking for more than an hour."

"Yes, but what about Mr. Sorrel. It seems he knew the Eagles and baby Jewel, and he was in the area. And you could have asked Mr. Sorrel for his time estimate."

"That's correct, your honour. But to leave the baby in the care of someone who has difficulty looking after himself would be equally negligent. And I can't say anything kind about any estimate he could make about time."

"Thank you for your assistance, counsel. Would you please stand, Mr. and Mrs. Eagle?"

They both rose unsteadily to their feet not knowing what to expect.

"I find that Child Welfare has not proven beyond a reasonable doubt that you abandoned your baby. I must warn you, though, that if you continue on this path, you are at risk of having your child apprehended in the future."

Judge Morrison stood and left the courtroom, leaving the clerk scrambling to shout "Order in court!" above the wails of Celia Eagle and the curses of Johnny, who had not realized that they were getting Jewel back. In their eyes, they had done nothing wrong, yet their baby was taken from them, and a man sitting above them on a bench had muttered some words which they didn't understand, then left in a hurry. What were they to think?

Stan Hewitt stood, with the aid of his walker, beside Celia and comforted her.

"It's all right, Celia. The judge said that Child Welfare made a mistake. You will get Jewel back."

Celia broke down and cried on Johnny's shoulder.

"Thank God, thank God," she wailed. "Thank you, Mr. Hewitt!"

Outside the courtroom, Stan gathered his legal team and his clients in a side room.

"Mr. Hewitt says we will get Jewel back," Celia said with a big smile.

"Yes. I did say that. And it's true."

"When?"

"Today."

Johnny and Celia both hugged Carter and Mary. They shook Stan's hand.

Carter shook the hand of the old lawyer, now well into his eighties, who walked with a bit of a stoop. His past was etched into his creased and weathered face.

"You're probably wondering why I allowed you to take this case fresh from your studies," Stan said to Carter, seemingly oblivious to Mary or the Eagles. "One of your professors, Tony Sheppard, is a friend of mine. He highly recommended you on the basis of your tenacious personality, and decent marks in the law of evidence. I think he was right. You're hired."

Stan suggested Mary accompany the Eagles to the registry. He and Carter said their goodbyes.

On the way to the office, Stan noticed Carter appeared to be in shock from the experience.

"I am pleased with the decision," Stan offered. "I had Mary prepare a Notice of Appeal in case it went the other way. Judge Morrison was a brilliant litigation lawyer and learned in the law, but his judging experience is limited to Vancouver. One has to live in the Cariboo-Chilcotin to understand the basic truthfulness of the Chilcotin people. By the way, Gilbert Sorrel's statement wasn't in the brief."

"I thought he should be called to support the Eagles' evidence," Carter stuttered.

"You took a chance. Who knows what he would have said on the stand? But you seem to have something that is essential in a barrister."

"What's that, sir?"

"Knowing the weakness in your own case," he smiled at his student. "That's the end of your first lesson."

Mary caught up with them as Stan was shuffling along with his walker. She slowed down to match Stan's pace. Feeling giddy from the events of the day and thankful for Mary's support, Carter smiled at her.

"I don't know what I would have done without your help," he offered. "Stan is fortunate to have a secretary with your skill." Seeing no response, he raised his voice. "You know, you should consider going into law."

Expecting a warm response for his generous praise, Carter was surprised when Stan stopped shuffling. The two young people halted beside him. Stan shook his head at Carter, then turned to nod at Mary.

"Do you know who prepared that brief?"

"You did, sir."

"Call me Stan, and no—it was Mary. She's completed her first-year law with honours at the University of Victoria Law School. She's a summer student in my office."

"Yeah," she said, "so from now on, don't be so fucking condescending."

13

On her second day at the cabin, Johanna settled into a routine of reading, thinking and writing. She was looking forward to seeing Mary, yet she was feeling apprehensive about what she was going to tell her daughter, never mind *how* she was going to tell it.

In *The Diviners*, Morag and her daughter Pique had a tempestuous relationship. Morag, like Laurence, was a writer who followed her muse above all other worldly considerations, including her marriage. As she read deeper into the novel, Johanna couldn't help but see parallels between Morag and Pique and her relationship with her own daughter. She began to wonder if her study of Laurence had given a subconscious push to tell Mary the truth. Johanna believed that Mary, like Pique, could live with the truth. On Thursday evening, with Mary coming for lunch on Friday, Johanna's mind still was not settled about whether she should tell her secret to her daughter. She kept asking herself, *How will Mary react?*

Flipping through the pages of the novel to find her place, Johanna noted with some pride that the pages were thick with her annotations on the margins. Her dissertation on the great Canadian writer was taking shape on the pages of the book itself.

Johanna didn't sleep well on Thursday night. Doubts continued to cloud the clear skies of her reason. She rose before the sun and rowed out into the middle of the misty lake. It was her last chance to reflect on the decision that would change her life, and the lives of those around her. Then the sun rose, piercing the mists and her misgivings alike.

Mary arrived in a flourish of youthful exuberance, excitedly talking about her week and drawing Johanna out of her deep introspection.

"You know, Mum, I am so glad that I decided to go into law. I can make a difference in people's lives. Stan is showing me how to be effective in cross-examination."

"Was your father in the office?"

"No, he had a trial in Prince George."

While they were chatting, they prepared lunch.

When lunch was ready, mother and daughter sat at a table on the porch under the shade of an umbrella, eating green salad and radishes with thinly-sliced rye bread and cold cuts.

"I met Stan's new student last Tuesday," Mary said. "His name is Carter Gordon, and Stan had him take a Child Welfare case right off the plane. He actually won custody for the Eagles on a brief that I had prepared. I was impressed by him until he told me that I should go into law—how arrogant."

"How did you react to that dear?"

"I told him to fuck off."

"It seems you like him," Johanna smiled.

"He's cute, but it seems he likes blondes. He saw Robin at the airport and was asking about her." After half a second of silence, she added, "It's good to have some time with you, Mum, but you haven't brought me out here just to hear me talk about Carter Gordon."

"Yes, dear. I want to speak to you about something that affects us all, you and me and Dad."

"I know you and Dad are not getting along. The silences at the dinner table are telling. And then you're so polite to each other." She bit her lip. "Are you going to leave him?"

"We haven't been talking much. Instead of slowing down at work, he tells me he's applied for an appointment to the bench. But it's more than that. It's a secret that I've lived with for a long time. It's important that you know it and I can't keep it to myself any longer."

"Are you ill, Mum?"

"No, dear." As an aside, she said, "I am making a mess of this." She took a deep breath and the words tumbled out. "The truth is that Malcolm is not your birth father."

Mary stood in a rush, threw up her hands and looked down at her mother as if she had lost her senses.

"What do you mean?"

"I mean, dear, that I had sex with a man other than your father and that you were conceived in that adulterous relationship."

"Who's my father, then?"

"Noah Hanlon," Johanna said timidly.

"Oh my God!" Mary sank into her chair. "I think of him as my uncle."

She held her head with both hands and slumped forward, trying to compose herself. After a while, without raising her head, she let out a low whisper.

"Does Dad know?"

Johanna had prepared herself for an emotional outburst and replied in soft tones to forestall it.

"If you agree, I'll tell him when I get home."

"What about Noah?"

"He doesn't know either. I had intended to tell him on Sunday."

Mary raised her head, disbelief written on her face.

"How is this possible?" she shouted. "That you kept this secret from the two men closest to you? And *why* did you keep it a secret?"

Johanna answered her daughter's anger with as calm an expression as she could muster.

"I learned after we were married that your father didn't want children. Your conception was an act of passion in a hotel room in Vancouver. It was the night of Noah's first successful art show. It was the one and only time. I didn't tell your father, and I don't believe Noah told Justine, because she carried on our friendship as always."

"Dad's not stupid. Surely he didn't believe it was immaculate conception?"

"Your. . . *Malcolm* was in Victoria at the time. Within the week, I joined him. A few weeks later, I discovered I was pregnant. I never thought of an abortion. I believed at the time—perhaps wrongly—that Malcolm would never accept you if he knew that you were not his child, and I so desperately wanted you . . . So I told him that I had made a mistake with my birth control, which was true, and that I was pregnant. He assumed that he was your father. When you were born, you looked so like me that there was no question of your parentage."

"What about Noah? Didn't he put two and two together?"

"We didn't see the Hanlons until we returned to Williams Lake a few years later. By that time, you were four and Noah and Justine were completely caught up with their children."

Mary was listening to her mother with one ear while look-ing at the lake and turning over in her mind a whole new sense of her own identity. She had overcome her teenage angst and had grown comfortable with herself in her early twenties. She had discovered she had a brain and could use it. She had a father who was distant, but was there for her, and a mother whom she adored. The Hanlons were good friends. With her mother's revelation, Mary's ordered world changed.

She stood and walked toward the lake without a word. She got into the rowboat, adjusted the oars, and took a few strokes before turning to her mother.

"You are nothing but a goddamn slut."

Johanna hadn't prepared herself her daughter's verbal attack. She watched her row across the lake to the far shore and disappear into the woods, her daughter's remark echoing in her head.

Mary didn't return 'til dusk. She walked calmly into the cabin and sat at the kitchen table in silence. Johanna sat down opposite her.

"I was worried about you, dear."

"I'm feeling better now," Mary replied, as if in a trance. "I walked down to the river. I watched it rush by me. I thought of Ta Chi, who is my grandmother. Noah often speaks of her. Her blood is my blood. My ancestors have stood on that very spot for centuries watching the river, the artery of the Chilcotin, flow by on the way to the sea. And the salmon that have sustained us from time immemorial swim back from the sea. What am I but a speck in the Chilcotin, the world, the universe? It calmed me."

"Darling, I know how upsetting this is," Johanna said in her most comforting voice. "I've been trying to find the courage to tell you who your father was for a long time. Then I re-read *The Diviners*. It gave me a new perspective on my life."

"I think Dad will take this hard. He's a proud man. You'll have to tell him."

"I will, dear, when I go home. You must be famished. Come. I've made some dinner."

They talked late into the night about the past, the recollection of which was now coloured by Johanna's revelation.

"I have lived with my mistake," Johanna told Mary. "Not the adultery—because you were born to me, I could never see that as a mistake. My mistake was not telling the ones I love—Malcolm, Noah and you—long ago. I can only find peace in your forgiveness."

Mary took her mother's hand and smiled.

"You know I love you, Mum."

Mary stayed overnight.

At breakfast, neither mother nor daughter seemed ready to continue the previous night's conversation, but Johanna had other news.

"I've been accepted by the head of the English Department at the University of British Columbia to read for my doctorate. I intend to write on Margaret Laurence. Another reason I've been re-reading *The Diviners*."

She showed her daughter the paperback copy she'd been reading. Mary took the book, opened it and saw her mother's annotations.

"I'd like to read it. Your comments on books have meant a lot to me."

"There is a hardcover edition in my library at home that you can have. After you've read that, we'll talk about it. Did you know that Laurence lived for a few years on 21st Ave. in Dunbar, near where I grew up in Vancouver?"

"I guess you haven't told Dad about you moving to Vancouver."

Her mother couldn't shock Mary any more than she already had.

"No, I haven't. I don't know how your dad will take all of this, but he's fully occupied with the law. I'm sure he'll cope. Since we'll both be at university, I was thinking that you could take your next two years of law at UBC and we could rent a place together in Dunbar."

"Mum, I'm still reeling from learning that Noah's my father. I need time to sort out my own life."

Later, on the porch, she hugged her mother.

"I'm sorry I said those things to you yesterday. It was selfish of me. I guess I had to know sometime."

Johanna kept her arms around her daughter.

"Will you be all right?"

"Yes, Mother. I forgive you, Mum. I'm sure the others will too."

"Thank you, dear. That means a lot to me."

"But I'm worried about you."

"I'll be fine."

Johanna watched Mary walk to her 1960's shamrock-green Volkswagen Beetle and wave as she drove off.

14

It wasn't a coincidence that Larson's troublesome neighbour on the other side of the ridge was building a house in the Chilcotin. It is a part of the human condition that an industrious man who is endowed with intellect and cunning, and who has little interest in morals and customs can, with application, rise quickly to the top of the business world. Once there, he is able to turn his attention from amassing a fortune to acts of philanthropy, or to fulfilling his personal fantasies. Vladimir Volk had no interest in philanthropy. His fantasy was Johanna.

Vlad did nothing by half-measures. His plan was to buy up the ranches on the benches of the Chilcotin River and create one the size of Douglas Lake Ranch, one of the largest ranches in North America. With the timber rights and the mineral rights, it was a good investment. He had bought his first property, Whiskey Glass Ranch, in the fall, soon after he met Johanna at the reunion. The sellers were a pioneer family, who agreed to stay on and manage the ranch for a year, but they didn't last 'til Christmas under Vlad's tight rein.

He had the cement foundations for his new house poured before the winter freeze. He had arranged for the log work to be done by Paul Laboucher, who was recommended by

Larson. Laboucher began work in the spring and by July, the walls were starting to rise.

In Larson's cabin, Johanna was dealing with her secret having been released. It took all Saturday for her to catch her emotional breath after confiding in her daughter. She had invited Noah for tea on Sunday on the pretext of finishing the portrait on which Noah was working. She knew Noah and Justine well enough to know that their marriage could survive her uncomfortable truth.

On Sunday, mid-morning, she had finished working on *The Diviners* and was mentally preparing herself for her meeting with Noah when she heard a crunch of tires on the gravel outside the cabin. She went to the window and watched Vlad step jauntily out of a red Jaguar. He was dressed in grey flannels, a John Brocklehurst English tweed jacket and a pink shirt with an ascot. Her hand touched her throat and the frog pendant. She hadn't included him in her plans for her stay at the lake. He had been discreetly pursuing her since their brush with romance in Vancouver last fall, and she had met him in Williams Lake during his business visits, where they had lunch. He had talked about buying property in the Chilcotin and building a cabin. He wouldn't say where. He wanted to surprise her. She was attracted to Vlad to the point of wearing his gift but, since their class reunion, she had so much on her mind in realizing her own life and career that she had no time to consider her relations with him.

Vlad brought lunch—two half-bottles of Mumm's champagne from his cellar, a salad, some cold meats and cheeses and a gateau for dessert. How could she refuse to see him when he was bearing gifts? She didn't.

Johanna appeared to Vlad to be in an unsettled mood, much different from the few times he had stolen a moment of her time in Williams Lake. In his experience with women, indecision meant an opportunity for him to take advantage of the situation. He poured the champagne into tall fluted glasses and brought them to where she was sitting on the divan.

"To the most beautiful woman in the world. And to us."

She laughed.

"Charlie, there is no *us.*"

"But there could be, my dear. There *should* be. Malcolm is a very nice man, a great lawyer, but he ignores you, and you deserve so much more."

"Yes. I deserve lunch."

"Your slave does your bidding."

He got up and prepared the food he had brought.

"What have you been doing since I saw you last?" he asked while mixing the salad.

"Oh, this and that," she replied, cautiously non-committal. Then her passion for Margaret Laurence overcame her reserve. "And I've decided to study Margaret Laurence at UBC."

She talked on and on about Margaret Laurence over lunch and he made a mental note to buy and read *The Stone Angel.*

It was getting on to two-thirty when Johanna's demeanour suddenly changed.

"It's time for you to go, Charlie," she announced. "I'm expecting company in an hour, and I want a nap before then."

"There's another half-bottle of champagne waiting to be drunk."

"Put it in the fridge. It'll keep. I'll think of you when I have a glass."

She rose from her chair. They were close and he took her in his arms and kissed her. She held her arms close to her chest and accepted the kiss tight-lipped, as she would the kiss of a cousin.

"We have an hour before your guests come," he whispered in her ear, "and I would like a nap too."

She broke away from him.

"Johanna, I'm in love with you."

Johanna unclasped the pendant from around her neck and rubbed it between her fingers.

"Charlie, I have to find my own way without you."

She handed him the pendant. He took the pendant from her and placed it on the kitchen table.

"Please, Johanna, keep it as a talisman. I'll be there for you in Vancouver and I'll be here when you return home from your studies."

"You must go now," she ordered.

He didn't argue.

"If you need me, I'm next door over the ridge, building my little surprise for you."

I've had enough surprises already for today, she thought to herself as he drove away, *and the day isn't finished yet.*

She went to the kitchen to make tea for her encounter with Noah. As he hadn't yet arrived, it occurred to her to bake some scones. A half-hour later, he showed up. She had the scones in the oven and couldn't leave them just yet. He walked across the lawn to look at the pond and set up an easel to work on Johanna's portrait. He stood with his back to the cabin, one hand waving in the air as if he was conducting an orchestra, but Johanna knew that he wasn't waving a baton; he was sketching the scene in front of him in his mind. He walked towards the cabin as Johanna took her baking from the oven.

Today, Noah was planning on finishing the sittings, sketching the pond and ridge in the background and doing some touch-ups.

"Hi," he smiled. "Those scones smell good."

"They're not just for smelling. You can have one after we finish the sitting."

He noticed Johanna's frog pendant lying on the kitchen table, shimmering in the sun where Vlad had left it. He picked it up.

"I've liked this jade frog piece. Would you put it on so I can include it in the painting?"

"If you think it is right for the portrait."

"If you don't like it, I can paint it out."

"All right," she said.

She took the pendant from him and fastened the clasp behind her neck.

"Go set up," she urged. "I'll bring scones."

After a half-hour of concentration and work, Noah stepped back from the painting.

"Come and have a look."

He started putting away his paints and cleaning his brushes.

"It's very flattering, Noah. I look about twenty years younger."

"Do you like the pendant?" he asked.

"Yes, I do," she said, touching the pendant around her neck and looking over at the painting.

"You look more rested than I've seen you in a while."

"It's the patience of the Chilcotin. When I talk, it listens. Let's have tea."

She went inside to boil the water. She came out with the tea and the scones and poured him a cup with milk and sugar and one for herself without.

"Noah," she began, "I asked you out here so I could make a confession under the open skies of our land."

"I'm an artist-shaman, Johanna, not a priest."

"You and Justine are my best friends."

"I know."

"I want to talk with you about that night more than twenty years ago when you and I and Stan went to Vancouver to exhibit and sell your paintings at the Stein Gallery."

Noah kept his eyes on the horizon. He was sure he knew what Johanna was going to say before she said it. He thought of Justine and how she would take it if Johanna now meant to tell her.

"I haven't mentioned it to anyone until this week when I told Mary. I don't think you ever told Justine for which I am grateful."

"Was it necessary to tell Mary?" he asked.

"Yes, Noah, it was," she sighed, "because, you see, you are her biological father."

Noah took a deep breath and exhaled quickly. He felt as if he had been punched in the stomach and the wind knocked out of him. He took another breath and exhaled slowly.

"Are you sure?"

"Yes, I'm sure. Malcolm hadn't planned on having children. I hadn't taken precautions on that night when liquor and your artistic success overwhelmed us."

"How did Mary take the news?"

"Mary was naturally angry and upset and she stormed off. She was gone for hours and when she came back, she was thinking about Malcolm and you."

"Does Malcolm know?"

"Not yet."

What will I tell Justine? was his first thought, and then gathering himself, he shook his head slightly and thought of the anguish that Johanna had gone through to bring herself to reveal her secret.

"I had so much guilt about that night," he confessed, "that I buried the whole evening in my subconscious. Bordy was a wild womanizer—I couldn't bear to think that I was just like him. I was afraid that Justine would leave me if I told her—just like Belle left Bordy. God, I hope this news won't ruin Mary's life."

Johanna spoke quickly as if she was explaining her actions to herself.

"I had to tell Mary. What if Mary had found out for herself? She would never have forgiven me for keeping it a secret. I felt I was living a lie. I owed my daughter the truth."

"I know. I'm not accusing you. You did the right thing. I didn't find out that Bordy was my birth father until after he died and, even now, I have difficulty coming to terms with it. I feel for Mary."

Noah rose to leave as if he was in a hurry to go, to leave this awkward moment. Standing, he looked at Johanna sitting, anxiously rubbing her hands together. He sat back down.

"I'm sorry," he offered. "I've been thinking about myself. This must have weighed on you for years. At times you must have cursed me. You must have had many hard days and nights wrestling with your decision to tell Mary."

"If it hadn't happened, Mary would not be here with us. Thank God she hasn't turned against me. I couldn't live with that."

"I understand. If Justine will forgive me, she may be willing to come and be with you."

"That's a kind thought, Noah, but why would she comfort the woman, her best friend, who she's just found had seduced her husband?"

Noah had no answer. He knew it was he who had done the seducing.

"No. I'm fine, Noah. Thanks for thinking about me."

He gathered his painting supplies and Johanna's unfinished portrait. He turned at the bottom of the stairs leading to the porch.

"You are my best friend," he said.

When he reached his truck, he turned to her. She had walked down to the dock and watched him from there.

"Wawant'x of the house of Raven," she shouted, "Frog continues to inspire me."

He last saw her through his rear-view mirror. She was sitting on the dock, holding a book and looking out at the lake. As he drove away, he thought about the influence of Frog on Johanna, which he had seen and believed, but an even greater influence on Johanna was Mary's future and he was now part of that future.

It was a long drive back to Tatlayoko Lake and Justine. Noah drove up to the house where Justine greeted him on the porch.

"How is Johanna? Did she like her portrait?"

"She's fine. She was pleased with her portrait."

They walked into the kitchen and he pulled a chair from the kitchen table and sat down, trying to appear calm. He spoke in a measured voice choosing his words carefully.

"That wasn't the only reason she asked to see me."

"Oh? What was the other reason?"

"Have a seat, dear. I'll tell you."

They sat down side-by-side, a middle-aged couple talking at their common table; the table around which lives were planned, dreams realized, and fears expressed— mundane talks that had confirmed the world and their place in it or talks that at times had changed their world or their perception of it. This was one of those times. Noah took Justine's hand in his.

"Do you remember my first showing in Vancouver? My coming home and you calling me a hero?"

"Of course."

"Well, I was a *false* hero. I had wanted to tell you that I had been unfaithful to you by sleeping with Johanna and I didn't."

As he spoke, he looked imploringly at Justine. She sat quietly listening for more without showing any emotion.

"I was twice wrong," he continued, "first in cheating on

you and secondly in not telling you about it."

Justine brought her hands together and lowered her head as if in prayer. After a while, she stood. She placed her hands on Noah's slumped shoulders.

"Yes, you were wrong," she said. "You hurt me, and you should have told me. But I am your wife. I knew at the time without you telling me that you had been unfaithful."

He turned and looked at her standing behind him.

"I am sorry, Justine. I thought by not telling, I would spare you. The truth is I didn't have the courage."

"In my heart, I have forgiven you and Johanna. I also knew you wouldn't do that again. And you didn't."

He stood and put his arms around his wife.

"You should be the *deyen*, not me."

Still holding her, he stepped back to look into her eyes, not having finished his story.

"That's not the end of it, though," he continued. "Johanna told me that I'm Mary's biological father."

Justine's intuition had clearly not embraced that knowledge. She bit her lower lip, her only outward sign of shock, before she spoke.

"I've thought of Mary as part of our family. We Chilcotins can always do with more children. We will just increase the size of the circle."

Noah had hurt Justine. He would have to show her that he was worthy of her forgiveness.

"I'm going to have to speak to Mary, and I would like you to be with me."

"I don't know if that's a good idea. But I'll speak to Johanna."

Noah slumped back into his chair. He was thinking about Old Antoine's faith in him as *deyen*. He had not only failed Justine, he had also failed Antoine.

15

On Wednesday, the day after their baby Jewel's custody hearing, the Eagles had left the Stampede Grounds where they had camped with all the Native participants who were now returning to their ranches and reserves on the plateau. They headed west on horseback to the Redstone Reserve. They figured it would take six days with visits with family at the Toosey and Stone reserves on the way. They were in no hurry. Jewel was strapped onto her mother's back, and they had a packhorse to carry the dry goods Celia had purchased and some building materials Johnny needed.

On the fifth night, a Sunday, they were conscious of not being able to return to Redstone for services at the church to give thanks to God for saving Jewel from the clutches of the Child Welfare. But they were tired and, at about two in the afternoon, decided to camp on a rise above the highway and the turnoff to Larson Road. There was a creek and some good pasture for the horses at a meadow below the rise.

There were a few vehicles going in and out of Larson Road. They didn't pay them much attention but either camping or moving slowly and deliberately across their land, as always, they took notice of all their surroundings: the wildlife, edible plants and the travellers on the road. The first vehicle was a red sports car heading out. Then a truck turned into the side road. Two hours later, Celia was pounding in some tent stakes when she called out to Johnny.

"Hey, isn't that Noah Hanlon's truck leaving Larson's?"

Johnny was playing with Jewel, but looked up.

"Yeah, that's him. I wonder what he's doing with Larson."

Then he saw a Cadillac drive into Larson Road. *Hmm, maybe's a party going on there,* he thought.

He began gathering sticks for a fire.

16

Johanna and Malcolm had grown more distant from each other in the last few months. So much so that Malcolm began to recognize it, which is not to say that he tried to narrow the gap. He had delayed sharing with Johanna his expectation of an appointment to the Supreme Court— what he had worked for his whole legal career and knew was deserved. He would be humiliated if he didn't get the appointment. There was some talk that a lawyer from Prince George, Brendan O'Brien, was the frontrunner on account of his connection with the sitting Member of Parliament. But Brendan, although a brilliant advocate, had a reputation for being a loud drunk, and if the choice was on merit and ability, then the appointment should be Malcolm's.

For the last month, Malcolm had sensed that there was something bothering Johanna. She had been preoccupied, yet he was too focussed on his appointment to bother to find out what was bothering her. On Sunday afternoon, he had a pleasant five-minute telephone call from the Minister of Justice telling him that the Cabinet had by order in council appointed him the resident judge of the Supreme Court of British Columbia at Williams Lake. He was told that he would be publically raised to the bench a week from Monday, but he would be sworn in and take up his duties on the coming Wednesday.

He decided to drive out to the Larson cabin and surprise Johanna with his news.

When he arrived at six, he drove slowly to the back of the cabin. Rounding the cabin on foot, he saw her on the dock reading under the shade of an umbrella. Without announcing his presence, he went into the kitchen and mixed her favourite drink, Pimm's Number 1 Cup and lemon soda on ice. Opening the refrigerator, he noticed a half-bottle of Mumm's champagne. There was another empty bottle on the sideboard. He wondered what Johanna was celebrating and made a mental note to ask her. He poured a splash of single malt scotch from a flask he carried for emergencies—and this was an emergency as Larson's liquor cabinet contained only blended scotch—into a glass with ice and carried the drinks down to the dock.

"Look who's here," she said, taking off her glasses and carefully placing the book she was reading on the dock.

"Hello. I brought you a pick-me-up."

"Your timing is good. I just finished reading *The Diviners*. I love the ending where Morag looks at the water—shallow, then deep—and returns to the house to write fictional words. Laurence's words are like chips of wood axed out of a Canadian forest—as honest and true as the call of the loon."

There was lilt to her voice as she spoke. Her face lit up with a smile as she lifted her head to greet her husband.

"I don't know the book," Malcolm replied coolly.

He gave Johanna her drink. He started to raise his glass in a toast to his appointment to the bench, his sole purpose for being there. He noticed that her brilliantly intense eyes were staring at him. He paused.

"Malcolm, I've made up my mind to go back to university this fall to study for my Doctorate in English at UBC."

There was a passion in her voice he couldn't remember having heard before. He didn't hide his disappointment. She took in his hesitation and his wry questioning look in his eye.

"You must have known," she raised her voice, "that my ambition to write on women's literature has been frustrated."

"I didn't realize you were serious."

"You've *never* taken me seriously." She knew that to be an exaggeration, but she was mad. "Now, you will have to!"

She broke off eye contact and looked out at the lake, ignoring him standing there awkwardly with a raised drink in his hand.

"What about Mary?" he asked, shocked.

"Ah, Mary," she sighed. "The more important question is what about you?"

He was unable to think of what to say. He felt ambushed. He had come to the lake to celebrate the realization of his dream of the bench and his future. He was met instead by Johanna's dream of her doctorate, and her flight to the city. What could he say? How could he answer? Should he offer to carry on and that they could see each other from time to time or should he avoid the question? He settled on his career.

"I came here to tell you that the Minister of Justice phoned me today. I have been appointed Supreme Court judge, sitting at Williams Lake."

"What wonderful news. I'm happy for you. You'll be able to retire to your den and ruminate on the law *all* the time instead of most of the time. For a moment, I thought you came to the lake to see me because you missed me."

This was not going well. She was the extrovert who enjoyed most people and the exchange of ideas. She looked after the social side of their partnership. He confined himself to his duties, which revolved around his clients and the law. He knew that they had muddled through their marriage for the last ten years and he realized they had come to the fork in the road. Perhaps this was his last chance to steer their lives in the same direction.

"Johanna, I have missed you. I need you here in Williams Lake with me."

Had he left it at that, perhaps Johanna would have softened her tone, but he carried on.

"You realize that as a judge I can't have any social contact with my legal friends or clients. I'll have more time for you."

"Malcolm, you don't understand," she sighed. "It's not all about you. I'm sorry. I've done what you have wanted me to do since we were married. Now I'm thinking about myself and Mary. This is very important to me. I've made up my mind. And besides, it's not flattering to be placed behind the lawyers and clients in your life. "

"But you don't have to stay in Vancouver for the whole term. You could come back here on weekends."

"If you want to see me and Mary, you can come to Vancouver on weekends."

He should have taken her in his arms. He should have said *To hell with it, I'll go to Vancouver every weekend.* He should have said *It'll be like old times.* But he couldn't discard years of caution and reason and work to achieve his just goal to spend so much time away. Instead, he sat down on a deck-chair opposite her.

"I thought Mary was going to Victoria for second-year law?"

"I'm renting a townhouse in Vancouver. And I'm hoping that Mary will transfer to UBC and stay with me."

"Do you think it is wise to interfere with Mary's legal education?"

Facing her husband, she let down her defences and spoke compassionately.

"Malcolm, I was going to tell you this when I got home and you were in the protection of your den surrounded by your law books and statutes. One of the reasons I came here by myself was to make decisions about my life. Which of course affects you. There's a secret that I have kept from you and Mary for over twenty years. I told Mary on Friday when she came to the lake."

"Aren't you being a *bit* melodramatic, Johanna?" Still smarting when he blurted this out, with unaccustomed anger, he followed it up with, "I think I know all your little secrets."

"Perhaps you're right, Malcolm. You usually are," she said in a voice laden with sarcasm. "I'll tell you when I get home. It will wait 'til then."

He stiffened, but he wasn't going to beg to be told.

"I'm sorry, Malcolm." She was modulating her tone of voice now. "It isn't my intention to hurt you. We seem to be going in different directions. I still have feelings for you and, if we work at it, we may be able to get along. As long as you understand that I have a life and a career too."

"Perhaps you could tell me," he said in icy tones, "if your secret is connected to the half-bottle of champagne in the fridge and the empty one on the sideboard."

"Vladimir Volk owns the ranch over the ridge. He brought the champagne for lunch."

"Well, perhaps he'll return and you'll drink the other bottle for dinner."

Malcolm turned, threw the contents of his drink onto the lawn and walked off towards his car.

"I don't want to interfere with your social life," he spat, before vanishing around the side of the cabin.

Johanna didn't move, looking across the water and into the trees as the car started and roared off into the distance.

What have I done? Johanna thought after Malcolm left. If she had kept her secret to the grave, she could have carried on with a life as a judge's wife, taught school 'til she was 65 and rejoiced when Mary found happiness in a career, marriage and children. Would that have been a bad thing? Perhaps not, but she couldn't have lived with herself. *No. I would wither and die if I had said nothing. I, like Morag and Margaret, have something to live for. I have something to give, and I want to do so with a clear conscience.*

Her eyes moistened as she reflected on the events of the last few days at the pond. A tear formed and trickled down her cheek. She wiped it away with her knuckle, stood up and walked resolutely to the cabin to prepare her solitary meal.

In the evening, under a full moon which lit the way, she rowed across the pond and climbed the ridge to the fence marking the boundary between Lar's and Vladimir's properties. From this height, she saw the great expanse of grassland sweeping down to the Chilcotin River and overlooking it all was a large half-built log mansion.

Charlie's surprise.

Not a small cabin by a brook, it was a colossus built by a master of the universe. She walked down off the ridge towards a bonfire and the lone seated figure of Charlie Black.

I have to return Charlie's Frog. No man has a hold on me.

17

At ten on Monday morning, Lars Larson drove up to his cabin. He looked out onto the lake and saw the white rowboat drifting swan-like in the middle. He opened the truck door.

"Johanna?" he called.

Not hearing a response, he walked hurriedly across the lawn and onto the dock to have a closer look at the lake. *The Diviners* was lying, cover up, on the planking. He raised his eyes anxiously scanning the lake and shore for any sign of Johanna and noticed something brightly-coloured amongst the dark green of the rushes a ways down the shoreline. He ran towards the dense tangle of rushes, keeping his eye on the colour which turned out to be a chartreuse blouse and white slacks. *Had Johanna discarded her clothes to go for an early swim?* He waded into the lake. He reached for the clothes. He saw Johanna's lovely lifeless face.

CHILCOTIN

18

Father Patrick Dolan entered the church vestry through a side door and greeted Johanna's family and close friends, the Hanlons', with words of condolence.

"I am sorry for your loss. Johanna was a wonderful woman. I pray this service will bring you closer to the peace of God which passeth all understanding."

"Thank you, Father," they murmured.

Mary embraced Justine. Noah took Mary's hand in his, placing his other hand on her arm in a reassuring gesture. Noah and Justine had, on hearing of Johanna's death on the radio, immediately called on Malcolm and Mary to offer their condolences, but no one had raised the issue of Mary's paternity.

The Hanlon children gathered around Mary, consoling her on the loss of her mother, while Noah and Justine exchanged knowing glances.

Noah had been brought up Catholic. Belle had seen to that. He had participated in the rituals of the church and had believed in the Holy Trinity—Father, Son and Holy Ghost—until the year that his birth mother, Ta Chi, led him into the Chilcotin wilderness and Old Antoine, the *deyen,* taught him the mysteries of the Creator and their land, and named him *deyen.* Now when Noah prayed in church, he offered his prayers to the Creator.

Malcolm, consumed with grief and remorse, couldn't face the idea of making any decisions concerning Johanna. He had asked Mary to take charge of the funeral arrangements.

Mary knew that her mother would have wanted Noah to say something at the funeral. She wanted to speak to Noah and her father about Johanna's secret, but now was not the time. She had phoned Justine to ask if Noah would give the eulogy.

The organist played a hymn as the church filled with relatives, friends and those in the community who wished to honour Johanna and to hear the comfort of words spoken in her memory. When the music stopped, the vestry door opened and the Kents and the Hanlons walked slowly into the nave. Malcolm and Mary glanced at Johanna's coffin in the aisle; the Hanlon children looked with wide eyes at the church filled to the rafters with mourners, and Stan, supported by his wife Belle, shuffled in and arranged himself in the front pew.

Mary had asked Father Patrick to read from the Book of Job at the beginning of the service.

"Oh that my words were written down!
Oh that they were inscribed in a book!
Oh that with an iron pen and with lead
They were engraved on a rock forever!"

Mary turned in her seat to look at her mother's coffin, nodded and smiled, then mouthed silently to her mother, *For you, Mum.*

Later in the service, Father Patrick gave Noah a sign to give the eulogy. Noah squeezed Justine's hand, and rose from his seat. Gathering himself, he walked hesitantly to the pulpit. He turned to face the congregation with a clear mind and vision, yet said nothing for a full ten seconds while the world turned on its axis waiting for his words, still slowly forming in his mind. To Mary, it seemed a lifetime.

"Johanna, our Johanna," Noah's voice echoed suddenly through the church, "you laughed at the laughter of the loon, you cried with the howl of a coyote. You were silent in the reflection of a full moon on a still Chilcotin Lake, and you challenged the spirits whipping the waves into frenzy."

He focussed his gaze on the mourners.

"Johanna's criticisms of my paintings made me a better artist. Her interpretation of Canadian writing gave me a better understanding of our land. Those of you here today have had the same experiences with Johanna as a teacher and friend. The land has reclaimed her. The laughter, the joy, the wisdom and the teaching she brought into our lives have been silenced, but not the memories."

He paused, casting his mind back to the lake.

"I last saw Johanna at Larson Lake the day before she was found. I had never seen her more radiant."

Mary brought her hands together and locked them, thinking of her radiant mother as Noah continued.

"It was as if a great burden had been lifted from her. When I left her that afternoon, she was sitting on the dock, cradled by the land she loved. It was a beautiful sight that I will always remember."

Malcolm suppressed a sob on hearing Noah's reflection, for his last encounter with his wife had been painful.

"Justine and I met Johanna and Malcolm in Vancouver and introduced them to the Chilcotin and to the symbol of Frog, which Johanna adopted as her own. They collected Native art and they were my greatest patrons. Johanna supported

Malcolm's career, raised their daughter Mary and taught English at the high school and college. She didn't live to see Malcolm elevated to the bench, a position which they had both earned. The Kents' greatest achievement has been raising Mary, Johanna's confidant and friend and Malcolm's pride and joy."

Malcolm felt a great relief on hearing the balm of Noah's words wash over him. Noah was not to know that he had told Johanna of his elevation at the lake.

Noah took his seat. He was followed by others who spoke about Johanna's influence on their lives.

Malcolm, sitting straight and unblinking in the front pew beside Mary, shut out the words, those heartfelt arrows of loss and sorrow spoken by her fellow teachers, students and friends. His thoughts turned inward as he remembered his last shared hours with Johanna at Larson Lake. Those memories tortured him. He was particularly remorseful for acting like a lawyer to his wife, who had wanted to tell him her secret at the lake. With the shock of Johanna's death, he hadn't asked Mary the secret yet. Then there was the neighbour, Volk. What was his relationship to Johanna? His thoughts were interrupted by Robin's clear soprano singing the haunting words of "Amazing Grace."

"Amazing Grace, how sweet the sound
That saved a wretch like me
I once was lost, but now I'm found
Was blind, but now I see."

Robin had phoned Mary from the Dawson Creek bar, where she was performing, as soon as she heard of Johanna's death from Mert. She had offered to sing at the funeral. Remembering her mother singing the song each year on

Robbie Burns Day, Mary asked Robin to sing "Amazing Grace".

*"When we've been there ten thousand years
Bright shining as the sun."*

Lars Larson squeezed his eyes shut to stop the salt tears from running down his cheeks during the song. He tried to stop his thoughts from wandering to the memories of the woman who was being eulogized, the woman whom he had idolized. He didn't know what to do with his hands the size of skillets and fingers like sausages as he stared at them resting on his knees. His mind was geared to looking at a stand of fir, calculating the board-feet measure he could extract from it in his mill and the cost of harvesting, hauling and milling it to a finished product, not to thoughts of romance and beauty. Neither his wife Gertrude, who sat placidly next to him, nor his son Cam, who fidgeted next to her, had any idea of the poetry that he was capable of. He had been devastated at finding Johanna's body floating in the lake.

"Was blind, but now I see."

The last line of "Amazing Grace" reverberated in the rafters as Mary stood. There was but six feet between the front pew where Mary sat and the pulpit, but to her it was an abyss. She hesitated before taking the first step. Love and obligation overcame her fear of publically accepting the death of the life that had given her life. Seeing no one, she saw all as one.

The first stanza of one of her mother's favourite poems suddenly came to her, and she repeated it as her mother had recited it to her over the years, her words echoing in the rafters of that intimate space.

"Because I could not stop for Death—
He kindly stopped for me—
The carriage held but just Ourselves—
And Immortality."

She paused a moment to let the words sink in. Seeing a few mourners nodding in their pews, she continued,

"My Mother, Johanna, was an English teacher who recited those words by Emily Dickinson to me and to her English classes. She shared her love of literature with me and her students. She kindled our interest in the eternal flame of the written word which to her was life itself.

"When she first came to the Chilcotin, she adopted Frog. She had Frog carved out of cedar on the lintel above our front door. It wasn't a surprise to me when my intellectual Mum, who turned forty-seven just a month ago, decided to wear a jade frog pendant. Mum wore it, not to draw attention to herself—wherever she went, she turned heads—but to express her zest for life.

"I was proud to walk down the street with my Mum and prouder still when people said I looked like her. I guess it was her colouring: jet black hair, olive skin nourished by the mists of the coast and jade green eyes. But for all that, it was her mind and gentle nature that caught the attention of those who knew her."

Mary looked out at her mother's silent mourners, those who knew Joanna. Foremost were her father and Noah sitting side by side, foretelling her future from different perspectives. There in the background was Carter, who was learning about her mother and the Chilcotin.

"Mum loved the Cariboo-Chilcotin, the people and the interaction between the two. By the turnout in church here today, you have shown your love for her. She and my father were patrons of the arts. She admired and collected the work of Bill Reid, Sonia Cornwall and Noah Hanlon. Our house is full of their paintings. She said that when you are looking at one of Noah's landscapes, it was possible not only to see the land but to taste and feel it. Because of her courage and her example, Dad and I will survive the tragedy of her death."

As she finished, she saw a stranger at the back of the church near the open door, elegantly dressed in a Savile Row suit. His clothes demanded a second look. They fitted him beautifully, but not the country. When he smiled at the appropriate times, his flashing teeth filled his large mouth. When he frowned at a sad detail movingly told of Johanna's life, his face turned to stone.

When Mary spoke from the pulpit about her mother, Vlad's heart stopped. For a moment, he thought he saw Johanna in the flesh. When Mary spoke of the frog pendant, the words strengthened his connection to Johanna's memory.

Sitting at the back of the church, Chief Inspector Ian Donaldson remembered Johanna as a delightful woman who attended RCMP dances with her husband and charmed the police and public alike. At official functions where lawyers, police and politicians mingled, Johanna's presence had made him want to make the effort to speak to her and experience the sparkle behind her eyes. She didn't just seduce men with her glance, she challenged them with her wit—and there weren't too many men who were up to the challenge.

Donaldson had been a staff sergeant in Williams Lake at the time and, as such, had a lot of interactions with Malcolm, who acted as Crown Prosecutor on the Criminal Assizes.

Donaldson had been promoted through the ranks and was now chief inspector for the Cariboo, stationed in Prince George. He attended the funeral as an acquaintance, but would have attended anyway in his professional capacity, paying his respects to the judiciary.

Sitting with Belle, Stan Hewitt strained to listen to the eulogies describing the strong ties that bound these people to this land. Stan was reminded that there was something that he had to say to Noah to set the record straight, something that his old friend Antoine had told him about Noah's father. He couldn't remember what it was just then, but he knew it would come back to him.

At the reception in the church hall after the funeral, the inspector paid his formal respects to the family and then retired to the sidelines. Later, when the crowd of mourners had thinned, he approached Mary, who he remembered as a young girl when he was stationed in Williams Lake.

"I'm sorry for your loss," he offered. "She was an exceptional woman. You look so much like her."

"Thank you, Inspector."

"At the service you spoke of her frog pendant. During my years in Williams Lake, I admired your mother, but never saw her wear jewellery."

"I received mother's effects from Corporal Melnick this morning before the service. I was looking for the frog, but it wasn't there. I was going to speak to the corporal. I'm worried, Inspector. It's such a small matter, but it means a lot to me."

"Who bought the pendant for Johanna?"

"I think Mother bought it herself when she was in Vancouver last fall. I saw it when I picked her up at the airport and when I asked, she just said she got it in Vancouver."

"I will look into it and get back to you."

"Thank you, Inspector."

"You do know that according to the autopsy, your mother's drowning was accidental?"

He said this to put Mary's mind at ease.

"Yes, I know."

After the inspector left, Mary was having a quiet moment when she was approached by the well-dressed man at the back of the church. He was sharp-featured and of medium height, with long blond hair combed back behind his ears. Mary's attention was drawn to his eyes, which were slightly slanted with a grey iris that was tinged with yellow. There was no hint of what was behind those eyes.

"Hello Mary. I'm Vladimir Volk. I was an old school friend of your mother's."

"I'm glad you came to her funeral, Mr. Volk."

"I'm building a house on my ranch next to Larson Lake, and I had lunch with your mother on the Sunday. She appeared to me to be in good spirits."

"Yes, she had everything to live for."

"Would you have lunch with me next week to talk about your mother? I would like to tell you about her early years. May I give you a call?"

"Yes, that would be fine. Thank you."

Well, at least I know who he is and why he's at my mother's funeral. I would like to know more about his relationship to my mother, she thought. She noticed Carter on the fringes of the crowd, and caught his eye. He walked towards her and she smiled.

Malcolm walked up to Volk and in a deliberate accusative tone introduced himself.

"Hello, I'm Malcolm Kent."

"Ah, Judge Kent. Vladimir Volk. I was a classmate of your late wife and have recently bought a ranch in the Chilcotin.

I wish I was meeting you under different circumstances."

Vlad's charm had no effect on Malcolm.

"I believe you were one of the last people to see Johanna alive."

"Yes, she was vibrant when I said goodbye to her after lunch."

Malcolm nodded.

"Perhaps we will meet again."

He turned and walked away.

"I'll look forward to that," Vlad said to Malcolm's back.

Malcolm heard Vlad's attempt at politeness and ignored it.

When I next meet him, he will have some explaining to do.

19

Mary's question about her mother's missing Frog nagged at Donaldson. He delayed his return to Prince George to the following morning. He woke early and was in the office by eight a.m. to the surprise of the staff sergeant. He pulled Johanna's file and stared at the summary of the autopsy report.

The cause of death was due to drowning. The manner of death was accidental. The date and time of death: July 8ᵗʰ 1985 between 12:00 a.m. and 1:00 a.m.

The police notes stated that Johanna drowned when she fell out of a rowboat while boating on Larson Lake. She was staying at Larson's cabin alone on the shore of his private lake and her body wasn't discovered until 10 a.m. by Larson. No one could say why she was boating on the lake that late.

Corporal Melnick, the investigating officer, had taken statements from her husband, her daughter, Larson and Noah Hanlon. Larson had "dropped in on her" at about 10 a.m. and found her body in the lake. He was asked why he'd dropped in and said he had been driving by on his way to one of his logging sites and thought he would see how she was doing. His new neighbour, Vladimir Volk, had been causing problems with the fence line between their properties and

Larson had wanted to find out if he had been bothering her.

Melnick had followed up and questioned the neighbour. Volk stated he'd had lunch with Johanna on the Sunday before her death and had left at about two p.m. since she'd said that she was expecting company for tea.

He was asked if he knew Johanna and replied that he knew her from their high-school days. He had learned from Larson that she was staying at his cabin. So the visit was both neighbourly and nostalgic.

Donaldson rifled through the other statements on file. The deceased's daughter had seen her on Friday for lunch. Hanlon had seen her on Sunday from three to five. The husband had visited her in the late afternoon to tell her of his appointment to the bench. He was there for an hour before he returned to Williams Lake to work on closing his files in preparation for taking up his duties. There were no marks on her body that would indicate a struggle. Death appeared to be accidental drowning as stated in the autopsy.

Melnick's report stated that when her body was removed from the lake, Johanna was wearing slacks, a blouse, a sweater and hiking shoes. A wedding band was on her ring finger. There was no mention of the necklace and frog pendant, and the list of Johanna's effects didn't include these.

That morning, Donaldson visited Judge Kent in his chambers at the courthouse. Donaldson was a brusque man with little time for pleasantries when he was on the job. He knew that the judge had the sharpest legal mind in the Cariboo and would want him to get to the point of his visit, so he skipped past condolences for his loss and congratulations for his appointment to the bench. They stood in the judge's chambers since he was gowned and was about to go into court.

"Very good to see you, Ian. Thank you for coming to Johanna's funeral. I'm sorry we couldn't talk at the reception."

"Yes, my lord," Donaldson nodded. "At your wife's funeral service, your daughter mentioned a pendant that your wife was wearing. Could you describe it?"

Malcolm was taken aback by Donaldson's businesslike attitude.

"As I recall, it was a fine gold necklace with what looked like a gold and green frog pendant."

"She wasn't wearing it when her body was recovered from the lake. Have you seen it?"

"I think she was wearing it when I saw her on Sunday late afternoon. But I was distracted by the news of my appointment to the bench and her news that she was going to take her doctorate in English at the University of British Columbia. You'll have to ask Larson if it's in the cabin."

"I will. I'm also arranging for a search of the cabin and the surrounding property."

The court clerk knocked quietly and after a pause opened the door.

"It's ten o'clock, my lord. The accused is in the prisoner's box."

"Excuse me, Inspector," Malcolm apologized. "The only way I can hold myself together is to keep working. I find peace in the law."

"I understand. Oh, one more question. Actually, two questions. When did Johanna start wearing the frog pendant and how did she get it?"

Malcolm swept out of the room, looking back over his shoulder briefly.

"I think I noticed it last winter," he said. "I assumed she bought it herself. Johanna was fond of frogs."

On the drive to his next interview, Donaldson compared the demeanour of Judge Kent with his own. They were both men of the law, driven by facts and with some understanding of the human condition. However, if his wife had died in such a tragic way he believed he would have shown more emotion than Judge Kent was showing. He found it strange that Johanna, who was so vibrant, and Malcolm, so dour, could have managed their age difference, let alone their marriage. Yet he wasn't aware of any hint of discord.

He came to the junction of Highway 97 North towards Prince George and Highway 20 West to the Chilcotin, and turned west proceeding down the hill to the flats and the sawmills which, along with the stockyards, kept the town alive. He headed towards the largest beehive burner, bringing his cruiser to a halt in front of the office of Larson Forest Products. As he opened the car door, the noise from the gang saws and the planer mill hammered his ears. He jogged up the steps to enter the relative calm of the office. Lars Larson, having seen him coming, greeted him as soon as he entered.

"Inspector, is this a social call?"

Larson was a barrel-shaped man with a booming voice and a friendly manner, but the inspector knew the Williams Lake forest district intimately. A small operator couldn't compete in the logging and sawmill business without having an angle, a chokehold on his competitors and an eye on the bottom line. Larson was already trying to call the shots by asking the first question.

"Can we go into your office, Lars? I want to talk to you privately."

"Sure. Come on in."

They walked into an office in the back, which looked out through picture windows onto Larson's whole sawmill operation.

"I guess you're here about Johanna's death?"

Another question. He was getting annoyed.

"Do you have any other queries or guesses, Larson?"

Lars waved his hands in the air in mock surrender.

The inspector nodded.

"At the funeral yesterday, Mary Kent mentioned that Johanna wore a frog pendant, and I have just talked to Judge Kent, who described it as a gold and green frog pendant on a gold chain necklace. Do you recall seeing it when you found her or later in the cabin?"

"No. I found her body floating in the bullrushes and immediately called the police and an ambulance. I couldn't watch them recover the body. I wasn't looking for the necklace in my cabin, nor did I see it."

"Had you seen her at the cabin before that day?"

"Yes, I mentioned to Corporal Melnick that I had driven her to the cabin on Tuesday and settled her in."

"Would you mind if we searched your cabin?"

"No, not at all."

"What was your relationship to Johanna Kent?"

"My wife and I were good friends with her and Malcolm."

"In your statement to Corporal Melnick, you said that your neighbour Vladimir Volk was causing trouble over the fenceline. What sort of trouble?"

"Well, he said that he had the property line surveyed and claimed that his property line came over the ridge. If he is right, then he could look down on my private lake and cabin."

Driving out of the mill yard, Donaldson passed a red Jaguar convertible with the top up. He looked back with a sense of envy before focussing his attention on the road ahead. He had always dreamed of driving a Jaguar convertible across Canada with the top down.

Larson was sitting at his desk looking out the window at his son Cam, scaling logs in the yard. Vladimir walked into Lars' office without knocking.

"The police were here. What was that all about?"

"Oh, it was a social call. The inspector from Prince George used to be a line officer in Williams Lake and he knows me."

"You may be a good lumberman, Lars, but you sure as hell are *not* a good liar. I have a large investment in your company, and we don't need the police to come snooping around."

"All right. If you must know, Johanna's necklace and frog pendant weren't found on her body, and they haven't turned up at her home. The inspector wanted to know if I knew anything about it."

"And *do* you know anything about it?"

"No, I don't."

Vlad left the office as abruptly as he had entered it, slamming the door behind him.

Lars considered his visitor. *I wish someone would rid me of this man,* he thought. Then he turned his attention back to his son. At his insistence, Cam had worked every outdoor job in his business. Larson's plan was that his son would run his company one day. Johanna's death had brought home to him the fact that life was short and now was the time to bring Cam into the office. He got on the intercom.

"Cam," his voice lumbered across the yard, "come to my office now."

Cam wandered in.

"What do you want, Dad? I'm busy."

"Sit down and listen. I want you to come into the office and learn the job of managing the company. Do you think you're up to it?"

"Of course. I've been waiting for the chance."

"All right. The first thing you've got to know is that we are short of cash and one of our biggest creditors is Volk."

20

At three in the afternoon, Donaldson parked his cruiser in the driveway of the Kents' waterfront home on the north side of Williams Lake. It was constructed of peeled pine logs intricately fitted together, quite unlike Paul Laboucher's style of stacked logs with white chinking in between. There were no windows on the entrance side of the house, only an imposing yellow cedar double-door. As Donaldson rang the doorbell, he was startled by two human-sized guardian ravens carved into the doors. On the fixed door, the raven's gaze was looking down. On the other door, the raven was unnervingly looking him in the eye. Carved on the lintel above the door was a painted green frog with golden eyes. He had been to the house ten years ago, consulting with Malcolm on trials they had worked on together and hadn't noticed the carvings then.

He was surprised when Noah opened the door.

"Inspector. Come in."

The instant Donaldson entered, he thought Noah seemed anxious.

"Hello, Noah. I'm here to see Mary."

"Justine and I just arrived a minute ago. Have a seat in the living room. I'll fetch her."

Donaldson had never been to this side of the house. Malcolm had always directed him to his private domain, the den, a cavernous room with no windows, lined with case reports and legal texts. In contrast, the south-facing living room was awash in sunlight, its walls adorned with Native art. Many of the paintings and some of the carvings were Noah's.

Donaldson was admiring the paintings when Mary entered the room with Noah.

"Hello, Mary," he greeted her. "I'm investigating the disappearance of your mother's jade frog."

"Thank you, Inspector. So do you have any news?"

"I've checked our files, and it's not mentioned in your mother's effects. I've spoken to your father and Lars Larson and am having my officers search the cabin, the lake and the surrounding grounds. I'm considering your mother's death as suspicious, and I'll keep the file open until the frog is found. If it isn't found, then I don't see any other leads."

On the surface, Noah was looking calmly out the window at the lake, but Donaldson still thought he seemed anxious. Noah wrapped his arms around his chest, bowed his head and rocked back and forth as the inspector spoke to Mary.

Donaldson turned to Noah.

"Noah," he asked, "do you recall Johanna wearing the pendant and necklace?"

"Yes. I was working on her portrait on Sunday. The pendant was on the kitchen table and I asked her to wear it. She agreed and I added it to the painting."

Donaldson made a note.

"Was there anyone at the cabin, or near the cabin, or on the lake, during the time of your visit?"

"I saw no one, but I did notice that Johanna was distracted. She kept looking into the trees across the lake. Oh, at the turnoff to the cabin from Highway 20, there was an encampment of my people. I didn't see anyone in the camp, but they could have seen me. The tent was pitched on some high ground. I first noticed it on my way out after I made my turn towards the west. Had I turned east back towards Williams Lake, it wouldn't have been visible as I didn't see it on my way in."

Donaldson made another note.

"A frog is carved over the front door and Johanna had a frog pendant. What's the significance of the frog and the ravens?"

"I was commissioned to carve that door ten years ago. I am a *deyen* of Clan Raven and our legends have it that I am a guardian of the Chilcotin. Johanna took an interest in Chilcotin and Haida myth and art. In both cultures, the frog is between worlds—probably best shown in Bill Reid's small carving of a canoe full of mythical creatures. Frog is half in and half out of the canoe between the water and the land. Johanna adopted it as her sign years ago after I told her the making of Frog in the Chilcotin creation story."

"Would you tell me that myth?"

The inspector had been sitting in a living room chair surrounded by the Native masks, paintings and carvings. Noah got up from his chair and sat cross-legged on the floor facing him. Mary sat on the floor beside Noah.

"This is part of the legend that was told me by Old Antoine my teacher . . ."

Noah told the inspector the same story with the same reverence that he had told Johanna in the hut at Acadia Camp years ago. When he had finished, the inspector thanked him for telling the sacred story, familiar with the ceremony of it all as he was. He got up with the intention of leaving, but turned back to Noah when he reached the door.

"Oh, and I would like to see your painting of Johanna wearing the frog pendant. Do either of you know who gave Johanna the frog?"

Noah and Mary shook their heads.

"No," Mary said reflectively, her suspicions about her mother's death growing stronger. "If it was a gift, someone must have admired her a great deal."

"The painting's outside," Noah offered. "In my truck."

The inspector followed Noah to his truck. Noah carefully removed the portrait of Johanna from the back seat.

"This is a gift from Justine and me to Malcolm and Mary. We intend to give it to them when Malcolm comes home tonight."

"It's a striking painting," the inspector remarked, taking in the portrait, "and the frog pendant is remarkable. Could you make a sketch of the frog for me and drop it by my office?"

"Mary has some watercolours in the house. I'll do better I'll give you a painting of it."

Back at the detachment office, Donaldson headed straight for the radio. He called Corporal Polanski, who was with the search team at Larson Lake.

"Have you found anything?"

"We searched the cabin and the grounds, sir. We haven't found the necklace. We *did* find a waterlogged book. A paperback. *The Diviners,* by Margaret Laurence."

"Where was it found?"

"It was under the dock."

"All right. Bring it in."

"It looks like a woman's book, Inspector. Do you intend to do some bedside reading?"

"Very funny, Polanski."

"Inspector, we also found a Lord Stanley High School yearbook of 1955 in the cabin. Johanna Barton's picture is in the graduating class."

RAVEN

21

Noah closed the front door behind the inspector; already his mind was elsewhere. He turned to face Mary, who burst into tears, abruptly leaving the room before he could speak. He needed Justine, finding her in the garden.

"That was Inspector Donaldson," he began. "He was asking questions about Johanna's death. Mary's upset."

Justine gave him a quizzical look.

"I think," Noah sighed, "he suspects that Johanna's death may not have been accidental."

"How's that possible? Johanna would never . . ." Justine raised her voice in disbelief. Then, realization hit. "What makes the inspector think that she may have been murdered?"

"He didn't say. He just said that it is suspicious. Johanna was wearing her frog pendant that day. The one that I painted in her portrait. It's missing."

"Where's Mary?"

"She went into the living room. I don't know what to do. Of course, I understand why she's upset . . ."

"Noah, did you tell her . . .?"

"I was going to. I don't know if this is the right time."

"We came here to speak to her," Justine prodded. "She needs our love and affection. Especially now. She needs to know that you accept her as your child."

Noah looked at the ground uncertainly.

"Okay," Justine's voice took on a soothing tone. "I'll speak to her and see how she is feeling."

Noah appeared relieved that Justine was taking charge.

Mary was sitting motionless, staring vacantly out the window when Justine entered the room. That morning Mary had been reading Shakespeare's *Hamlet* from the viewpoint of Ophelia, who, in a fit of madness, had drowned herself in a pond. As Justine entered the room Mary was comparing her mother to Ophelia and wondering, *Who was Mother's Hamlet?*

Justine sat beside Mary and took both her hands. The poor girl had held herself together through learning that she was Noah's child, the tragedy of her mother's death and her mother's funeral. The possibility that her mother might have been murdered was understandably too much.

"Noah told me about the inspector's visit. I know how upsetting that is."

"I had accepted that Mum died accidently," Mary whimpered. "Now I'm not sure. I can't believe that anyone would have harmed her."

"We don't know that," Justine reassured her. "I promise you that we'll find out what happened."

Mary relaxed a little on hearing this.

"Noah was at Larson's on Sunday to finish your mother's portrait," Justine confided. "Your mother told him her secret. Noah told me and I have forgiven him, but we never realized ... We have always thought of you as family and we still do."

Mary gripped Justine's hands tightly and nodded, crying.

"Noah wants to talk to you. Do you feel up to it?"

Mary nodded, letting out a weak, "Yes."

Justine stood and walked a few steps towards the kitchen.

"Noah," she called quietly, so as not to alarm Mary.

Noah entered the room. He'd been waiting for her summons. Mary stood.

"It seems," she stammered, "I have two fathers, four sisters and brothers, and no mother."

Justine felt a tide of empathy.

"I'll be your mother," she murmured.

Noah put his arm around Mary.

"Justine and I are here for you. We'll do all we can to help you through this terrible time."

"Dad doesn't know," Mary said, suddenly revived. "I'll have to tell him tonight."

With a questioning look, her eyes moved back and forth between Noah and Justine.

"Would you stay over for dinner? I'll need your help," she begged, again sounding like a lost little girl. "For the first time in his life, I think he feels vulnerable."

Justine caught Noah's gaze, and he nodded.

"We will stay for dinner," she asserted, "but you and your father will have to talk in private about your mother's secret. Noah being your birth father."

Mary nodded. Noah gave her a reassuring nod and Justine put her hand on the young woman's shoulder.

She's been through so much, Justine thought. *Only the Creator knows what will become of this child if she finds that her mother was murdered. But she is part Johanna's child and part Chilcotin. She'll pull through with our help, and that of the Creator.*

Justine couldn't think of anything else to say. She squeezed Mary's hand, hoping the girl could feel her conviction.

22

Malcolm arrived home at six exactly.

Mary was the kitchen, preparing dinner with Justine's help. She had decided to cook the dinner in memory of her mother, using her mother's recipes. Tuna fish casserole was the main course with apple strudel for dessert. Mary froze like a startled deer when she heard her father's car outside. She looked at Justine, who smiled reassuringly, and they both looked up to see Malcolm open the kitchen door and greet them.

"Hello, Mary," he smiled warmly, nodding to Justine. "Good to see you, Justine."

Mary knew had she been closer, he would have given her a hug. His recent displays of affection towards her had been uncharacteristic. She thought that this was his way of dealing with his grief. She had never doubted that he was fond of her, even loved her in his own way. He just hadn't shown it much up until now.

Noah joined them in the kitchen and Malcolm shook his hand.

"Mary has been neglecting you," he said good-naturedly. "Does anybody want a drink?"

He poured a beer for Noah, a gin and tonic for Mary and a single malt scotch for himself. Justine settled for water.

Scotch in hand, standing in the middle of the kitchen, Malcolm announced, "Inspector Donaldson was in my chambers today. He was questioning me about Johanna's frog pendant."

"He was here too, Dad. The frog is not with Mum's personal effects. I'm worried." She paused. "I think Mum was murdered."

"I don't know, dear," Malcolm said as he approached Mary standing at the sink. "The autopsy says it was accidental and your Mum wasn't a good swimmer."

He put his arm around his daughter's shoulder and she placed her head on his shoulder.

"The frog was Johanna's good luck charm," Noah offered. "I painted Johanna wearing it when I was working on her portrait on Sunday afternoon."

"We would like to see the painting. Do you have it with you?"

"I've just about finished it. It's in my truck."

"Dinner's ready, Dad," Mary interjected. "Noah can fetch the painting after we eat."

The Hanlons were usually good company, with lots of stories to tell when Johanna was alive. Not that night. Mary was quiet, caught up in second thoughts, *I'm not looking forward to telling Dad about Mother's secret. Perhaps it should remain a secret between me and the Hanlons for now.*

It was left to Malcolm, whose only concern was Johanna's death, to keep the conversation going. This had been one of Johanna's strengths. She could draw people out or amuse them at the dinner table and there would be no awkward pauses. Malcolm tried to lighten the room with anecdotes drawn from his cases.

It was with relief that the apple strudel was brought to the table, tasted and subjected to critical acclaim. In the more relaxed atmosphere, Malcolm remembered the portrait.

"Noah, I'd like to see Johanna's portrait. Could you show it now so that we can admire it over coffee?"

Noah left the table and returned with the portrait, resting it beside Johanna's chair at one end of the table.

"Perhaps we should wait until after dinner and we could unveil it in the living room."

"Nonsense, I want to see it now," Malcolm commanded. "Why don't you place it in Johanna's chair so that we can all see it."

"I don't think this painting does justice to Johanna," Noah said, following Malcolm's direction. "But when she saw it last at Larson's cabin, she said she liked it."

In oils, the portrait showed Johanna with an enigmatic smile, seemingly at peace with herself and the world. Noah, as if the unveiling let him see his work for the first time, flashed back to Larson Lake on Sunday—she had looked exactly as she did in the portrait. Were it not for the circumstances, he might have taken pride in his work. She was wearing her frog pendant, sitting at the edge of Larson's pond with the treed slope and bare rocky ridge as a backdrop—half of the background was the water of the pond, the other half the land of the Chilcotin. Frog was the intermediary.

"There's an evil force in the Chilcotin connected to Mum's missing frog," Mary blurted out suddenly. As the others turned to her, she cited Ophelia's mad scene from *Hamlet*:

"She is dead and gone, lady,
She is dead and gone;
At her head a grass-green turf
At her heels a stone."

"Now don't be superstitious dear," Malcolm cautioned, uncertainly. "The frog could have fallen into the lake."

The tension around the table slowly dissipated under Johanna's portrait's serene gaze. They each found themselves watching it, feeling her presence, and the outburst was quickly forgotten.

"I'll get coffee," Mary said suddenly.

Over coffee, it was Malcolm who became agitated.

"At the cabin," he announced, "Johanna said she wanted to tell me a secret, a secret that she had lived with for years. In my usual high-handed way, I said something I regret about her being melodramatic. She told me that the secret would wait 'til she got home."

Malcolm stared at the painting. The others exchanged surprised glances. They had no idea that Johanna had mentioned the secret to Malcolm.

"Mary," he continued, looking up at his daughter, "she said she had told you."

"Mum did tell me. I'll tell you tonight after the Hanlons leave."

"The Hanlons are our dearest friends. We wouldn't be here in the Cariboo-Chilcotin if it weren't for them. I don't see why they shouldn't know."

"They *do* know, Dad."

"All the more reason you should tell me now."

"Malcolm," Noah interceded, "it's a matter that should be discussed privately. Between you and Mary. There'll be plenty of time later for Justine and me to talk to you."

"Please indulge me," Malcolm urged. "My pride has put me in this position of hearing my wife's secret from my daughter and my friends. I was a fool. I must pay the price of embarrassment."

Mary looked at her mother's portrait, trying to gain the courage to speak.

"Mum told me at the lake that when you and she moved to the Chilcotin you had not wanted children because of your age, and your concern about finances in the early years of setting up practice in Williams Lake."

"That's right. But when you were born, I found out how wrong I was."

"You've been a good father, Dad."

"I've tried. I know I've sometimes been neglectful," he replied. "Mary dear, I'm leaning on you to help me survive Mum's loss. What has this got to do with her secret?"

"Dad, the secret that Mum told Noah and me, and had wanted to tell you, is that I'm not your natural child."

Malcolm's expression didn't change as he listened to his daughter. If he had had his bench book in front of him instead of his dessert plate, he would have been writing down Mary's words as if they were evidence in a trial.

"Who then," he whispered blankly, "is your birth father?"

There was a long silence. Mary, who was sitting opposite Noah, shifted her gaze to him as if to say it wasn't her place to answer. Noah took Justine's hand in his.

"I am," he announced.

Malcolm's gaze turned to Noah, still blank.

"It happened," Noah continued, "when I had my first commercial success in Vancouver. Johanna and I were both drunk and we regretted it. I didn't tell Justine until recently, but she had divined that I was unfaithful that one time. I didn't know that Mary was conceived from that until Johanna told me at Larson Lake where I saw her last. Ironic as it seems, it was a wonderful day for you and Johanna the day that Mary was born. You have raised a beautiful and talented daughter. Nothing will change that."

Malcolm turned to the portrait of Johanna, then immediately broke down sobbing into his napkin. He cried for the first time in the memory of anyone there. His famous reserve, his aloofness, all that had held him together was shattered. He hadn't cried when he heard the news of Johanna's death, nor at her funeral. His built-up grief was too much to hold back now. Mary put her arm around her father's shoulder. Justine poured him a glass of cold water. No one said anything, trying to make out words from the sounds that punctuated his sobs.

"Dear, this changes nothing between you and me," he suddenly announced clearly. "I shall always be your father."

"And I, your daughter."

"I'm not crying because I feel cheated. I'm crying because I realize how much in love I was with your mother. I didn't show it or speak it, yet despite my neglect, she stood by me. If I had had my way, you would never have come into my life. But Johanna made it happen, and here you are, and I love you."

He dried his tears and took a sip of water. He turned to Justine.

"Justine, I know how you feel," he offered. "If Johanna was here, she would have told you that she was sorry that she has caused you so much heartbreak. She would have asked for your forgiveness as you have forgiven your husband."

"I would have given it freely," Justine replied. She turned to Mary. "Mary, you have to know that as well as being your father's daughter, you are now part of our family."

"Thank you, Justine."

Malcolm looked at Noah.

"Noah, my friend," he said. "I'm experiencing pain and joy. You have betrayed me, yet you have been my salvation, for Mary is my balm and reason for living."

Silence followed. Mary rose from her seat and faced the painting. She raised her wine glass.

"To Johanna, my mum, Dad's wife and the Hanlons' friend. May she live in our hearts and memories forever."

The others rose. In unison, they said, "Johanna forever."

23

In the morning of the following day, Noah set up a makeshift easel. With Johanna's painting before him and brushes and paints to hand, he painted a likeness in watercolour of Johanna's jade frog as it appeared in his earlier oil painting. That the watercolour was two steps removed from the pendant was not lost on Noah. As he painted, he thought of Johanna, of how she looked when they had first met, of the time he told her the Chilcotin legend of how Frog was created. Her words—*"I don't think Frog is ugly"*— resounded in his mind, so he gave life to his watercolour frog and made it beautiful.

On their way to their ranch at Tatlayoko, Noah and Justine stopped at the RCMP detachment to deliver Noah's watercolour. Their next stop was the Larson Lake turnoff to check out the encampment Noah had seen on the day he had visited Johanna. They stopped near the raised clearing.

"It was always a joy to be in Johanna's company," Justine said wistfully. "Remember at the stampede? She was talking about your series of portraits."

"I hadn't been very pleased with them, except the portrait I painted of her."

"She praised them all."

"She was generous that way," Noah nodded.

Justine placed her hand on her husband's knee as they drove up to the clearing. He stopped the car, leaned over and kissed her on the cheek. He and Justine clambered to the top of the rise to where he had seen the encampment. There were the remains of a fire and the grass had been trampled and flattened where a tent had been pitched. He was looking for signs to show which family had camped there. It would have been the week after the Williams Lake stampede, and they would probably have been returning home. Noah and Justine found nothing on the ground that suggested the identity of the campers.

Back on the road, he turned slowly onto the highway towards the west and Tatlayoko Lake.

"I remember three horses tethered on that patch of grass over there. They may have belonged to the people in the encampment."

The ground had been soft in the low-lying meadow and then hardened with the dry weather. There were clear hoof marks from three tethered horses. Noah noticed that the right front shoe of one of the horses was a bit broader than the others, which would make it easier for him to trace, should he see it again.

Ta Chi would have known where to find the horse and its owner, for she had known every grass meadow and every creature that moved on the Chilcotin's vast openness. She had joined *Lendix'tcux,* the transformer and his sons, who after they had made the animals, birds and fishes of the plateau had transformed themselves into *Ts'il?os*—the mountain that overlooked their land. Ta Chi was now herself part of the legend and mythology. Noah often thought of Ta Chi when he was alone sketching on the plateau. She had lived by herself, a nomad of the Chilcotin. She had considered the whole territory her home by hereditary right. When she died, they buried her on Potato Mountain. Since then, he paid his respects to her every year at harvest time. Her spirit continued to shape his thoughts.

Returning to the truck, Noah eyed Justine. She knew the look meant unfinished business.

"When I ride with Joel next month, I'll keep an eye out for that horse."

24

Since her mother's death, Mary's role in the family had changed.

She had intended to travel with friends to Haida Gwaii in August. She thought that her mother would have expected her to stay in Williams Lake and help her grieving dad, who had immersed himself in the law. She felt the need to keep their small family unit together until she went back to the University of Victoria in the fall. She would keep house and continue to work part-time as a summer student at Hewitt and Bates, her father's old firm.

Carter Gordon being the articled student in the firm may have played a part in her decision. Her interest in Cam Larson had ended in late summer last year when he had attempted to force himself on her.

The revelations of yesterday about her mother's death changed her plans. She decided that, if she had to, she would even delay her return to the university in the fall until she found out how and why her mother died, by following the clues no matter where they led. If that meant missing a year of university, then so be it. In the meantime, she would take an English course at Cariboo College on Shakespeare's tragedies.

The following morning, Robin dropped by for a visit. Mary told her what had happened since her mother's funeral. They were washing the dishes from last night's dinner when the phone rang. She picked it up on the third ring.

"Hello."

"Mary, this is Vladimir Volk. It is such a lovely day I thought you might want to go for a ride in my plane."

"Mr. Volk, you own an airplane?"

Robin cocked an eyebrow, suddenly intrigued.

"Yes, it's a Cessna float plane."

"Well, that would be interesting. Could I bring Robin?"

"Who's Robin?"

"Robin's the girl who sang at Mum's funeral. She's visiting me."

"All right. I'll land on the lake and pick you up at your dock in an hour."

The neighbours crowded onto their front decks as the float plane taxied up to the Kents' dock. Mary and Robin were waiting.

Vladimir cut off the engine and drifted in. He got out of the cockpit, stood on a pontoon with a paddle and used it to cushion the plane's contact with the wharf.

"Vladimir, this is my friend, Robin."

"I heard you sing at Johanna's funeral. You have a beautiful voice."

"Thank you. You have a good ear for music," she said sardonically. "I sing for a living."

"Where are we going?" Mary asked.

"I thought we might fly to Chaunigan Lake for some fly-fishing and lunch."

Vladimir followed the Chilcotin River to the Chilco River where it joined the Taseko, then over the Brittany Triangle to Nemiah Valley and Chaunigan Lodge. There, they fished with Oliver, a guide from the lodge. Within a few hours, they had a good catch. Over a lunch of pinot gris and pan-fried rainbow trout—noted for its pink flesh from eating lake shrimp—Vladimir explained his relationship to Johanna.

"We were old school friends and just getting reacquainted when Johanna had that tragic accident. She introduced me to the Chilcotin and she was one of the reasons that I bought the ranch. I'm building a house on the property, which I may occupy in my lifetime if my log-builder Laboucher ever finishes it."

"Your log-builders are my mother and father, Paul and Mert," Robin chirped in.

Vlad nodded and held his tongue.

"What were your other reasons for buying the ranch?" Mary asked, her suspicions growing the longer she spent with this charming man. *He says he was close to my mother, but Mum never mentioned him.*

"The Russian in me was drawn to the benches. We call them the steppes of the Chilcotin. I'm an investor, with my head office in Vancouver. I was planning on living at Wolf Ranch, for a part of the year. What about your life and plans?"

"I'm enrolled in second-year law at U Vic, but I think I will take some time off to look after Dad." Then she looked Vladimir squarely in the eye. "And to find Mum's killer."

Meeting her eyes, Vlad answered with the utmost, unctuous sincerity.

"I too think your mother's drowning may not have been an accident. You can count on me to help."

Vladimir broke eye contact with Mary, abruptly turning to Robin, who was quietly listening and just as quietly polishing off a bottle of wine.

"Do you have anything to say for yourself?"

"You're damn right I do," was her loud, tipsy response.

"I'm looking for my big break in the music world. It's the same old story—talent needs a financial backer. 'Til that happens, I'll be playing bars in Western Canada. So what do you say to that, Vlad?"

"Good luck."

Mary wasn't to be put off by her friend's drunken strong-arming of the conversation and broke in before Robin could be more explicit.

"Mother had a jade frog pendant that has gone missing. Do you know anything about that?"

"She was wearing it when I saw her at the lake on Sunday. That's all I know."

Mary seemed to accept that answer but thought, *There is something more to this man than meets the eye.*

It was after four when they boarded the Cessna. Robin, who had retired to the bottle of wine for the balance of lunch, had to be guided to the plane by Mary. On the flight back, Vladimir flew over his ranch and half-completed house. Robin roused herself to look down and could see her mother and father working on the logs.

"There's Ma and Pa."

Mary looked down on Larson Lake and Lars' cabin less than a mile away. She noted how close the two houses seemed from the air. Vladimir landed the float plane in front of Mary's home. As she stepped out, he waved goodbye and promised to call again.

For the next month, not a week went by that Vladimir didn't call or see her.

25

Paul Laboucher placed a stalk of grass in the leaves of the book he was reading to mark the page. He turned off the kerosene light and lay on his back, hands behind his head, listening to the rain striking the canvas directly above him. The Williams Lake librarian had recommended Nietzsche's *Beyond Good and Evil* after he had told her he wanted to read up on evil. She was the only person who knew what he was reading. To look at him, to hear him speak, you'd think the deepest thought he had was measuring a log for cutting and that, if he read anything, it would be a story by Paul St. Pierre or Louis L'Amour. But as he lay there in his bedroll next to Mert, his thoughts were philosophical. He was mulling over a line from the book: *So cold, so icy, that one burns one's finger at the touch of him!*

He went to sleep considering the truth of nihilism, the denial of established beliefs and values in morality and religion. The quote and the philosophy both seemed to fit Vladimir Volk.

When Paul opened the tent flap next morning, he looked over a field of wet-cut hay lying limp in windrows, steaming under the morning sun. He set his mind to musing. The hay would have to be turned again before it was baled, else it wouldn't be worth feeding to the cattle. The ranch manager had quit a few months ago, and the ranch hands were not up to the job. His tent was in the shadow of a half-built log building, the biggest he had ever constructed. His head was bursting with architectural drawings, which were foreign to him. His plans were sketched on a scribbler. The buyers were usually pleased with what they got.

Mert roused herself and stood beside him. Both looked at what they had wrought in three months of solid work, relieved only by the weekly run into town for supplies, drink and gardening. The days had been packed. He hadn't the time to play the fiddle.

"*Sacré bleu*, Mert, this is no cabin. I'd call this a fort. I figure Volk is trying to house his huge ego."

"I dunno, but whatever it is, it's going to kill us. Yesterday, I was an inch from being flattened by that log you was hoisting."

"I know, I know . . . anyway I hired Henry Lalula and his two sons full-time. They're coming over this morning. You can go back to peeling logs."

After lunch, the five of them worked on the fort. Paul was on the highest log, wielding a chainsaw. He watched as Vladimir's convertible left the highway and began its uphill climb towards the building, past the herd of Black Angus cattle, which were there as much for show as for sale. Paul wasn't looking forward to this meeting with Vladimir and his architect. The car stopped, facing the front of the house as Paul climbed down from his sculpture.

The two men didn't get out of the car. They sat and talked while Paul waited for them and Mert worked away patiently peeling the pine logs with a draw knife and a small axe. They got out of the car and approached Paul.

"You haven't made much progress, Paul," Vladimir shouted.

Usually, Paul would have launched into a broadside of explanations, excuses and evasions. With Vlad, he held his tongue for he knew he wasn't dealing with a warm-blooded being.

"Oh, we're getting there."

"What does that mean?"

"I've put up another round of logs in the last week. I figure at a round a week we'll be finished 'bout the end of September. The roof should be on afore the snow flies."

"I brought Lewis along for a close look at what you've done."

Lewis spread his blueprints out on the hood of the car and motioned Paul over.

"I'm afraid you haven't followed the design for the porch. It should be seven feet wide and it's only six."

"Well, the fact is the logs I got only allow for six feet so I thought that would do."

"I'm afraid you will have to undo it."

Paul didn't know what the architect was afraid of, but there was no damn way it would be undone.

"Ah ha," he grunted.

After a few more picky comments, the architect finished with Paul.

"I'll be back in a month's time. Pay more attention to the details."

As they were leaving, Paul gave Vlad a soiled, hand-written bill.

"This here's my bill for the work done the last month. Did you bring your chequebook?"

Vlad looked at the bill, and then gave it to Lewis before turning to Paul.

"Come and see me at my office."

With that, Vlad and Lewis got in the car and drove off.

Paul made a mental note to be in town on Friday to pick up his cheque and weed his corn. Mert would get to watch her favourite television program.

On the way back to Williams Lake, passing the turnoff to Larson's cabin, Vlad wondered to himself, *Why am I staying on in this country now that my love has been ripped from me?* A moment later, the answer came to him.

"The Chilcotin will pay for my loss," he said aloud, to no one in particular.

"Who is this Chilcotin someone?" Lewis asked.

"It's ironic," Vlad muttered, to no one in particular. "I came here to conquer this country and now it's claiming me."

26

Every year since they married, Noah and Justine rode up to the flat ridges of Potato Mountain at harvest time in July for the gathering of the tribes, and in remembrance of their ancestors who had made the same journey from time immemorial. They also rode to celebrate their marriage on the mountain.

Noah had learned from the teachings of his mentor Antoine and the example of Ta Chi that nature carries the language of the Earth which must be learned by listening to the trees, water and everything in creation. That language is harmony and balance. The Chilcotin gave him the direction and the limits of his search for meaning. When he was on the land, he saw its interconnections with the plants and animals and felt its pulse. When he wasn't traversing its meadows, mountains and valleys, he was communicating with it through his painting. He used this knowledge to feed his spirit, his mind, his memory. He went to the mountain as a parishioner would go to church to seek absolution and redemption for his trespasses. There he would ask Raven what happened to Frog, and to hunt for her killer.

The Tsilhqot'in National Government was meeting and had asked Noah to speak.

It was a windy morning. Noah, Justine and their children saddled up at the ranch as a lone thrush heralded the dawn. With Angus, their blue heeler, trotting behind, they headed along the south shore of Tatlayoko Lake, rode through the lakeside meadow where they left the lake behind and headed to Halfway Meadow, where the pioneer Bracewell family had a wilderness lodge. From there, it was a three-hour steep switchback climb to the flat ridges of Potato Mountain.

Noah reined in his horse, sweating and breathing hard from the climb, and surveyed the scene laid out in front of him as a gourmand would look at a feast spread out on a table awaiting his pleasure. He saw the Creator's amphitheatre: the wild, white potato flowers appeared as snow on the hills surrounding the stage, a bare grass-covered area with two small lakes set side-by-side, glistening in the afternoon sun. In Noah's mind, they were the eyes of the mountain—a connection to the spirits of their ancestors.

Noah dismounted and set up his easel to sketch the land-scape. Justine took photographs to help him remember the colours which, when in his studio, he would transform into a painting as *Lendix'tcux* had transformed beasts into animals for the benefit of the Chilcotins and then transformed himself and his sons into a mountain to overlook what they had created.

The children rode down the hill at full gallop to meet their friends from the Chilcotin reserves and ranches. In the following days, there were feasts of venison, wild potatoes and onions, hooshum berries from the land and fish from the rivers and lakes which they shared with their neighbours. People they hadn't seen for a year were eager to tell what had happened in their lives. Stories were told and songs were sung at night when the drums beat for the dancers circling the fire.

During these days there was talk of their nation. The

hereditary chiefs, the elected chiefs and the elders were there representing the six reserves: Tl'esgox (Toosey), Tsi Del Del (Redstone), Tletinqot-t'in (Anahim), Esdilagh (Alexandria), Yunesit'in (Stone) and Xenigwetin (Nemiah).

On the fourth day, the circle of elders and chiefs formally met in the space between the two small lakes to settle the philosophy of their government to be written down and remembered. The chiefs sat to the south of the circle, and the elders were in clusters on two sides. Noah faced the chiefs. Those who took a close interest in their nation's affairs were to the east and west. Noah was not involved in governance, nor was he a hereditary chief, an elected chief or an elder. He was recognized as *deyen*, chosen by Old Antoine, who had preceded him, as was the old man's right. He was the natural son of Ta Chi, the embodiment of the land and an artist who was telling the Chilcotin story through his paintings. He sat amongst them as an equal, one who had earned his right to be there.

In the speeches on Potato Mountain, there was much talk of belonging, acceptance, sharing and respect. Noah sat cross-legged in the circle and listened. The sun was on the descent and the cooking fires were being lit when Mabel Twoshoes, the spokesperson with the eagle feather, looked at him. She called out, using his Chilcotin name given him by Ta Chi and Old Antoine.

"Let us hear from Wawant'x, the *deyen*, who has travelled the paths of our ancestors and recorded our land and people on canvas, wood and metal."

She rose from her seat and carried the feather to Noah, handing it to him.

Noah raised his left hand with the feather and looked upwards to the west, to the setting sun. With his right hand, he gathered a bit of parched earth on a piece of fossilized rock that he had picked up on the mountain—this had the impression of an ancient seashell etched on its surface.

"Amongst the waters of our lakes and rivers, amongst the sun and the parched earth, amongst the mountains and the valleys, the Creator made the Chilcotin and its people, the people of the ochre river who hold it in trust for our children. The seashells we find around us as numerous as wild potatoes are proof eternal of life eternal. Today, looking about me at our people, the Dene, I feel in the wind the presence of our Creator and our ancestors. On Potato Mountain, I see our land stretching out in every direction. With my hands, I touch the land that sustains us and nourished those before us. You see me with my easel, canvas and paints in every season and in all weather. You saw Ta Chi when she roamed our land and lived as our ancestors lived. I am but one man seeking to strengthen the bonds between our people, our Nation and our land."

Noah's next words were drowned by the engines of a helicopter. The shape of a dragonfly, it crested the ridge to the east of the mountain bordering Chilko Lake. It hovered over the circle, remaining there for a brief period, whipping the air. Then, it rose again and darted to the north, where it settled a hundred yards from the circle. The children, naturally curious, ran towards the insect as the blades slowly wound down. Noah saw a blond man emerging from the machine who he vaguely recognized as being at Johanna's funeral service.

Suddenly, a Native sitting to the west of the circle stood and walked quickly toward the blond man. They met and shook hands. They both ducked their heads as they approached and entered the helicopter, which then rose vertically, banked and headed back east towards Chilko Lake.

Mabel Twoshoes apologetically raised her voice as the noise died down.

"My cousin Raymond apparently has some business to attend to."

She looked at Noah, inviting him to continue.

Noah had taken in the scene before him: the interruption, the interference, the insolence of the machine swallowing the Aboriginal Raymond Twoshoes and removing him from the circle. He changed the tone and substance of his message to the assembly.

"I have spoken to you of our Native philosophy, of sharing and honouring our ancestors, and our land, for that is what and who we are. Now I speak to you of the other's philosophy spoken hundreds of years ago by a white English philosopher or *deyen* named Locke. He said that, 'land that is left wholly to nature, that hath no improvement of pasturage, tillage, or planting, is called, as indeed it is, waste.' That is the way the whites view our land. Those words were written by a man who gave birth to the American constitution. The whites have a different philosophy than us. We must understand their philosophy and try to soften it. To keep faith with the land, we must educate our white brothers to respect the land. When that man Locke spoke, he knew nothing about the Chilcotin. We are the land and the land is us. We are not waste."

27

Noah and Joel left the next morning. Father and son would continue east on a sketching and teaching ride along the trails of their ancestors all the way to Williams Lake. Noah had made the same journey with each of his children when they turned sixteen. Justine and the other children would return to the ranch. From there, Justine would return to the nursing station, Elizabeth to the Aboriginal Friendship Centre in Williams Lake and Joel's two older brothers to work putting up hay for the winter. That evening in the Hanlons' camp, the children were talking.

"I'm taking Angus with me," Joel announced.

"Hey, we need Angus at home. He's the only cow dog we can trust." Brent, the eldest brother raised his voice. "Besides Angus doesn't like to take time off. He's a working dog."

"Dad said it was a good idea."

"Yeah, go to Dad," Liam chimed in. "You're his favourite. You get to holiday while we have to stay at home and put up the hay."

The two older boys got Joel into a playful headlock.

"You had your time with Dad," he protested.

"Boys, will you shut up? I'm trying to read," Elizabeth commanded.

Noah and Justine didn't hear the tumult among their children. They were walking on the mountain and planning the next month, when Noah and one of the children would be retracing the journey he and Ta Chi had made across the Chilcotin plateau. Every time Noah parted from Justine, he felt diminished for a short time until he began to look forward to seeing her again and sharing the stories of his adventures with her. For as much as he revered the land that he roamed and painted, he knew that Justine and he were one.

In the early morning, Noah and his youngest son descended the eastern slope of Potato Mountain to Chilko Lake, which was spread out before them.

At noon, they heard Raven's song. Angus, following on the hooves of their horses, barked and ran off into the bush towards the cawing. Noah thought Raven might be signalling a bear and motioned Joel to fall in behind him as he removed his rifle from its scabbard.

"Angus, come! Leave that critter be," Noah called.

They followed the dog's bark into a small clearing. The dog stood over the carcass of an animal. There was movement in the bushes beyond. It looked like a wolf to Noah, who shot above it to scare it off. Angus gave chase. They rode closer. The kill was a Hereford calf with the Hanlon Bar 5 brand on its right flank. They had no choice but to follow the dog chasing the wolf, who could be leading it to the pack and certain death. Angus returned spent, but unharmed. Wolf was alone.

They camped on their first night off Potato Mountain at Henry's Crossing near where the Chilco River drains Chilko Lake.

"Dad, you've told me stories of how *Lendix'tcux* and his sons made our land ready for the Chilcotins. Elizabeth says that Raven told you to change your way of painting for an exhibition in Vancouver."

"Yes, that's right. I went to Antoine's cave above the Homathko River without provisions except water and some dried salmon. Every day, I asked Raven the same question: Should I unlock the secrets of our ancestors and of my spirit for the greater world to see? After the third day, when I was getting weaker, I added another thought: If the answer is yes, what should I paint?"

"Did Raven answer?"

"Be patient, son," he chided. "It was on the seventh day. I was weaker still. I was annoyed at Raven perched near the cave, cawing without stop, interrupting my meditation. I was about to throw a stone at him when I remembered the story of Raven that Antoine had told me in that very cave. Antoine's voice seemed to come back to me repeating the story.

In the old days before my time, it was dark. There was no daylight. There was only one man in the world who had light, and he would not give it to the other people. So one day, Raven decided to try to get it by trickery. He went to the man's house and waited near the place where he drew his water. When Raven saw the man's wife coming down to drink, Raven turned himself into a fir needle and went into the water, and the woman swallowed him as she drank. Soon the woman became pregnant and gave birth to a child. Now, this child was Raven.

The child grew very rapidly, and used to cry continually to play with the box containing the daylight, which the man kept hanging in the roof of the house. The child cried and cried, but they would not let him have the box. At last one day, to quiet him, the man gave him the box to play with. Immediately, he stopped crying and began rolling it about on the floor. Finally, when the man was not looking, he rolled it out of the door and, turning himself into a bird, flew away with the daylight.

Soon he came to a place where a woman was picking berries and he asked her for some to eat, for he was hungry. At first the woman refused, but Raven said if she would give him berries, he would give her daylight. The woman replied that she wished to see it first. So Raven opened the box a little way, and it was twilight, and the woman gave him berries. And many other women came and gave him berries. Finally, he broke the box and it was light all over the country. But the people grew tired of daylight all the time, so Raven said to the light, 'Half the time you are to be dark, and half the time light.' And that is the reason it is first night and then day.

Joel looked at Noah, staring in a trance into the fire.

"That's a good story, Dad. Raven has a lot of power."

"Raven is my crest and Antoine's before me. And it will be yours."

"What was Raven telling you, Dad?"

"It was a sign to exhibit my paintings in Vancouver to throw light on the Chilcotin for the world to see."

There followed a silence between father and son, soon broken by the sounds of a squirrel chattering in the tree above them.

"Was Raven right?"

"Maybe. I painted our land from the heart and my paintings hang on the walls of the world. Many people who see my paintings know about the spirit of the Chilcotin only through them. I want the others to feel the land that I paint the way our people feel our land. Raven gave me the light. It's for others to say if Raven was right."

"Isn't Raven a trickster?"

"Yes, he is."

"Did he ever trick you?"

"No, I tricked myself. Your mother and I have told you about your grandfather, Bordy."

"Yeah, he had a mean streak in him."

"He was mean to Belle and me and to the cowhands, but mostly he was mean to himself. He cheated on Belle and she left him. I tried to get along with him, but I couldn't accept his ways with women and I made up my mind not to be like him. And your mother and I have been happy together."

"That's good, Dad."

"Except once."

"Oh?"

"It was at the time of my exhibition in Vancouver. I made a mistake and, on that one occasion, I slept with another woman. Your mother has forgiven me, and I wouldn't be telling you this if Johanna hadn't given birth to Mary, who is your half-sister."

"Oh."

"Mum and I think you and your brothers and sister have a right to know. Mum is telling them back at the ranch. You're of an age now where you have to learn to control your emotions. Bordy had no control. I thought I did. I hope you will be able to."

"Okay, Dad."

They let the fire burn down and Joel fell asleep under a starry night. The telling of the Raven story brought buried memories to Noah of the time before the Vancouver exhibition when he was modest about his art. He had decided that for the exhibition he would paint smaller scenes than the larger canvasses that he was known for. His subjects were as varied as the Rainbow Range of mountains to the Northwest, Dante's Inferno near Hanceville and even as remote as Ralph Edwards' Lonesome Lake, the home of the whistling swans.

Noah's preoccupation was the play of light on his subjects. In keeping with Chilcotin thinking, these landscapes were really portraits of the land. The land was personified and the spirit of Ta Chi and *Ts'il?os* continued to guide his hand.

Noah's thoughts were disturbed by the howl of Wolf calling from across the river. Wolf had swum the Chilko River into the Brittany Triangle, the range of the wild horse herds. Their tethered horses stirred and Angus, the blue heeler, yelped.

"Are you awake, son?"

"Yes, Dad."

"You heard Wolf?"

"Yeah."

"Raven tells me many things. Tonight, he tells me to follow Wolf. We must also keep our eyes open for a misshapen right front horseshoe. The owner may know something about Johanna's death."

28

In the morning, Noah, Joel and Angus forded the Chilko River at Henry's Crossing. It took them over a week to ride through the Brittany Triangle, the land lying to the east of Potato Mountain between the Chilko and Teseko rivers.

As they rode, Noah observed a number of wild-horse bands, each guarded by a white stallion. There was one band in a meadow that they watched for a day. The mares were nursing their foals and the stallion was chasing off a young stallion who was trying to cut out a few mares from his band. Noah sketched the movement of the stallion—not its flaring nostrils, nor the wild eyes found in many cowboy paintings, but rather the spirit of the beast.

He wanted to capture it with the power of a brushstroke in the manner of the Palaeolithic Age and the Lascaux cave paintings of horse and bison. Those hunters thought that if the animal was drawn, the hunter could catch it. Sonia Cornwall's elemental painting of the rust-coloured, white-faced Herefords bunched in a corral came to mind.

The wind shifted, causing the stallion to sense the intruders. It pranced and snorted towards them, while the lead mare gathered the band in a bunch. Noah and Joel stood their ground. The lead mare took the band into the trees, where they vanished in a thunder of hooves followed by the white stallion, leaving an empty stage and an awestruck Joel.

"Horses act different in the wild, Dad."

"So do humans, son."

In the following days in the triangle they pushed on through the pine and meadow. Noah was interested to see that patches of the Brittany pine forest had been recently logged. He had thought that this was a nature preserve.

Camped on the banks of the Teseko, Angus was acting up. Again, they heard Wolf howl.

"I don't know if we are chasing him or he is leading us," Noah said, "but I figure we are going to meet again."

They continued east, keeping south of the Chilcotin River for the next week, living off the land and sketching. It was well into August when they crossed over the bridge west of Alexis Creek to get supplies and camped on the bank of the river downstream a few miles.

That evening they dropped in on a rancher, Hugh Sherriff, a friend of the family. His ranch house was built in the style of an English manor house with wainscoting in the major room and intricate wood carving on the staircase and banisters.

Over coffee in his kitchen with some fellow ranchers, Hugh talked to them about wolves.

"Felker, a sheep farmer up the road was sounding off about a lone old grey wolf the other day," he recalled. "He figured the wolf is the largest he's seen around here. It killed half a dozen lambs on his summer meadows and one of his guard dogs. Felker saw the wolf. It had a silver coat with a black upper muzzle. He fired at it, but couldn't get a good shot away. He expected that it would scare off then, half an hour later, it was back."

The men around the table had never heard of a wolf that wasn't gun-shy.

Ableman, a small rancher living near Riske Creek, shifted a chaw of tobacco from his left cheek to his right and spat before he added his two bits.

"I had trouble with the same wolf. It dragged down and killed one of my calves last night. Before he could make a meal of it, the dogs scared him off. He's hungry and's got the smell of my herd in its nostrils. I think another one of my calves is next on his menu. Yep, I'm thinking of setting up a blind, staking out a yearling and waiting for that one."

Noah nodded.

"It's being forced east by wolf packs that don't want it poaching on their territories," he explained. "It's getting bolder, feeding on domestic stock. We're tracking him. We were planning on moving, but we'll overnight here and give you a hand setting the trap."

They staked a yearling heifer in a small clearing on Ableman's ranch. The weather was clear, the wind steady from the west. Noah built the blind downwind about fifty yards from the heifer. If it was going to work, he would have to be in the blind with Ableman, who had a rifle. Joel shadowed his Dad, who let him come to teach him patience, but Angus was left behind. Ableman was a fidgety man and if on his own would have given himself away and Wolf wouldn't take the bait.

A three-quarter moon lit up the clearing as the two men and boy waited. Long before Ableman heard anything, Noah held up his hand. Five minutes later, in the moonlight, he saw a slight movement on the other side of the clearing, which Ableman didn't see. The heifer started bawling as it sensed the predator, and they saw the silver timber wolf run straight for the animal. The heifer raced to the end of its tether and was jerked off its feet as the wolf struck at its haunches. Ableman brought his gun to his shoulder and fired. The movement was too hurried, without proper aim.

He missed. Wolf loped away. Before it reached the trees, Ableman squeezed off two more rounds. Wolf vanished into the brush.

"I think I hit him."

"We'll see."

The heifer was slashed on its left back leg, but would live. They followed Wolf's tracks to the edge of the clearing, and found there was blood on the ground. Not *much* blood—the wound was superficial, but it would slow the cattle killer down for a while.

Many years earlier, on the shores of Tatlayoko Lake in the dead of winter, Belle had read to the young Noah the myths of ancient Rome where a she-wolf had suckled Romulus and Remus, the founders the city that spawned that great Western Empire. As a child, he had difficulty accepting this story and feared the wolf pack howling at the winter moon. Later, he learned from Ta Chi, as would be reinforced by Old Antoine, that Chilcotin wolves were to be feared by the people and that contact with wolves resulted in nervous illness and death, confirming his childhood instincts.

Sitting beside the fire that morning, Noah sketched the spirit of Wolf to help in the hunt. Wolf would be hungry and would strike again.

They rested for a few days before pushing off mid-morning, keeping to the north of the river.

"Why are we taking this trail? I thought we were going to retrace your journey with Ta Chi across the bridge over Farwell Canyon?" Joel asked.

"We will, but we are hunting Wolf now, and Wolf is on this side of the river."

On the south side of the highway, opposite Whiskey Glass Ranch, they were riding on the Aboriginal trail and were stopped by a newly-erected fence and signpost:

YOU ARE TREPASSING ON WOLF RANCH

Noah cut the fence with wire cutters and took the time to put in a slip-wire gate.

"Why is there a fence here?" Joel complained. "It's blocking the Native trail."

"Some ranchers don't respect our ancient rights," Noah replied.

He didn't know who owned this spread, but it took them a good part of the morning to cross it. They stopped at a partially-built log structure with the dimensions of a Hudson Bay trading post. Letting their horses graze, they walked around the building.

Out front, facing the river, was a large field of cut and wind-rowed rotting hay. No effort had been made to put it up for silage and an expensive herd of Black Angus cattle were foraging among the rows. He shook his head.

"You know what Bordy would have said about the owner of this place?"

"He's a goddamn gentleman farmer!" was Joel's immediate response.

It was one of the worst slurs one could say about another in the Chilcotin.

Men were working on the roof. Noah recognized Paul Laboucher, Leonard Lalula and his sons.

"Paul," he shouted good-naturedly. "Watch it or you'll fall off and get yourself killed."

"You mean he will get *me* kilt."

Noah looked down and saw Mert carrying some materials up the ladder. He waved.

"I've got to keep going before the snow flies," Paul yelled down from his perch. "There's plenty of time for hibernating after that."

"Who's the owner?"

"Vladimir Volk."

"Is he around?"

"*Tabernac,*" Paul growled, "that son of a bitch is prowling about somewhere near. I expect him soon."

Below them, on the fields fronting the river, a doe and her fawn were eating the cut grass. Man and boy dismounted and walked to the fence bordering the field to look at the doe and late fawn, which was trying to drink from its mother's teat.

Five minutes later, Volk's truck pulled up to the house. Volk didn't get out of his truck. He raised his binoculars and watched the deer for a while. Then he got out, a hunting rifle in his hand. Ignoring Noah and Joel, he walked to the fence, some one hundred and fifty yards from the feeding deer and raised the rifle, sighting the telescopic lens on the deer.

"I'm Noah Hanlon and this is my son, Joel. This is not hunting season, and the doe has a fawn."

Volk adjusted his aim and squeezed the trigger. The gun kicked and barked. The sound bounced off the house and echoed in the valley. It was a clean kill. The fawn crumpled to its knees and fell. The doe leapt out of sight behind some firs.

"Dad, look!" Joel cried. "He killed the fawn."

Noah didn't flinch as Volk walked back to his truck.

"I'm Vladimir Volk," he said over his shoulder. "I own this place. I don't like trespassers. And I don't like deer eating my grass."

Noah, who was standing by the horses, didn't look at Volk. He kept his eyes on the field below, upwind from the dead fawn. He walked over to his horse, took his hunting rifle out of its scabbard and sighted through the telescopic lens. Joel ran screaming up to Volk, catching up to him as he was opening his truck door to stash his rifle.

"That was a fawn," Joel yelled. "An innocent baby. Are you going to shoot us too?"

His back to Noah, Volk looked down at Joel and softened his stance.

"I heard a lone wolf cry last night. There was no answer from the pack. I saw that it's on its own and lame. It needed some help hunting. Besides, it was a late fawn and it wouldn't have survived the winter."

Noah saw the outline of Wolf's black muzzle in the tall grass as it lifted its head to smell the air. His shot echoed off the house. He lowered his rifle and turned to Volk.

"Wolves that hunt alone kill livestock. This one's been causing trouble. There're lots of rabbits and squirrels around to shoot. I wouldn't concern yourself with the welfare of a rogue wolf."

Noah's tone, the lesson, the obvious contempt in Noah's voice, saying that Vladimir shot squirrels, was too much for the Russian count in Vlad. He looked closely at Noah for the first time.

"Thank you for your sage advice," he said, his voice dripping with sarcasm. "Look, I would invite you in, but as you can see Paul is taking his time with the roof. I wouldn't want to interfere with his work."

He turned and walked to his truck, and drove off.

29

Noah and Joel had lunch looking over the panorama, then Noah sketched the scene while Joel tended the horses. In the afternoon, they mounted and moved east towards Larson Lake. Following a creek, they neared the fence line, where they came across a patch of pine which had been thinned. Between the thinned trees, camouflaged from the air by their branches but freely receiving the sun, were rows of cannabis plants in plastic containers. Perhaps this was why the owner had allowed a working ranch to run down.

It was a five-minute ride off a steep ridge to the west shore of Larson Lake. At dusk, they looked across the lake to the empty Larson cabin. Noah's mood became darker as they skirted the lake. They camped on a rise above the highway and Larson Road. Noah was quiet when they led the horses down off the rise to a meadow and tethered them near the stream. Joel provided for and cooked supper, which they ate in silence. When they were done, Joel eyed his father.

"What's bugging you, Dad? And why have you picked this spot so close to the highway for our camp?"

"Remember what I told you about keeping an eye out for a misshapen hoofprint."

"Yeah. I did, but I didn't see any."

"Well, the meadow where we tethered our horses is where I noticed the hoofprint. The police inspector needs proof that Johanna was murdered and by whom. I think the owner of that horse may be able to give us that proof."

"Why would anyone want to murder Johanna?"

"I don't know, son."

"When they find him, I hope they kill him."

"No, that's not what we do. There will be a trial. And if he is found guilty, he will be sent to jail for a long time."

"But that's not right, Dad."

"We Chilcotin have learned that revenge destroys the tribes that seek it."

"But I'm talking about our friend, Johanna."

"Two hundred years ago, before a white man set foot in this country, a war was fought between the Chilcotin and the Carrier, and the reason was revenge."

"Tell me about it, Dad."

"It was a bloody war."

Noah got up from the log he was sitting on and put another piece of wood on the fire, which blazed in response, showing the concentration on his face.

"Before my time," he began, "before the whites, in the mid-seventeen hundreds, a Chilcotin notable was killed by the Carriers, and the Chilcotins let it be known they intended to avenge his death. A few years later, a large Chilcotin war party descended on the Carrier village of Chinlac at the meeting of the Nechako and Stuart Rivers, near present-day Fort St. James. They practically annihilated the village at dawn, killing everyone they could find.

"Only a few were able to run. They, and those who were away from the village, survived. Among the latter was the chief of the village, Khadintel, who was checking his snares downriver when he spotted the war canoes bearing down on him after the raid. He beached his canoe and shouted to his two companions, 'Chilcotins are after me. Run up the bank and flee for your lives. I am the one they want.' He remained on the beach and dodged a volley of arrows aimed at him.

"Khalhpan, the captain of the war party, ordered a suspension of hostilities. Then he said, 'Khadintel, you have the reputation of being a man. If you are such, dance for me.'

"Khadintel started the dance of *toeneza*, the chief's dance, on the beach of the river to show that his heart was above fear and emotion. When he finished, he warned his enemy that, in the course of a few years, he would return their visit.

"Proceeding on to his village, Khadintel found it bathed in blood. He collected and burned all the bodies and collected the bones, which he placed in leather satchels and entrusted them to the care of their few remaining relatives. Then he prepared the vengeance due such a crime."

"Dad, I fear this did not turn out well for Khalhpan."

"You'll find out, son," Noah growled. "Two years later, Khadintel, with his war party, reached the Chilcotin valley at a place not far from here where Anaham now stands. They passed the night undetected on the higher steppes of the valley overlooking the village.

"Kun'qus, brother of Khalhpan, was a strong warrior. He was expecting reprisals, but even he was overwhelmed by the force of the raid. He fought to the last with his little son between his legs. He was protected by his double armour of dried rods of hardened wood, over which he spread a sleeveless, tunic-like armour of mooseskin covered with a coat of glued sand and gravel.

"His son was killed, pierced by an arrow. 'Kun'qus was surrounded but, with a stone dagger attached to the end of a stick, he held them at bay for a while. Under a heavy stroke from a war club launched on the forepart of his head, 'Kun'qus fell dead. He was cut to pieces. I won't go into the details, Joel, but the Carriers did to the Chilcotins what was done to them by Khalhpan a few years earlier. The women and children were massacred and the men died fighting. Those that survived were tortured before they were killed. Khalhpan was not in the village at the time. He came upon the war party, which was leaving by canoe with his daughter, and he broke down in sobs across the water from them, begging his adversary to spare her life."

As his father finished the story, Joel stood up and stirred the dying embers of the fire with a stick. His father stood beside him and put an arm around his son. With tears in his eyes, Joel looked up at his father,

"Dad, did they spare her life?"

"I'd like to think so, son."

Joel wiped the tears from his eyes and they sat silent for a while.

"I told you this story," Noah said, finally, "to show you that vengeance follows vengeance. Johanna's killer needs be found and tried and jailed. That's the white man's law, and that's the Chilcotin law now, and it's a good law.

"I see, Dad."

They arrived in Williams Lake in late August having spent a month on the ancient Chilcotin trails. Noah had heard Raven's song and followed Wolf to Volk's ranch. The Queen's law would need more than that to charge Volk for the murder of Johanna Kent.

30

The higher elevation ranches, the ones not blessed with land on the San Juan, Chilcotin or Fraser river valleys and benches have one hay crop a year. Depending on the weather, this is harvested in late August or early September.

On this year, in the last weekend in August, most of the hay was up, and it was time for the Halversons' barn dance. Between the stampede on the July first weekend and the end of August, a lot of sweat and blood was shed and a lot of curses uttered by the farmers and ranchers. It was time for a party, and the Halverson barn dance provided the excuse and the venue. Each prepared in his or her own way for the event which, this year, was featuring 'Robin and the Redfords'.

Paul and Mert had returned from Volk's partly-finished log shell to see their daughter perform, and to do some business on the side. There was heavy traffic heading north past their shack on the Horsefly–Likely road that led to the Halversons', and many of the revellers knew where to stop for weed. Paul was his usual gregarious self. His French–Canadian accent was more pronounced when trading his baggies for money, which he was short of, as Vlad had not made good on his promise to pay him that weekend.

Elizabeth Hanlon and Cam Larson were going to the dance and Elizabeth had asked Mary to go with them. Mary was back on speaking terms with Cam, who had told her at her mother's funeral that he was learning how to run his father's forestry company and disliked reading novels. Mary invited Carter Gordon, who was living at a boarding house in town and dividing his waking hours between the courthouse law library and the Hewitt and Bates law office. Mary had forgiven him for his putting her down. She had to persuade him to come.

"I don't know, Mary. Bates wants me to read the transcript of a trial he's taking to appeal next week."

"Oh come on, don't be a dull boy. You need the break."

"I'd like to, but . . ."

"Robin will be there; she's the star of the show."

"It seems you won't take no for an answer," Carter beamed.

On the way there, Cam drove his Ford Mustang into Laboucher's yard . . . "just to say hello."

The others stayed in the car. Mary and Elizabeth were talking and Carter, sitting in the back seat next to Mary, appeared to be following their chatter though his mind was focussed on meeting Robin, whom he had wanted to get to know before she vanished on her northern tour.

It wasn't long before Cam was back with his pockets bulging. Mary knew what he was up to, but didn't let on to Carter. Carter was quiet, not paying any attention. She figured he was thinking about a point of law that he had left behind.

Back on the road, Cam's red Mustang outran all the pickups, trailers, campers, cars and trucks on the road, their occupants shouting encouragement as they passed. He pulled into one of the cut hayfields that was being used as a parking lot. The revellers were streaming out of their cars and finding places by the Horsefly River to set up picnic tables and light fires as they readied themselves for the dance.

Carter wandered amongst the campfires, listening to the guitars and laughter. He hadn't been fully accepted by the country or its people, nor had he accepted them. There were no fights yet—the beer and heat after supper had made everyone lazy. He met up with some 'old boys' in black Stetsons. He knew one of them had done some time and another was a city cop. They were all Cariboo boys telling tall tales.

Soon, someone got out a Frisbee and it was being flung around close to the river, inevitably landing in it. The game turned into water Frisbee as the men stripped off their clothes to pursue the disc. The women moved downriver around the bend and modestly stripped to their panties and bras.

As the sun was going down, Carter, naked and wet, heard the warm-up band, the Beaver Valley Boys, amping up in the barn. The men ended the game and began towelling off, sharing whatever towels were to be found, before slowly getting into their best jeans and high-collared shirts. Their hair slicked down, they started moving towards the silver-roofed building. Again, modesty held the women back. They waited in the willows and watched their men stroll by in the buff.

The women took longer readying themselves for the dance. Among them were Mary and Elizabeth, who raced to their clothes and towels, quickly got dressed in their finer clothes, then ran to join up with Cam and Carter.

"We saw you watching from the willows. I hope I didn't scare you," Carter said with a smile.

"Naw, I've seen better," Mary bantered back.

The group, in an excited state, ran into Noah and Justine, who had just arrived, at the entrance to the barn.

"This is Carter," Mary said. "He's the articled student who insulted me on his first day on the job."

"Hi," Carter smiled. "My intentions were honourable. I meant to praise her."

"Mary can look after herself," Justine responded. "Whether it's an insult or praise."

"Yes, I found that out."

They moved into the barn with the rest of the crowd. The band was playing, couples were on the dance floor, and squares were being formed. Cam drifted off and Elizabeth started talking to friends.

Mary asked Carter to partner her in a square dance. He had never attempted the dance, but agreed. They joined a square with Noah and Justine. He soon got twisted in the first set and ended up paired with Noah to everyone's amusement. Mary and the Hanlons patiently moved him around. By the third set, he was performing to the calls of allemande left, half-promenade and hold-your-hands, as well as doing the Canadian Breakdown and the Red River Valley. They were into the fourth square of the set when Carter twirled Mary and performed a do-si-do. The music stopped and Paul entered the barn.

"Who is that man?" Carter asked Mary. "The one over there that Cam saw on the way here?"

"That's Paul Laboucher, Robin's dad."

Carter took an immediate and closer interest in him.

"Would you introduce me to him?"

The band took a breather and Carter began moving slowly through the crowd towards Paul with Mary close behind. Just then, a group of people walked into the barn demanding everyone's attention. In the centre was Volk, dressed in designer Western gear, the kind a city boy pretending to be a cowboy would wear, and a white Stetson, like those worn at the Calgary Stampede. He was with an entourage of two couples who appeared to be outliers. The men were dark-skinned but not Natives. They wore matching white Stetsons but would have been more comfortable in sombreros. Paul began moving towards this glitter as Carter was trying to get closer to Paul with Mary in tow.

This was Paul's night. His daughter was setting up on the stage playing to a hometown crowd. Earlier, he had done a brisk business in supplying many patrons with weed, and he was feeling the effects of it himself in a happy way, which loosened his tongue. Paul's progress through the crowd toward Volk was slowed by talking up customers and friends.

"Hey dere, Lemieux, put on a smiley face. My dotter's singing soon. Your sour face could turn the milk in a cow's udder." And to another, "Hey, Cram, the last I heard from you was a fart in church."

Closing in on his quarry, he spoke in a loud jovial voice so all those around could hear, including Carter, who was right behind him.

"Hey dere, Mr. Volk, you owe me five thousand dollars for a month's work. Cowboys pay their bills, ya know."

Volk's face hardened. The two men with Volk moved forward, one on each side of Paul. Volk looked past Paul at Carter, then over Carter's shoulder at Mary.

His hand came up in a sign of peace.

"Come by my office tomorrow," he said to Paul, "and pick up your cheque."

The two men fell back and took their position by Vlad's side. Vlad walked by Carter as if he wasn't there, making a beeline for Mary.

"Hello, Mary," he smiled. "May I buy you a drink?"

"Thank you, Vladimir."

Mary, who hadn't been able to hold Carter's attention by

being nice to him, decided to try a different approach. She and Vlad went off, leaving Carter to introduce himself to Paul, who was listening to Robin sing a Patsy Cline song.

It only hurts for a little while
That's what they tell me, that's what they say. . .
But I will hurt 'til you come back to me.

In the lull between songs, Carter walked up to Paul and put out his hand.

"Hi, Mr. Laboucher," he said. "I'm Carter from Mr. Hewitt's law office. And a friend of Mary Kent."

"You don't say." Paul ignored Carter's hand, instead putting his arm around his shoulder. "I'll be needing your services soon. How about a reefer?"

He stuffed a joint into Carter's shirt pocket.

Robin finished her set with her band twanging around her as she sang the title song from her new album *Sagebrush Blues.*

My heart's breaking, my soul's aching
I'm a nothing since you've gone
I'm singing the sagebrush blues
Thinking of your charms
And of the times you held me in your arms.

Robin came down from the stage flushed with the crowd's cheers as the Beaver Valley Boys returned to the stage with a screech of fiddle and stomp of feet leading into a square dance. On the dance floor, she was met by Mary and Vlad, who was holding his white Stetson and deferentially nodding.

"Hello, Mr. Volk. How did you like my song?"

"I know talent when I see and hear it," he crowed. "Why don't you join Mary and me for a drink and talk about how I can finance your career? You should be singing in Nashville, not in a barn outside of Williams Lake."

Carter was drinking beer to keep himself afloat as he made his way through the well-wishers, arriving at Robin's table just as Paul did. They were both greeted by the sight of Vlad being affable to an excited Robin. She shouted to Paul over the crowd noise.

"Paul, Vladimir's going to be my new agent."

"Well, I'll be damned! We'll see about that," he shouted back.

Mary consoled Carter on the loss of his songstress by dragging him on to the dance floor where she held him up on a set of slow dances. Through the fog of his drunkenness, he was beginning to understand why Cam had fallen for her.

"I think that *Catcher in the Rye* is a children's fairy tale," he challenged, out of nowhere.

She stopped dancing, looked at him and shook her head.

"Spoken like a drunk, illiterate, articled law student."

With that, she left Carter swaying unsteadily on his feet.

The last Carter saw of Mary, she was dancing with Cam. Before he passed out, Carter had one clear thought.

I'm no longer a stranger in this country.

THE RULE OF LAW

31

The lawyers of the Cariboo Bar Association met every year on a date set by a committee of one to accommodate his or her own calendar. At these meetings, they conducted their business, told war stories of their wins—never their losses—all the while discussing the finer points of law and justice in the northern part of the province. The purpose was mostly social, a thin veneer spread over the law that enabled lawyers to rest for a short time from their legal combat. The judicial district of the Cariboo County extended from Ashcroft to the Yukon border and from the Coastal Mountains to the Alberta border, an area the size of France.

It was Acton Bates' turn to be the committee of one, and he decided that the meeting would be held on the second weekend in September at Wells, an old gold mining town, now an artist colony, a few miles from Barkerville and one hundred and fifty miles by road northeast of Williams Lake.

Bates also had the responsibility of providing Carter Gordon's articles as Stan was only in the office one day a week, and on that one day took a nap after lunch. Stan had a practicing certificate, but he didn't actually practice law. He acted more as a tuning instrument to the county's legal orchestra, while entertaining his old friends and clients.

Stan suggested that Bates stir up interest in the annual bar event by enacting a mock trial at the Richfield courthouse of one of Sir Matthew Baillie Begbie's famous cases in the very building where the judge, who had brought law and order to British Columbia in the 1860's, had dispensed harsh but fair justice. Stan insisted on honouring Begbie because of the physical and spiritual connection that Begbie had with the land and with the law of the province. Begbie, known as 'the Hanging Judge', had brought the rule of law to the outer reaches of the nascent province on horseback and canoe.

Bates had sent out the notice of the meeting to the profession in June. It was now September, and Bates, who had been overwhelmed with work since Malcolm had been appointed a judge, had done little except to hire two actors. There was a decision to be made on which of Begbie's trials to stage and then the writing of the script, all before the bar met in two weeks. Bates called Mary and Carter into his office, with Stan, to discuss which one of the many murder cases that the chief justice had presided over would be appropriate. The professional actors were to play the part of the lawyers arguing the case.

"Where can I get the BC Law Reports?" Carter asked Bates. "I haven't seen them in the courthouse library."

"Malcolm Kent has a complete set in his home library," Stan offered, "and I have the biography of Begbie by David Williams, *The Man for a New Country*. You should be able to find something in there."

"Carter," Bates said, "you and Mary find a case that we can use, write a script for counsel addressing a jury and have it on my desk by the end of the week. And Mary, would you ask your father if he would play Begbie?"

"I'll ask him," Stan interjected. "He can't refuse me."

Carter took William's book and skimmed it that afternoon.

He and Mary met for dinner to discuss what cases he had found, decide what case would be presented and start thinking about the script.

They took a back table at Sam's, a Canadian-Chinese restaurant, and ordered egg foo yung, chicken fried rice, vegetables in black bean sauce and beer. Carter pulled out the red-covered David Williams biography that Stan had given him.

"Begbie was an extraordinary man," he said. "Do you know that in cases where there were no counsel, he acted as prosecutor, defence lawyer and judge, three roles in one? He did it because he had to, and no one questioned that justice was done. Old Hewitt is a lot like him. Who else would have trusted me with a trial right out of law school?"

"I wouldn't have."

Ignoring her jibe, he continued.

"The best case for the mock trial that I've found is *Regina v. Barry*. It's the case of the death's-head pin."

Mary shivered involuntarily.

"Well, that sounds dramatic."

"Barry," Carter explained, "was an American accused of murdering Blessing, a fellow gold miner and countryman, for his money. He was suspected when a barber, Moses, a black man who had been with the two men on their journey to Barkerville, persisted in asking for Blessing when Barry came into his shop for a shave. The answers he got were evasive. Later on, a hurdy-gurdy girl paid Moses for a hairdo with a death's-head pin, which had been Blessing's good luck charm. Blessing's body was later found, and Moses told the police about the hurdy-gurdy girl. She told them that Barry had given her the pin. Barry was found guilty and was sentenced by Judge Begbie to hang, and the sentence was carried out along with another criminal on the same gibbet."

"'Gibbet' I know," Mary noted. "What's a hurdy-gurdy girl?"

"She's a dance girl. You pay to dance with her and buy her drinks. The two hangings in August 1867 were the last in Barkerville. Judge Begbie had tamed the gold fields. What do you think?"

"Perfect."

Bates approved of the case and they set to it. It took them the better part of the week to write the script in the evenings after work. Mary wrote the prosecutor's address to the jury while Carter wrote the defence lawyer's. They found an account of the case by Higgins in *The Passing of a Race*. It described the other convict, the one who shared the gibbet with Barry, as a Native named Paskel.

"At least in death, there was equality between white and Native people," Mary commented drily.

Mary made the suggestion of creating an Exhibit A—the death's-head pin which would be placed in a white envelope and revealed at the trial. Carter provided an old gold-coloured key chain. They were finished late on Thursday, the night before the Cariboo Bar meeting.

"It's time to call it a night," Carter declared, stretching.

Out on the street, Mary stopped, a thoughtful look on her face.

"I'm going back to the office to type a good copy of our speeches," she announced. Then, as an afterthought, she added, "Oh, I've found someone to play the accused."

"Let me guess. Is it me?"

"You would be my *second* choice. My first was Mr. Volk."

"How did you get him to do it?"

"I asked him nicely."

He laughed and mussed her hair.

"You're a devil."

"I know," she smiled.

On Friday morning, Celia Eagle came by the law office

to get some legal advice from Carter, as the supervisor of children was bothering her about Jewel. Celia was dressed in a simple but colourful flowered maternity dress with cowboy shirt and belt, carrying Jewel on her hip. He asked her to sit down in his private office and smiled.

"When is the baby due?"

"The doc says mid-October."

He was about to ask the purpose of her visit when he noticed that Jewel was playing with a pendant dangling from a gold necklace around her mother's neck: a jade frog pendant. It looked suspiciously like the frog pendant Mary's mother was wearing in Noah's portrait.

"That's a beautiful frog pendant, Celia."

"Thanks. Can we talk about Jewel now?"

A few minutes later, Mary arrived after her Shakespeare course at the college. Carter saw her as she went by the open door of his office.

"Mary, come in and say hello to Celia and Jewel."

Mary came in with a broad smile, hand outstretched.

"Celia, it's been a while, how . . ." Her eyes rested on the pendant. "Where did you get that frog?"

"Johnny found it. We was riding near a big house getting built a few months ago, and it was lying by the trail."

"Celia, that's my mother's necklace. We've been looking for it."

After explanations, Celia reluctantly gave up her treasure for the promise of a replacement. Mary saw her to the door.

"Where will you be in the next few days, Celia?"

"We're heading back to Redstone."

In Carter's office, Mary stared at the necklace. Carter stared at her.

"What are we going to do?" she asked, not looking up.

"We have to turn it over to the inspector," Carter responded firmly.

Mary rose from her chair, shut Carter's door, and sat down opposite him.

"When you found Judge Begbie's death's-head pin trial, I immediately thought of Mother's pendant. I think that one or more of the people who saw Mother on the last days of her life know something about her death and aren't talking."

"What are you thinking?" Carter asked, with suspicion.

"At the mock trial," she replied slowly, "I want to place Mother's pendant in the Exhibit A envelope. Maybe it will shock someone into saying something that will lead us to Mum's killer."

"The people you're talking about are your father, Noah Hanlon, Vladimir Volk and Henry Larson—all powerful men in the Cariboo-Chilcotin."

"Yes."

"You suspect your father?"

"In my mind, nobody is above suspicion."

"And you want me to go along with this charade?"

"Yes."

"It may be the end of my career."

"Remember what Hamlet said to the players?" she urged.

"The play's the thing," he said, bemused. He clapped his hands together. "Fine. I'll do it."

She slipped the pendant into her pocket.

"Acton has asked the inspector to speak to the Cariboo Bar in Wells this weekend. Inspector Donaldson will receive Mother's pendant in a roomful of lawyers. What could possibly go wrong?"

Vlad agreed to play the accused. Mary didn't mention to him that the trial ended in a hanging or that the accused allegedly spent his victim's money on fancy clothes. Nor did she mention that when Stan had asked Malcolm to play Judge Begbie, he agreed to do so on the condition that Vlad play the accused, Barry.

32

At 6:30 a.m. on September 18th, a schoolbus left Fort St. John in the northern reaches of the province, heading south towards Dawson Creek—an hour's drive away. The bus wasn't crowded with schoolchildren on an outing, but it held an equally excited group. They were lawyers and their spouses headed to Wells and Barkerville for the annual Cariboo Bar meeting and to witness the beginnings of law and order in the province, featuring the exploits of the first Chief Justice, Sir Matthew Baillie Begbie. The event had been eagerly awaited by the lawyers for, as past meetings had shown, anything can happen when Cariboo lawyers collide on these occasions.

The first stop was Dawson Creek, where four more couples boarded and were greeted with good humour and the opening of the bar. Prince George would be the next stop on the journey to Wells. The four hours seemed to melt away the ice in their drinks before the pulp mills indicated that they were within twenty miles of the northern hub of the province. Their numbers swelled from the Prince George contingent, and the bus burst into song on the hour's drive to Quesnel, on the promise of only a further hour's drive to Wells. The talk was of what had occurred in the intervening year.

Brendan O'Brien spoke, in what he thought to be a muted voice, to the lawyers at the back of the bus closest to the makeshift bar, but it was more of a bellow. He was lamenting that he wasn't appointed the resident Supreme Court judge.

"I have more murder trials under my belt than any lawyer in the Cariboo." He paused for effect. "And more acquittals. I thought the appointment mine. David Thorpe thought so too. Then what happened?"

He paused again to take a drink from his double martini. Everyone knew what happened, Thorpe was their Member of Parliament and had assured Brendan he was a shoo-in for the appointment, but only Brendan could add his own colour to the story.

"I'll tell you what happened. They appointed what I was told was 'a lawyer's lawyer', whatever that means. I'm a 'peoples' lawyer' and proud of it."

A crown prosecutor from Dawson Creek took him on.

"Malcolm Kent knows his law and has been a bencher. He was an asset to the bar and will make an excellent judge."

Brendan had the last word, as he usually did.

"May I quote your brown-nosing when next I appear before him?"

The spouses sitting nearer the front were remembering Johanna. Anne Jenkins from Quesnel spoke of the good times at the annual meetings.

"As I recall, it was Johanna's idea. The meeting was in Prince George and we decided to put on a show as hurdy-gurdy girls. We made costumes and did the whole routine including dancing the can-can. God, that was fun."

Others joined in, telling stories about Johanna, some spurred by memories sparked by her name, others simply not wanting to be outdone.

The bus pulled up to the Wells Hotel at five in the afternoon and the merry group of travellers poured out to be greeted by their counterparts from Williams Lake and 100 Mile House. The work of registering, informing and directing fell to Carter, Elizabeth and Mary. The guest speakers from Vancouver, the president and CEO of the BC branch of the Canadian Bar, and the Treasurer of the Law Society had to be fluffed and fussed over. Inspector Ian Donaldson had been added to the speakers' list at the last minute.

After dinner and a curling contest between the north and south Cariboo, most of the lawyers settled in for the night, knowing the next two days were going to be busy. Some of the lawyers remained with Brendan to officially close the hotel bar. The annual general meeting on Saturday morning would look after the formal business, but even that tame exercise of appointing the executive committee of one and conducting the society's business had led to raucous debates in the past.

The program after lunch called for the mock trial in the Richfield courthouse, with the role of Chief Justice Begbie played by Judge Malcolm Kent. The prosecutor and defence lawyer were to be played by the members of the Barkerville Actors Guild. A surprise was that the role of the accused was to be played by a stranger, Vladimir Volk.

Vlad only knew that his role was non-speaking. Since Vlad's life was an act to him, this was but another role, another mask, another way of ingratiating himself to the Cariboo-Chilcotin before, as he had promised himself, making it pay for Johanna's death.

Carter had arranged for the inspector to sit in the back row of the courtroom beside Larson. Lars had accepted Mary's invitation when she mentioned that Vlad was playing the accused murderer. Robin was there; she had been hired to sing at the dance with her father and his pick-up band.

Stan Hewitt gave the opening remarks. It cost him a great deal of his precious energy to attend the Cariboo Bar meeting. Noah and Justine had driven the old couple from Wells to Barkerville that morning. From there, they had taken a horse-drawn wagon to Richfield. The lawyers assembled at the small courtroom in Richfield on the outskirts of Barkerville, the gold miners' town which was now a tourist attraction. They were unaware that Mary saw the trial of Barry as an opportunity to put the four men who had last seen Johanna Kent alive—Malcolm, Vladimir, Lars and Noah—through a trial of her own, inspired by her reading of *Hamlet*.

The able-bodied lawyers walked the half-mile uphill to the courthouse while a horse and wagon brought the others. Carter acted as clerk of the court. He and the paid actors were dressed in traditional lawyers' gowns and the now-discarded fashion of wigs. Vladimir was in the prisoner's box.

Stan stood with both hands on his walker, under Belle's watchful eye, and addressed his fellow lawyers.

"Today, we are going to re-enact with a great deal of awe and respect a trial that occurred 121 years ago in 1867 in this very courtroom. Chief Justice Begbie presided over the murder trial of Barry who, it was alleged, murdered Blessing for his money on the way to the goldfields of Barkerville. You may know of this as the *Death's-Head Pin* case."

An excited murmur went through the crowd. A few hands started into applause before they were shushed.

"Mr. Justice Kent is playing the chief justice. Mr. Franklin Johnson, a professional actor, is playing the prosecutor, Mr. Crease. Mr. Jack Hawkins, also of the theatre, is playing the defence lawyer, Mr. Richards. Mr. Vladimir Volk, a local businessman and rancher, has volunteered to play the accused. The clerk is my articling student, Carter Gordon. We are thankful that the court reporter, Bernie Freeman, has volunteered his services so that we will have a record of this historic event."

He then motioned to the full house of lawyers in that small whitewashed room.

"You, my learned friends, will be the jury. Let the trial begin."

Belle sidled over to help usher him to a seat.

"Order in court, all stand," the clerk called out.

The robed, bewigged and precise figure of Judge Kent entered the courtroom to the scraping of chairs. He waited 'til the hubbub ceased.

"*Her Majesty The Queen v. Barry*, my lord."

"Yes, Mr. Richards. We have heard the evidence, and now I believe you have something to say to the jury for the defence."

"Thank you, my lud," Mr. Hawkins said.

"Please, sir, no affectations in my courtroom. It's 'my lord'."

There was a titter from the crowd, and the judge glared. He was obviously fully engaged in his role. In contrast, Vladimir, sitting in the prisoner's box, took a relaxed attitude to his role, lounging around, quite unconcerned about his fate.

"My apologies, my lord. May I begin?" Mr. Hawkins continued.

"It seems that you already have. The jury is all ears."

Hawkins turned to the audience, spreading his hands wide to engage them.

"Members of the jury, my client William Barry is a gold miner, not a murderer. He came to this new territory, as you all did, to dig for gold, not to kill for it. On his way, he fell in with another miner, Mr. Blessing, a fellow American. They travelled together as companions, sharing food and drink and shelter. On their journey, they came upon Mr. Moses, a barber, who was returning to his shop in Barkerville, and he was invited to join them. During their time together, there were no fights, no quarrels or disputes. All was peaceful. Mr. Moses gave evidence that, one night, Blessing showed them his pin with a gold nugget, which had the peculiar shape of a death's-head."

The 'jury' up to this point had been quietly attentive, but now they showed signs of real interest, led by O'Brien, who nodded his head vigorously. Caught up in this active interest, Hawkins responded with more passion.

"On their arrival in Barkerville, Moses went on his way to the barber shop and didn't see either Blessing or Barry until sometime later, when Barry came to his shop for a shave. I pause here to refer to the law. The Crown must prove its case beyond a reasonable doubt. In other words, if there is another reasonable explanation for Blessing's death, then the Crown has not met that test and you should acquit. And there is another burden of proof on the Crown. The only evidence that has been presented in this trial, to which you and the walls of this courtroom have borne witness, is what the law calls circumstantial evidence."

The actor in Hawkins couldn't resist colouring his performance with this theatrical reference to the walls in order to enliven his lines from the dry law.

"Here again, if there is another reasonable explanation for Blessing's death, then the Crown has not met the test. In the evidence put to you by the defence, there is a reasonable explanation.

"In the barbershop, Moses enquired after Blessing. Barry said he had no knowledge of that man's whereabouts. There is nothing sinister in that. They weren't friends or partners; they weren't intending to mine together. In short, Barry was not Blessing's keeper. They were travelling companions, that is all.

"The Crown has introduced evidence that Barry spent

money in the weeks after he arrived in Barkerville. Again, that is not unusual. Miners come to the gold fields with a grubstake, and there is no evidence to show that this money wasn't Barry's. The whole weight of the Crown's case rests on the death's-head pin, which was given to the hurdy-gurdy girl by Barry. But Barry's evidence is that the pin was given to him by Blessing. The crown says my client killed for the trinket, but there is another reasonable explanation of how it came into Barry's possession—that it was given as a parting gift. Its value was minimal as evidenced by Barry's gift of it to the hurdy-girl for a dance and a drink.

"Moreover, if Barry had killed Blessing, why would he take a trinket that was sure to link him to the victim and make a gift of it? The very fact that he gave it to the hurdy-gurdy girl speaks of his innocence. Members of the jury, I submit that the Crown has not proven its circumstantial case beyond a reasonable doubt. I urge you members of the jury to let an innocent man, my client Barry, walk out of this courthouse a free man."

Richards had raised his voice to a controlled shout and left the words ringing in the 'jury' members' ears.

Vladimir was moved by his counsel's speech and flashed on his caption, *'Born to be free'*, in his graduation yearbook. He looked at Mary and, for a moment, saw her mother sitting behind him and smiled. The lawyers in the jury seemed to admire the actor's style and words, especially as he shouted "a free man" in an oratorical style suited to the times.

The chief justice broke the spell following the oration.

"Members of the jury, you have heard from the defence counsel, Mr. Richards. Now, listen carefully to Mr. Crease for the prosecution."

"Thank you, my lord. Members of the jury, on many occa-sions, to.my knowledge and on my reading of the law reports, accused are often convicted on circumstantial evidence, for it is not often that the courts are afforded an eyewitness account of the crime. This case is no different in that respect. In this case, you have been shown an overwhelming build-up of irrefutable evidence, all pointing to that man sitting in the prisoner's box, the accused, Barry."

Here, 'Crease' paused for effect, pointing directly at Vladimir, who smiled and raised his bejewelled hand.

"First of all, the accused and the victim Blessing were not friends. They happened to be travelling together when they fell in with Moses, whom I suggest is an honourable man and a credible witness. He told you of Blessing showing both himself and Barry the death's-head pin, which he had fashioned out of a gold nugget, and which was his good luck charm, as it had brought him riches in the California gold fields—a detail that my learned friend in his remarks failed to mention. You can take from that that Blessing would not have voluntarily parted with it. A few weeks later, Barry, dressed up in new fancy clothes, showed up at Moses' shop for a shave."

The actor broke away from his lines to pause and point at Vladimir.

"You will note, members of the jury," he continued in a suggestive tone, lowering his voice, "how well-dressed the accused is today. You will remember that, when Moses asked about Blessing, Barry was evasive. Later, the hurdy-gurdy girl came to Blessing's shop for a hairdo and showed Moses the pin, which she said she got from a customer, whom Moses identified as the accused. On the promise of more hairdos, the girl gave the pin to Moses, which he kept until the body of Blessing was found in the bush just off the road to Barkerville by the shore of a pond."

Mary smiled to herself. Although there was no evidence

for the reports of a pond, she had been unable to resist adding that detail to the script.

"The coroner's evidence was that he died from wounds received by a sharp object, like a knife. He had neither money nor the death's-head pin on his person. Moses then went to the police.

"I submit that all the evidence points directly to the accused. The Crown has proven its case beyond a reasonable doubt. And to dispel any doubt whatsoever, I wish you to consider in your deliberations Exhibit A in these proceedings, the death's-head pin which is in this white envelope I am handing up to the clerk."

Mary had written the last sentence in the prosecutor's speech and had prepared Exhibit A. She was keeping a close watch on her father.

Vladimir had no smiles for Mary after the prosecutor's address. All eyes were on Chief Justice Begbie. No lines had been fashioned for the judge. In the stage direction, Mary had given him, he was to open the envelope.

Malcolm Kent, who had never approached a courtroom without being fully prepared, had read David Williams' outline of the case and had read Begbie's address to the jury in the BC Law Reports. He knew the inevitable outcome.

Carter, who held Exhibit A, stood to perform this duty, but unaware of Mary's stage directions to her father, he gave the envelope to the jury foreman, Brendan O'Brien. The chief justice interrupted him.

"Wait. Mr. Clerk," he admonished. "Hold on to Exhibit A and take your seat. I have not delivered my address to the jury."

He then raised his head.

"Ladies and gentlemen of the jury," Malcolm spoke to the rafters extemporaneously and completely caught up in his role, "you have patiently heard counsel's submissions. It now falls to me to tell you the law and summarize the case."

Malcolm eyed Freeman, the court reporter, and was pleased that he was furiously taking down his every word.

"You needn't be too timid about the law," Malcolm continued. "It is a simple matter of deciding whether the accused is guilty beyond a reasonable doubt, which means that you should be sure of his guilt. You have heard of circumstantial evidence from both counsels, who express only their own opinions. I am here to give you the law which you must follow. It is here also that your robust reason comes into play. The question you must answer in coming to your verdict is whether there is any other reasonable explanation for the death of Blessing other than by the hand of the accused. My comments on the evidence which I am about to give are for the purpose of refreshing your memory for, of course, whether you believe the evidence is entirely for you to decide.

"The issue seems to boil down to this: how did the death's-head pin, that unique trinket and Blessing's good luck charm, come into the possession of the accused? Was it by fair means or foul? That is for you to decide, but it seems to me that it would be highly unusual, given the evidence, that Blessing would have given it up voluntarily. Now the prosecution has handed the clerk a white envelope which has been marked Exhibit A. Would you hand me the envelope, Mr. Clerk?"

Carter handed Malcolm the envelope.

"Thank you. I shall now open the envelope."

Mary had a clear view of her father and scanned his face for any reaction. Carter, who was a willing participant in Mary's play within a play, was sitting beneath the judge's bench and shared his perspective, looking at the jury, Larson, Noah and the accused Volk. The judge opened the envelope marked Exhibit A and withdrew its contents. Dangling from his left hand was Johanna's gold necklace and jade frog pendant.

"I'll be damned!"

"What cruel joke is this?" Vladimir shouted from the prisoner's box. "That's Johanna's necklace."

Noah, sitting beside Justine, was impassive. Larson, sitting next to the inspector, took a quick intake of breath through pursed lips.

Mary didn't suspect her father or her birth father, but she thought that the shock of seeing the frog pendant might have the effect of their being perfectly frank when answering the inspector's inevitable questions. As for Vlad and Lars, they had more to answer for, given the spot where Celia Eagle said it had been found: on the border between their two properties.

Malcolm stood and strode, without a word, jade frog in hand, to his chambers, then slammed the door.

"All rise," Carter immediately announced. "There will be a five-minute adjournment."

He motioned to the inspector and Bates to join him and Mary in the judge's chambers.

33

"What's the meaning of this?" Donaldson demanded. "How could this happen?" Malcolm added.

"It was my idea," Mary said. "I knew you would be here, Inspector, and while I realize this was taking the law into my own hands, I put Mum's necklace in the envelope to see if the killer would reveal himself."

Malcolm's face betrayed his shock.

"Where did you find it?" Donaldson asked.

"Celia Eagle, a client of Carter's, said her husband found the necklace on the trail from Vladimir Volk's ranch to the Larsons' property. He gave it to his wife, Celia, who gave it to us yesterday morning."

"I'm equally responsible for this," Carter said.

"I'll take possession of the necklace," the inspector interjected, sweeping the necklace off the table and into his pocket before turning to Mary. "Do you realize I could charge you for tampering with evidence and your law career could be over before it's begun? You too, Gordon. "

"Inspector," Malcolm said calmly, thinking of his daughter and taking his role as judge to heart. "We are all under a great deal of stress. The important thing is that the necklace has been found. Now, we have a courtroom full of lawyers out there all wondering what's happening. What do you suggest we do, Bates?"

"If you're up to it, Malcolm, the show should go on. Our lawyers are getting restless."

"All right," Donaldson said to Malcolm, "but I want to see you here afterwards. Bates, tell Hanlon, Volk and Larson not to leave Wells before I have had a chance to speak with them."

Bates and the inspector left through a side door while Carter re-entered the noisy courtroom.

"Order in court," he shouted.

The crowd quieted down. Judge Kent entered and sat on the bench. Everyone's attention was focussed on the empty envelope in his hand. Malcolm's posture said that he had returned to his role.

"Ladies and gentlemen of the jury," he intoned, "the contents of this envelope need not concern you."

The crowd shifted in their seats, reintegrating themselves into the courtroom of the past.

"Someone's imagination was working overtime. All that need concern you members of the jury is the law, which I have given you, and the facts as outlined by the statements of learned counsel. It is now up to you to bring in your verdict."

Judge Kent stood and went back to his chambers. Vladimir stepped down from the prisoner's box and was ushered into the jury room. The jury room was too small to house the enlarged jury, who remained in the courtroom for their deliberations. Mary followed Vlad.

"What's going on . . . ?"

He could be heard speaking sharply to Mary.

Brendan, the foreman of the jury, took charge by stepping up to the bench and sitting on the judge's chair, which he thought fitted him very nicely.

"Since our jury numbers have swelled from the usual

twelve to thirty, the rules will be relaxed so that instead of a unanimous verdict, we will accept a majority opinion. We will take a straight vote by show of hands. Speaking for myself, the Crown has not proven its case. Forget history and consider the facts before you today. All those in favour of conviction, raise your hands."

Twenty-eight hands were raised.

"All those against?"

Two hands, including O'Brien's, were raised.

Vladimir sat in the jury room with Mary, waiting for the verdict. Although it had pleased him to perform this little calculated act of kindness for her in remembrance of her mother, his tone of voice betrayed his annoyance.

"You didn't tell me that this was a hanging offence."

Carter opened the door.

"The jury has reached its verdict," he announced.

34

Vladimir followed Carter out of the jury room, mounted the steps and stood in the prisoner's box. Carter opened the door to the judge's chambers and, turning to the courtroom, announced the judge's presence.

Malcolm entered and glared at the crowd. They settled quickly.

"Mr. Foreman, has the jury reached its verdict?"

Brendan stood and looked up at the judge.

"We have, my lord."

"And what is your verdict on the count of murder in the first degree, guilty or not guilty?"

"Not guilty, my lord."

With that pronouncement, the courtroom erupted in protest because it had been plainly evident that the vote wasn't even close—the majority had clearly favoured a guilty verdict, the same outcome as the original trial.

Judge Kent hammered his gavel to silence his courtroom. He glowered at the prisoner.

"Do not leave the prisoner's box just yet, and remain standing. I have a few words to say."

He turned to the jury.

"Ladies and gentlemen of the jury, in all my years on

the bench, I have not encountered such a perverse verdict completely unsupported by the evidence. It is a verdict, that I do not accept. I am taking this trial away from you and pronouncing a verdict of guilty as charged."

The judge paused for a theatrical moment while his words were being transcribed by the scribbling Bernie Freeman and digested by the stunned audience. He took a black hanky from his pocket and placed it on top of his white wig. He then locked his eyes on Vladimir, who was confused and still standing in the prisoner's box.

"Having found you guilty, Mr. Barry," he said in a stiletto voice, "I hereby sentence you to death. You will be taken tomorrow morning at six a.m. and hanged by the neck until dead. May God have mercy on your soul."

Vladimir's rage, for the first time in his life, a life governed by self-interest and reason, was uncontrollable. He seemed to have forgotten that this was only a play, a re-enactment, and that he was but a mute bit player. Since he had arrived in this country, this Chilcotin, he was finding that, unlike the city, the Cariboo-Chilcotin did not play by his rules, and this was but another example. He personally felt that there had been a gross miscarriage of justice.

"The jury's verdict of not guilty," he protested in a barely-controlled voice, "can't just be overturned by the judge as if it were nothing. And furthermore, Exhibit A cannot be tampered with by the judge."

The court reporter stood.

"Stop!" he shouted. "You're speaking too quickly. I can't get this down."

This interruption struck Vladimir as another attack on his dignity and he reddened.

"Exhibit A was taken from the courtroom by the judge without showing it to the lawyers or to the jury. Or to me.

What he had in his hand was a necklace and a frog pendant, not a death's-head pin. That charm was Johanna Kent's, a woman whom I would never harm. I demand to see the contents of the envelope marked Exhibit A."

During Vladimir's impassioned speech, Lars was smiling. He seemed to be enjoying Vlad's discomfort.

"Order in court," Judge Kent hammered his gavel again. "This trial is over."

35

The first of the Cariboo Mountain snowflakes fell on the crowd exiting the Richfield courthouse, cooling off the hot tempers raised at the trial. They left in twos and threes, heading back to the Wells Hotel for the dinner and dance.

Mary and Vladimir walked separate from the others. Vlad was still upset.

"I have never been so humiliated, to think that I could be spoken to in that manner by that insulting little man."

"You're talking about my father. It was a play. He wasn't sentencing you. He was following the script."

"No. No, he left the script when he opened the envelope. That was your mother's pendant. There was something going on there, and I don't like it."

"Just calm down, I'll explain everything later."

She led him into the hotel.

Malcolm had been instructed by Donaldson to remain at the courthouse. Bates had advised the others that the inspector would be questioning them on his return to the hotel.

Judge Kent faced Inspector Donaldson in Begbie's historic chambers.

"Judge, I am conducting a police investigation into the circumstances surrounding your wife's drowning."

"I understand."

With the formalities complete, the inspector began questioning a judge as a possible suspect on a murder investigation. Something he had never done in his long career.

"Is there anything more that you can tell me about your relations with your wife?"

"Inspector," Malcolm sighed, "when Johanna and I met at the lake for the last time, we had words. She told me that she intended to take her doctorate in English in the fall in Vancouver. I had received word of my appointment to the bench in the Cariboo. Our careers were diverging. She was going to tell me a secret. I behaved badly before she told me. I was rude and overbearing, and she said the secret would wait. I left her in a huff."

"When did you find out her secret?"

"The day after Johanna's funeral," Malcolm paused for breath, "I learned from Mary and Noah that Noah is Mary's birth father. Johanna had told them both at the lake."

"How did you deal with that?"

"It came as a shock to me. After the surprise wore off, and after speaking to Mary and Noah, I have come to terms with it. Strangely, the knowledge has drawn me closer to Mary. Noah and Justine remain my friends. But," he stumbled a bit, his jurist demeanour giving way, "I can tell you that when I opened Exhibit A in the courtroom today and held Johanna's jade frog in my hands, it pierced my heart in a way that words had failed to do. It seemed to me that at that moment I was holding Johanna in my hands."

"Is there anything more you can tell me about your last hour with your wife?"

"When I was in the cabin mixing a drink, I noticed an empty half-bottle of champagne on the sideboard and another unopened bottle in the fridge, which I thought rather odd.

That was Vladimir Volk's champagne. He'd had lunch with my wife."

"Do you think they might have been having an affair? That he may have given her the necklace?" the inspector asked.

"I wouldn't have thought that. I wasn't a jealous husband. Perhaps I should have had the measure of it. I should have been more attentive."

The inspector thought for a moment that he had found the person behind the lawyer.

"I can tell you this," Malcolm continued, "it gave me great pleasure to sentence Volk to death."

"Did you see anyone on your way there or heading back to Williams Lake?"

"No."

"Did you kill your wife?"

Tears welled in Malcolm's eyes, which he wiped with the back of his index finger.

"No."

Donaldson noted that the judge did have an emotional core.

When Donaldson was back at the hotel, Corporal Lum brought Vlad to Donaldson's room.

"Thank you for coming, Mr. Volk."

Vlad approached the interview with disdain — was he not a wealthy man of the world and the inspector but a country policeman?

"Of course, Ian."

"I am questioning you formally in the death of Johanna Kent."

"I am aware of that. Am I a suspect?"

"Yes," the inspector said with emphasis. Vlad was testing his detachment. "I have your statement that you gave Corporal Melnick concerning Johanna Kent's death. You were friends in high school, I believe."

"You believe correctly."

"You said in the courtroom that Exhibit A was Johanna's necklace."

"Yes."

"How did you know that?"

"Because she was wearing it when I had lunch with her. I noticed that the jade and gold suited her."

"Did you give her the necklace?"

"No."

"Hmm," the inspector wondered out loud, letting Vlad know he doubted his answer. "It was found on your property. Do you know how it got there?"

"No."

"Were you her lover?"

"No," he hesitated. "But I was in love with her. I want to find her murderer as much as you do."

"Did you kill Johanna Kent?"

"No."

"Is there anyone you suspect of killing her?"

"Perhaps her husband."

"Why would he kill her?"

"I find him to be a very insensitive man."

"Thank you. Please give me your contact numbers and don't stray far from Williams Lake."

The inspector made a note that there was no love lost between Judge Kent and Mr. Volk.

"I'll need to travel to Vancouver for business. I'll keep you informed. "

Mary entered the inspector's room as Vlad left.

"Am I a suspect in my mother's death?" she asked.

"You were in possession of your mother's necklace."

"Yes, it was found by Celia and Johnny Eagle and I took possession of it to give to you. Carter knows that. He was there. You were coming to the Cariboo Bar meeting and so were the others who saw Mother in and around the time of her death. I thought the shock of seeing it in the context of the murder trial might reveal some truths."

"Did it?"

"It's hard to say. Perhaps in time it might work its magic."

"You're not a suspect, Mary."

She rose to go, but the inspector raised his index finger and she sat down.

"But in the future, Ms. Kent, leave the policing to the police. If you have any questions or ideas, my door is open."

Lars had no questions for the inspector when he was ushered into the room by Constable Lum.

"Have a seat, Larson. What did you think when you saw that necklace in the courtroom?"

"I didn't think anything."

"Did you recognize it?"

"Yes, that's Johanna's."

"Are you sure? Have a good look at it."

Donaldson placed it on the table. Lars didn't look.

"I am sure."

"It was found on the Native trail between your place and Vladimir Volk's ranch. Do you know how it got there?"

"No. Who found it?"

"That's not your concern."

The inspector paused for a moment, sizing up Larson.

"Did you give Johanna the necklace?" he continued.

"No."

"Were you her lover?"

"No."

"Did you kill Johanna Kent?"

"I did not. She and Malcolm are friends with me and my wife."

"Do you have any idea who might have killed Johanna?"

Lars hesitated for the briefest time.

"No, I don't."

"Fine. Please don't leave the county."

Corporal Lum opened the door for Lars and shut it after him.

"Corporal, would you bring Noah Hanlon?"

A few minutes later, Noah entered the room.

"Noah, did you know that Johanna's necklace had been found?"

"No," he shook his head, "but I recognized it as soon as Malcolm removed it from the envelope. I see it on the table. May I look at it?"

The inspector nodded and Noah picked up the necklace, examining it carefully.

"Johanna had mentioned that it was costume jewellery, but this is a work of art by a master jeweller," he concluded. "Now that I have a closer look at it, the jade is very high quality. The gold looks like fourteen-carat. This piece was made by a West Coast Native craftsman—the use of abalone for the eyes is typical."

"Do you think that it would be a piece of jewellery that Johanna would have bought for herself?"

"I can't say. She did not wear much jewellery, but the jade frog suited her so well."

"Did you give it to her?"

"No."

"Do you have any idea who did?"

"No. Where was it found?"

"It was found near the boundary line between Volk's ranch and Larson's property, on the Native trail."

"I was there with my son three weeks ago. We were on that Native trail riding from Potato Mountain to Williams Lake. It must have been found by a Native."

"I haven't had the chance to speak to the person who found

it, but I believe that it was found soon after Johanna's death."

"I saw a camp of our people on the Sunday. They would have used the same trail."

"Were you Johanna's lover?"

Noah wasn't prepared for that hard question and it took a moment for him to respond.

"Johanna and I slept together once, over twenty-one years ago. When I met her at the lake to finish her portrait, she reminded me of that night. I had put that behind me and I thought that Johanna had done the same. I regretted my infidelity. I hadn't told my wife. Then on Sunday, Johanna surprised me by telling me that Mary was my daughter. You will understand that that was a bittersweet moment."

"What do you mean?"

"Bitter in the sense that it reminded me that I had cheated on my wife, sweet in that Mary was born and is now an accomplished young woman."

"I have to ask you this. Did you kill Johanna?"

"No. Justine and I were very close to Johanna. We introduced them both, Johanna and Malcolm, to the Chilcotin. She loved her adopted land."

"Has Justine accepted that you had fathered a child by Johanna?"

"That happened a long time ago and Justine and I are still in love. When we found out about Mary, how could we turn our backs on that wonderful woman?"

"When did Justine know about your relations with Johanna?"

"Although I hadn't told her, she had guessed that I had been unfaithful with someone on that trip to Vancouver, but she didn't know about Mary until I told her later on Sunday."

"Do you have any idea who would have killed Johanna?"

"I am a shaman," Noah said, straightening taller in his chair. "During my summer ride with my son across the

Chilcotin plateau, I asked Raven to help me find Johanna's killer. Raven led me to Wolf and I followed his killing trail for a month from Potato Mountain to Vladimir Volk's ranch. There, in Vladimir's presence, I shot the wolf that he was protecting. I believe that Volk has something to do with Johanna's death."

"That's interesting," Donaldson said in a disinterested tone. His tone changed to warning. "If he has, you may be at risk."

"Whoever found the necklace is at greater risk than me," Noah countered. "My people were camped by the road and may have seen vehicles moving in and out of Larson Lake. If they can identify those vehicles, then you would be closer to the killer. They also could be suspects. They were camped within a mile of the cabin."

Donaldson recognized the truth in Noah's words.

"You will have to leave that investigation to me."

When Noah left the room, Donaldson rang the Williams Lake RCMP detachment office.

"Melnick," he ordered into the phone, "I want you to pick up Johnny and Celia Eagle and hold them for questioning in the investigation of Johanna Kent's death. They should be at Redstone Reserve. I will be in Williams Lake in the morning."

At the dance that night, as it would be for years afterwards whenever the Cariboo Bar met, Brendan O'Brien's motives for saying "not guilty" were discussed and debated. The consensus was that Brendan was getting back at Judge Kent for allegedly stealing Brendan's appointment to the bench. If that was Brendan's plan, it failed, for by putting Brendan in his place at the mock trial and dealing unflinching justice on the head of the accused, Malcolm had clearly demonstrated amongst his peers why he merited his appointment to the bench.

That evening, Judge Kent and his legal colleagues gathered

for dinner in the Wells Hotel to speculate on the motives of the mock trial *Regina v. Barry* and the beginning of another Cariboo Bar legend. The judge accompanied Mary and sat next to her at the table.

Halfway through dinner, Malcolm whispered to his daughter.

"Do you suspect me of murdering your mother?"

"Dad, we're all suspects."

He tried to shrug off her comment.

"You're partially right. I don't suspect you."

The man whom Mary's father had sentenced to death was very much alive down at the other end of the table, sitting with Robin and her unhappy parents, who had arrived for the dinner and dance. Vlad was enjoying a bit of notoriety from the lawyers who admired his extemporaneous speech from the prisoner's box.

In his cups, Brendan O'Brien proposed a toast.

"To the Hanging Judge."

The toast was repeated and glasses were raised. The noise subsided as they awaited the response.

Malcolm Kent slowly rose to his feet and replied in his role of Chief Justice Begbie.

"In this year of 1867, in the preamble to the BNA Act, the constitution of the Dominion of Canada, to which our province will soon be joined, the Supreme Being and the rule of law are recognized." He raised his glass. "To the rule of law."

He thought it would be presumptuous to toast God.

On that happy note, everybody except the judge and the inspector moved to the ballroom for the dance. These two retired to their rooms, the judge to work on a judgment and the inspector to think about the murder of Johanna Kent and to read Johanna's annotated book, *The Diviners*.

Donaldson had sent the waterlogged copy to the RCMP lab in Saskatoon to be restored. It had taken the restoration experts over two months to treat each page and then reassemble the book. He had received it back from the lab before the meeting and had started to read it and planned to finish it on the weekend.

Bates had put him at the end of the program on Sunday morning, to talk about crime statistics after breakfast so that the lawyers would leave for their homes on a sober note. Donaldson wouldn't mention the possible murder of Johanna Kent. Up until the frog necklace was found, her murder was only a suspicion and the investigation was a long way from proving there was a murder, let alone who the perpetrator was.

In the morning light, after the events of the Begbie trial, that suspicion had grown to a probability. Perhaps he had too hastily dismissed Noah's shaman divination of linking the wolf to Vladimir as the prime suspect in the murder as questionable. On reflection, he had to acknowledge that he had acted on hunches or gut feelings in this case and others during his long career. Perhaps these were no different from Noah's shamanistic insights.

Donaldson had read the first chapters of Johanna's heavily annotated copy of Laurence's novel before the missing necklace had suddenly appeared and Judge Kent told him of his encounter with Johanna at the lake. He now knew from the judge why Johanna had the book at Larson's cabin. He couldn't rule the judge out as a suspect just because he had come forward. He considered whether Noah could possibly be a suspect. He said he had been at the lake between three and five p.m. But when he left, Johanna was alive and in good spirits according to the judge, who had arrived at six p.m, and left just after seven. *But what about after the judge said he left? Noah and any one of the other suspects could have returned. The Eagles may have the answer.*

After midnight, he could hear the faint sounds of the last of the revellers downstairs. He was at page 266 and was beginning to doze off. His interest as a reader picked up on a possible sexual encounter between the main protagonist Morag and a man named Chas, who was a friend of Fan, Morag's landlady in North Vancouver. Chas said that he came to Fan's house not to see Fan, but to see Morag. Anticipating trouble for Morag, Donaldson's eyes shifted from the bottom of the left-hand page to the top of the next page. Instead of an assault, which he expected, he read that Pique, Morag's daughter, was still asleep upstairs. He looked at the page number—it was 269. A leaf, pages 267 and 268 had been torn from the book. His interest as a policeman was as intense on discovering the missing two pages as a reader's feelings in discovering what happened to Morag.

Perhaps Johanna had left a clue in those missing pages? He would go to the Williams Lake library tomorrow, after the bar meeting, to copy the missing pages, to find out what Johanna Kent, the English teacher, was trying to tell him.

36

The consensus amongst the lawyers around the Sunday breakfast tables in Wells was that the Cariboo Bar tradition of the unexpected had been met, and some thought surpassed. Surely it was up there with the vote years ago to ask the chief justice to remove a sitting judge. Because of the meeting's success, Acton Bates, the committee of one, was toasted with mimosas. He deflected the praise to his young staff—Carter, Mary and Elizabeth. Immediately following Inspector Donaldson's speech on crime statistics in his district, the lawyers' bus left for the return trip to Fort St. John.

Paul and Mert had left before breakfast, heading back to Vladimir's log mansion on the steppes above the Chilcotin River. Snow on the Cariboo Mountains had reminded Paul he had a building to finish. He would need a few more weeks to nail on the shakes.

Paul had the closest contact with Vladimir Volk since he'd descended on the Chilcotin from the steppes of Russia. To others, Vlad appeared charming. Not so to Paul, whom Vlad treated like a serf—strong-arming him, lying to him and making wild, and so far unkept, promises to his daughter. Paul would have given up the building contract except that he owed the Lalulas money for their work on the house. In Paul's mind, Vladimir wasn't bound by the social glue that held the Chilcotin together, and Paul had learned not to cross him. Since the Halversons' barn dance, Vladimir had kept him on a short leash. Vladimir was always late on wages and the holdbacks were not the usual 10%—they were 25%. Once the roof was on, Paul would be finished and free of his menace, leaving only the matter of Robin's career on hold. To a free man, and everyone has his or her ideas of freedom, it was unbearable to have to dance to the tune of a madman, a man who was intent on imposing his will on him. With these troubling thoughts, Paul pulled his truck off the highway at nine a.m. and climbed the road to the house. He was hoping that Lalula's crew would be there. The front door opened, revealing Vladimir's grim face.

"You'd better get to work," he said. "If that roof isn't on before the snow flies, don't expect to get paid."

Vlad brushed by, continuing on to the back of the house where his four-wheel drive truck was parked.

Vlad headed west, back towards Williams Lake. He stopped at Larson Road, got out of his truck and walked up to the rise overlooking the turnoff. The sight of Johanna's necklace in the Richfield courthouse had unnerved him. He recalled that the morning after he had visited Johanna at the cabin, he was at his construction site when a Native couple, the woman with a baby strapped to her back, had ridden their horses through the meadow fronting the river. He had shouted at them and was walking over to tell them they were trespassing when Paul had hailed them as if they were old friends.

"Where ya heading?" Paul had asked.

Vlad had held his tongue.

"Heading to Potato Mountain for the jamboree." the man had shouted.

After Paul had had his talk with them, and they had passed out of sight, Vlad had rounded on Paul.

"I want you to tell all your Native pals that this is private property and they are not to cross it."

Those must have been the Natives that he had seen camped at the turnoff to Larson Road as he drove back to his ranch from seeing Johanna. He came down from the rise to his truck thinking he must ask Laboucher about those Indians, but then he remembered why he was going to Larson Lake this morning. He was late for a rendezvous.

Vladimir drove to the clearing on the small lake. There was a curl of smoke from the chimney of the cabin and a yellow pickup truck with a 'Larson's Lumber' logo parked outside. Larson had arranged the meeting with Vlad at the Wells Hotel before the dinner, to which Larson had not been invited. Larson had hinted that he was interested in offering Vlad a partnership in his company. Lars was looking out the front window onto the lake when Vlad entered.

"Where was it," Vlad asked, without preliminaries, "that you discovered Johanna's body?"

Lars appeared startled by the question.

"It pains me to think about it. She was in the reeds to the left of the dock. Shall we get down to business?"

"You were fond of her?"

"Yes, I thought she was a remarkable woman."

"I thought so too."

"She wouldn't be your type."

"Oh, you've heard that opposites attract, haven't you?" Vlad's dislike of Lars had grown over the summer and he prodded Lars. "Perhaps you could describe your Johanna's attributes?"

"Now boast thee, Death in thy possession lies a lass unparalleled."

Lars delivered this line movingly and without hesitation, as if he was a Shakespearian actor declaiming to an audience what was said of Cleopatra.

To Vlad, these sentiments coming from a rough woodsman seemed odd, but maybe not. Johanna had that effect on men.

"Wherever did you run across that quote?"

"Johanna taught an adult education course on the works of Shakespeare. It's from *Antony and Cleopatra.* I've always associated it with her. Shall we get down to the purpose of this meeting? You've seen my books, you know my business. I need financing for the winter season, and the banks don't seem to be interested. I thought you would make a loan to the company."

"How much do you need and at what rate of interest?"

"A million dollars at one percent below bank rates."

"I'll lend you five hundred thousand. At double the bank rates."

"That's not on the table."

"Then I can't be of any help to you." Vlad rose. "By the way, you shouldn't be cheating on the logging scales, and I believe that logging cedar on Crown land is against the law, not to mention logging in the Brittany Triangle."

With that, Vlad opened the door to leave.

Lars, visibly upset, physically forestalled him. The two protagonists came face-to-face, neither giving way until Lars spoke through gritted teeth.

"Let me tell you a story about cheating and rejection which will change your mind about the loan."

"I don't think so."

"It concerns you and Johanna."

"You know nothing about my relationship with Johanna."

"My story won't take long. On the night Johanna drowned, I saw her hand you her frog necklace. You refused to take it, and there is no doubt in my mind that you were her lover and she was rejecting you."

"Why are you telling me these lies?"

"Inspector Donaldson would like to know. He *needn't* know if you lend me six hundred thousand dollars at one percent under bank rates for five years."

Vlad considered Larson's blackmail for a moment.

"Where do you say this happened?"

"In front of your trailer by your half-completed house. You were lit by a bonfire, and I had an excellent view."

"No one would believe you, but that aside, I'll agree to your terms. Have your lawyer draft the documents and bring them to me when they're ready for signature. In the meantime, do you mind if I use your cabin? I'm finding it a bit cramped in my trailer."

Larson handed over the keys.

"You'll find that your loan is a good investment."

Vladimir stood at the door waving goodbye, a beautiful broad smile on his face as if Larson were his best friend, not his blackmailer.

37

The inspector opened the passenger door to the squad car idling outside the entrance to the Wells Hotel and sat in the warmed vehicle.

"Back to Prince George, sir?" his driver, Corporal Lum, cheerily asked.

"No, we're going to Williams Lake."

There was little talking during the two-hour drive as the inspector finished reading Margaret Laurence's novel. Aside from the novel being an important piece of evidence, he was engaged in the story. He would recommend it to his wife—that would surprise her. He wished that the police had a diviner on staff.

On their entry to Williams Lake, he directed the corporal to the library. With the help of Lillian Mack, the librarian, he found that the library had two editions of *The Diviners*, and one had been checked out. What was left was a well-used hardcover edition, the same edition that Johanna had. He turned to page 267 and read that, although the sex was consensual, the brief encounter ended in violence by Chas, a brutal man.

The pathologist had not conducted a rape test. There was no evidence in the autopsy report that Johanna had had intercourse in her last hours, nor were there any signs of physical trauma to her body.

He looked deep in the binding of Johanna's copy of the novel and saw that the leaf was torn out hurriedly, leaving jagged edges. He wondered about Johanna's state of mind at the time. If she had removed the leaf, she must have had a reason to tear it out. The missing leaf wasn't found in the cabin, but they hadn't been looking for it. It might still be there. At his request, Lil copied the two pages from the book and gave them to him.

Copies in hand, he ordered Constable Lum to take him to Larson Lake so he could look for the torn pages.

There was a truck parked outside Larson's cabin which the inspector imagined belonged to Larson. He wouldn't have to break in. He had obtained Larson's agreement to search the cabin back in July, yet there was some doubt if the agreement was still valid.

There was no movement inside the cabin. He got out of the car, and knocked on the back door. There was no answer. He turned the handle. The door was unlocked. He ordered Constable Lum to go inside and search for the missing leaf. Then he walked around to the front of the cabin which looked onto the lake, carrying Johanna's high-school yearbook. Volk was standing on the shore facing the lake, watching a bufflehead duck paddling near the reeds. A breeze ruffled the water.

Donaldson was a bit of a dandy. He noticed that Vlad was dressed for the change in the weather in a Louis Vuitton coat. Vlad had to have been aware of their arrival, and of the inspector approaching him on foot, but Vlad was completely indifferent to his presence and remained fixed, unmoved. The inspector said nothing until he came abreast of the lone man.

"I find it so peaceful in this virginal landscape," Vladimir said without turning, as if speaking to the wind.

"You are looking at the scene of a murder."

"Ah, Inspector, I thought it might be you. Are you sure it was a murder?"

"Why are you here, Volk?"

"Lars allows me the use of his cabin from time to time while my house is under construction."

Vladimir turned, looked the inspector in the eye and gave him a dazzling white-toothed smile. Donaldson was the same height as Vlad but weighed twenty kilograms more.

"What connection do you have with Lars?"

"I'm a venture capitalist and Larson Forest Products is a business investment."

The inspector opened the yearbook to the page for Vladimir Black opposite that of Johanna Barton.

"Your picture appears as a mug shot with the words, *Born to be Free* and in handwriting, *To live a life of crime.* Is that your handwriting?"

"Yes."

"Have you lived up to your promise?"

"Ah, that was the utterance of a callow youth. My blotter is clean, Inspector."

"I'm sure it is."

"Inspector, I only wish I had provisions here so I could offer you some refreshment. Next time, eh?"

Constable Lum now joined them. The inspector raised his eyebrow in a questioning look, Lum shook his head and the inspector abruptly marched off to the parked police cruiser.

"You'll be hearing from me," he curtly told Vlad. "Remember keep me informed of your whereabouts."

Vladimir accompanied the officers to their car. Before the inspector opened the door, Vlad, standing at his elbow, fixed him with a glance.

"I believe as you do, Inspector," Vlad's voice was different now, deep and serious, "that Johanna was murdered. As I told you, she was a bright woman with great promise—which I learned from attending her funeral service, had been realized here in the Chilcotin. Call on me if you need any help."

Donaldson nodded, closed the door and turned to Lum.

"You didn't find the missing pages?"

"No, sir."

As the squad car pulled away from the cabin, Vlad was waving goodbye. Vladimir Volk, the Russian Wolf, was firmly on the inspector's list of suspects.

38

Stan and Belle arrived at their house in Williams Lake, driven by Noah. They had bought the house ten years ago so that they could spend six months of the year within walking distance of Stan's law office. The other six months they spent at the ranch at Tatlayoko Lake. The law and Belle were the only things that gave Stan an interest in life. Belle's sacrifice was that she was separated from her Bechstein grand piano. It had accompanied her from Scotland when she married Bordy Hanlon, it had travelled with her to Victoria, where she lived for a few years, and back again to the ranch at Tatlayoko where it had been her constant companion ever since. In Williams Lake, she made do with an upright piano and gave piano lessons to a few students.

On their arrival, Belle insisted that Stan take to his bed. He didn't resist. She fussed over him. He bridled a bit at that, especially in front of Noah. They left him alone to rest and Belle fixed lunch. Stan usually had a nap after lunch. Today, he was desperately tired, but he had to speak to Noah alone. Noah came into his room and shut the door.

"There is something troubling me about what Antoine said to us," Stan sighed. "I was thinking about it at Johanna's funeral."

Stan had kept returning to Antoine's last words over the years as if it was a mantra, and each time he did it, reminded Noah of the mantel of *deyen* passed on to him by Antoine. Noah humoured the old man.

"That was a while ago."

"I know, I've thought about it a lot. Remember Tatlayoko Lake? Antoine in his lean-to?"

"You mean the day he died?"

"Yes. He told you who your father was."

"Yes."

"You took his words to mean that it was the Chilcotin itself. I believed that Antoine said it was Bordy."

"You told me that in Vancouver years ago, and you've reminded me of it from time to time."

Noah said this to his failing friend in a gentle voice, asking Stan's meaning.

Stan said nothing for a while. He was breathing slowly and his eyes were closed. Noah sat in a chair by the head of the bed, leaning over Stan to catch his words.

Belle began playing Beethoven's *Pathétique,* Sonata No 8 – 2nd Movement in A flat major in the adjoining room, and the music roused the old man.

He opened his eyes and looked at Noah, he took Noah's hand in his own, gripped it, and picked up as if there had been no silence.

"Now, at the end of my life," he said softly, "that's pretty well all I think about. It's taken me this long to figure out Antoine's meaning."

There was another pause.

"Antoine's meaning," he repeated. "Yes, Antoine's meaning was that both Bordy and the spirit of the Chilcotin fathered you."

Noah smiled. It had taken Stan, the white man, to the end

of his days to understand the meaning of the Chilcotin: this duality of nature's agent and the human agent which Noah had instinctively understood. He squeezed Stan's hand.

"I know."

39

It was 9:30 on Sunday when Mary, Carter and Elizabeth checked out of the Wells Hotel. They were surprised, when settling up the accounts for the entertainers, to learn from the clerk that Robin had checked out at five-thirty a.m., and the Labouchers had left at six.

Driving through Williams Lake with Carter at the wheel, on that quiet Sunday, they approached the Rendezvous Café. Robin was out front talking to Wheelchair. Standing there in the cold, she looked dishevelled, and as they drove closer they could see that she had been crying.

"Pull over. Something has happened to Robin," Mary ordered.

Carter parked the car beside Robin, and Mary jumped out.

"What happened to you? You look terrible. Are you all right?"

"Can we help you?" Carter asked, coming up beside her.

"I'm fine," Robin said, the tremor in her voice and lack of eye contact betraying her. "And I'm talking to Wheelchair."

Carter nodded to his old witness, who gave him a smile of recognition.

"We were told at the hotel that you left in the early morning."

"Oh," Robin laughed nervously. "I got a ride with Vlad. He had some important business to look after and he left me here."

She sniffled and wiped her eyes, then laughed.

"I know I look a mess. I'm not used to getting up at five-thirty in the morning, but he was going and I wanted to talk to him about my career. He didn't seem interested. My ambitions have been crushed."

"Look, we can't leave you here," Mary said. "You come home with me. You'll probably want a rest."

Mary took her by the arm and steered Robin to the car. She was about to get in when Wheelchair whistled for attention.

"Hey, pretty one," he called out. "You forgot your baggie."

He wheeled over and he handed it to Robin.

"Thanks, Wheelchair," she smiled.

"See you again soon."

At the Kents' house, Mary took Robin into her bedroom and shut the door.

"All right," she asked, "tell me what happened."

Robin looked down at her hands.

"I couldn't sleep. I got up about five and went down to the lobby. Vlad came down at five-thirty and I asked for a ride back to Williams Lake. On the ride back, he seemed agitated, almost spooked."

Mary drew back at this, but recovered and gestured to Robin to continue.

"'I had to be out of there before six,' she said. I remembered that your dad had said at the mock trial that he was to be hanged at six, and I said, 'Vlad, don't be so superstitious.'"

She looked up at Mary.

"He never gets mad. It's as if he has no emotions. He just gets quiet and gives you a weird look. On the trip to town, he and I had as close to an argument that you could have with Vlad."

She seemed unsure whether she should continue.

"Go on," Mary assured. "It's okay."

"He said that he had to find out who killed your mother. That he had been humiliated by your father. He was driving to his ranch so I asked him to drop me off at the Rendezvous Café. Wheelchair showed up and he kept me company over coffee until you arrived."

"I didn't know Wheelchair was a dealer?"

"Yeah," Robin sniffled. "He deals for someone in town."

40

Vladimir watched the inspector's car vanish into the trees.

He realized that he was not just a person of interest, but was now the prime suspect for the murder of the only woman he had ever loved. The last time he had faced such humiliation was when his father had banished him from the family after Boris had discovered that he and his half-sister had had sex. Consequently, it had taken him twenty years to rise to wealth and respectability. He was not prepared to be put on trial by a two-bit country policeman for Johanna's murder.

He waited five minutes for the inspector's car to reach the highway, then got in his truck and headed west towards his ranch for another talk with the Labouchers. When he drove up, four men were on the roof, hammering shakes. Mert was clambering up and down the ladder, supplying them with fresh material.

"Laboucher," Vlad shouted to Paul. "Come down here. I want to talk to you."

Paul slowly made his way down the ladder.

"It looks like you might finish after all."

Vlad's tone, his demeanour was almost jovial. Paul wasn't

sure what was going on, but he was going to ride this pony as far as he could. He looked up at the roof.

"Yeah, it will take another week. They're hoping to do some hunting before the season's over." Sensing this was as friendly as he was likely to see Vlad, he added, "And when you pay me, they will get their paycheques sooner, too."

"That's fine with me. Do you remember those Indians who rode through my property in July? I told you to tell them not to trespass again?"

"Yeah," Paul nodded, now a bit suspicious of Vlad's mood. "I didn't see them again."

"You knew them. Who were they?"

Paul wasn't about to go out of his way to answer any question from Vlad. He scratched his head.

"Are they causing you any trouble?"

"No."

"I don't know their names. We Métis just like to keep things friendly with the Native folk."

Mert passed the two men with a bundle of shakes and Vlad hailed her.

"Say, Mert, you remember those Indians that trespassed on my land in July? What were their names?"

Mert missed the signal from Paul to plead ignorance.

"The girl is called Celia."

"Is she from hereabouts?"

"Yeah, she lives on the Redstone Reserve."

He looked at Paul.

"You've been smoking too much pot. And get rid of those plants you're growing near the ridge."

41

Donaldson had stayed overnight in Williams Lake. In the morning, he sat at his desk at the local detachment of the RCMP, staring at a treasure trove of evidence laid out on his desk. The notes that he had gathered during his weekend at Wells were there, as well as the statements made by those who were close to Johanna, the necklace with the jade frog pendant, the hardcover edition of Margaret Laurence's *The Diviners* with two pages missing, photocopies of the missing pages and Johanna's high-school yearbook.

He compared the jade frog pendant with Noah's watercolour painting of it drawn in turn from his oil portrait of Johanna wearing the pendant the afternoon before she drowned. The likeness was striking, from the gold clasps holding the jade right down to the gold backing and legs, and the abalone eyes. These collected pieces of evidence gave him the feeling that Billy Barker would have had on discovering gold in his pan at Williams Creek. Now all Donaldson had to do was to discover what Billy Barker discovered: the motherlode.

After reviewing and pondering the evidence for an hour, he still couldn't say that Johanna was murdered—yet his instincts said she was. Three people had travelled the Larson Road that day: Vladimir Volk, Noah Hanlon and

Judge Kent. Then there was Larson, who owned the cabin and discovered Johanna's body, and the Eagles, who had camped nearby. The judge was the last person who had admitted to seeing Johanna alive, and he was an unlikely suspect. He had just been appointed to the bench. Why would he jeopardize his lifelong ambition? There was no doubt in Donaldson's mind that Johanna's death had had a profound effect on him. It had made him more empathetic, a role that he'd previously delegated to Johanna, but now that she was no longer there, he had to assume himself.

Donaldson's immediate concern was Johanna's annotated copy of *The Diviners*. It needed to be deciphered to see if Johanna had provided any clues about her murderer besides the missing pages. His first reading of the book had been a quick skim of the text itself. It would take him days to read the annotations and relate them to the text. He would have to enlist someone to help, someone who knew Johanna intimately, who could read her notes and divine her message. He came to that conclusion after reading, with difficulty, Johanna's last note, which would require a dictionary to begin with, for him to fully understand.

It seems to me, The Diviners *is as close as a writer would want to get in fiction to her own life, short of calling it an autobiography. Peggy, if I may call her that, has created a mirror image or doppelganger effect. I am beginning to feel a personal affinity for ML.*

Mary came to mind as the diviner of her mother's work. Time was of the essence so he thought of the unorthodox step of enlisting Mary to read and interpret Johanna's annotated edition at the detachment offices.

Melnick arranged for Mary to attend at the detachment offices that afternoon. The inspector himself met her in reception and brought her into his office.

"Would you like a cup of tea?" he asked.

This was a much different interview than the one she had in Wells when she was told by Donaldson to mind her own business.

He ordered tea and picked up *The Diviners* from his desk. He shook it as he would a rattle.

"This is your mother's book that we found in the lake," he offered. "You see that it has been badly water-damaged, but our lab has salvaged it. What I am about to tell you is between you and me. You mustn't tell anyone."

"I recognize it," Mary replied, surprised. "I held it in my hand when I last saw Mother alive. I've read a copy of it that mother had in her library."

"I've read the book too and I believe that your mother left us a clue in this book. There is one leaf, pages 267–68, torn from the book that refers to an assault on Morag, the main character, by a man named Chas. The book is heavily annotated in your mother's handwriting, which is difficult to read. And part of it is her own shorthand."

"I can read her shorthand."

"I was hoping you could," he half-smiled, "because, you see, I would like you to read the book at the detachment and give me your summary of anything in the book that might relate to your mother's death."

"When would you want that done?"

"By tomorrow morning," he said. "If there are any further clues in the book, I want to know about them as soon as possible."

She picked up the book from the desk where Donaldson had placed it and held in her hand as if it was a fish and she was judging its weight to determine the time it would take to cook. Then she flipped through the heavily-annotated pages and finally said.

"I'll try."

Since the mock trial in Richfield, Donaldson's hunch was now a full investigation. He was now the lead investigator on a sensitive case which involved the wife of a judge, and Corporal Melnick was up-to-date for the purpose of assisting him in the ongoing investigations.

42.

On Monday evening, Vlad built a fire with the firewood that Lars had thoughtfully provided. He sat in front of the flames nursing a glass of Larson's scotch and reflecting on his change of fortune since Johanna's death. He didn't enjoy liquor, but now he needed it to dull his pain. Up to the time of his high school reunion, he had acquired all that the city had had to offer: first wealth, then with wealth came respect, with respect civic awards. Then he'd met Johanna at the reunion and she had drawn him to the Chilcotin. *Like the sirens who had tempted the sailors in the Odyssey,* he thought.

He had given Johanna his heart—something that he had given no other woman, but he found that she'd had her own dreams. After a few more sips of Larson's scotch, he felt uneasy.

Something isn't right in the room. Someone or something is between me and my thoughts of Johanna.

He looked around and noticed that Larson had three original oil paintings hanging on the living room wall. He got up from his chair and looked at the signature: Noah Hanlon. Of course it was Noah — the guardian of the Chilcotin. Noah had given the eulogy at the funeral. Noah had shot Vladimir's wolf. Noah had witnessed his humiliation at the vindictive hands of Malcolm Kent in the mock trial.

Vlad poured himself another scotch and studied the paintings. They appeared to be identical 3' × 4' oil paintings of a lone pine standing in the middle of an endless clearcut. They reminded him of Monet's series of haystacks. He saw that the angle and intensity of light on the living pine cast an altered shadow in each painting, signifying a movement of the sun and the passage of time. He removed the paintings from the wall and carried them to the fireplace. He thought, *This would be a good way to rid me of Hanlon.* He threw the first painting into the fire, smiling at the flash fuelled by the oily canvas lighting the room.

His downed the scotch in a swallow. He filled his empty glass with scotch and studied the second painting. The lone, living tree in the sun-drenched clearing looked different. It seemed to be a small message of hope amidst devastation. This thought warmed him a little. He recognized this warming as a weakness but, as long as it wasn't overindulged, it could cause him no harm. He hesitated and, in that moment of indecision, the second painting slipped from his hand into the fire.

"Damn, I didn't intend that."

Then he laughed.

In the flash of firelight, he examined the tree in the third painting more closely, and noticed a green seedling amid the pine cones at the base of the tree. From devastation, there appeared in the painting a small hope of creation. He stayed his hand.

The painting said to him that, if one stands one's ground—if he stood his ground in the Chilcotin—like the Natives, like the pine tree, he would prevail and so would the Chilcotin. He wouldn't attack the Chilcotin, he would caress her. She would become his ally, not his enemy.

The hot flames fuelled by the paintings died to ashes,

leaving the skeletal frames. He hung the last picture back on the wall and, for the first time since he was told by his mother as a child that his father had left him to return to Russia, he cried. He had come so far from his father-less childhood. He had proven to his father that here on the steppes of the Chilcotin, he was an equal to a Russian count on the steppes of the Volga. He had his *dacha*, his fields and his peasants. He had everything, yet without Johanna he had nothing. But then he had what Johanna had—the Chilcotin—and he would, like Noah's pine tree in a desolated landscape, stay and face the future.

Donaldson phoned the judge at the courthouse and asked if he had read any of Margaret Laurence's novels or short stories.

"I know who Margaret Laurence is," Malcolm answered defensively, trying to cover his lack of knowledge about his wife's passion. "I've read about the controversy around *The Diviners*."

"Oh? what controversy?"

"I believe a number of people in the small Ontario town where she was living took exception to the sex scenes in the novel."

"Did you disapprove of your wife's subject for her doc-torate?"

"Heavens, no. To be honest, my disagreement with Johanna was that she was going to move to Vancouver for a number of years, when I needed her in Williams Lake. My conduct was selfish and mean-spirited, and we parted for the last time in a bad way. I will have to live with that for the rest of my life."

The judge paused. The inspector did not fill in the gap with another question so, uncharacteristically, Malcolm decided to share a personal moment with the quiet lawman.

"Ian," he confided, "Mary has been my salvation since Johanna's death. I used to think that as long as I had the law that I was impervious to fate and fortune. But the rule of law doesn't embrace emotions. I've discovered since Johanna's death that if I don't have Mary's love, I have nothing."

"Do you have any enemies?"

"Not that I am aware of."

"What about Johanna?"

"No, a few people were jealous of her talents, but that's all."

"Were *you* jealous of her talents?"

"No, she was my wife. She was a good woman. My error was that I took her for granted. And when she called me on it, my response was irritation at her not being enthusiastic about my being appointed to the bench."

ENDGAME

43

Mid-Tuesday morning, September 23rd, Melnick reported back to the inspector.

"Mary Kent spent most of the night reading *The Diviners*. It was a big job. She's given us a typed report on her findings. Her mother's annotations are written in a shorthand that Mary was able to read. The notes were mostly academic and cross-referenced to Laurence's other writings, but Johanna also wrote some personal things in the margins. One of the more interesting details is that Vladimir Volk was at one time was called Vladimir Black."

"I know, his picture faces Johanna's in the high school yearbook. Here it is."

Donaldson thumbed through the yearbook and found the page of Vladimir Black, *'Born to be free'* printed beneath, then in handwriting *'To live a life of crime.'*

"I put it to Volk at the lake and he acknowledged that it was him."

"Mary also had her boyfriend search the change of name registry, which confirms that Volk was the student named Black. He also dropped his middle name, 'Charles'."

"Melnick, that's the clue that Johanna left us. Chas in the *Diviners* is Vladimir Volk!" the inspector shouted.

"Very good, sir."

"And who do you mean by Mary's boyfriend?"

"Carter Gordon."

"Just because they conspired to make the frog pendant the centrepiece in the Richfield trial doesn't make them a couple, Corporal."

"Yes, sir. On a personal level, Mary found that Johanna had serious reservations about her marriage. And Johanna was thinking of living with Mary in Vancouver while she was studying for her doctorate."

Donaldson nodded.

"Mary also found, in her mother's notes, parallels between their relationship and that of the mother-daughter relationship in the book."

"If that's all, Corporal, pick up Volk for questioning in the death of Johanna Kent. Have you found the Eagles?"

"No, sir. Constable Roy, stationed at Tatla Lake, went to the Redstone Reserve and was told that the Eagles had gone fishing. No one knew or would tell the constable which of the thousand lakes, rivers and streams in the Chilcotin they were fishing."

"Melnick, has it occurred to you that the Eagles' lives are at risk? They may be able to identify the killer. They were in the vicinity of Larson Lake when Johanna drowned. We have to assume that the killer is aware of that."

"Yes, Inspector, but no Native is going to tell the police where to find the Eagles."

"We've got to find them. We don't know what role if any they played in Johanna's death. They were by the lake that night. They found the necklace; they could be witnesses or they could have been involved. Their neighbours would tell Noah Hanlon how to find them. Contact Hanlon and bring him to me. I'll personally give him instructions to locate the Eagles."

Late Tuesday morning, Noah was at the hospital when Melnick located him. Stan Hewitt had suffered a stroke and was in a coma. Noah and his family were at Stan's bedside. Noah left his stepfather in the care of Belle and Justine and called on Donaldson, who asked him to find and speak to the Eagles.

"As soon as you find the Eagles," Donaldson said, "get their story and phone it back to me. Don't waste any time."

Noah decided to bring Carter along with him—he was someone the Eagles trusted. He picked Carter up at his law office and they headed out to the reserve in Noah's truck with a horse trailer and two horses. They drove into the chief's yard. He came outside to talk to them.

"Afternoon, Joseph," Noah said.

"Noah, who's you got with you?" he grunted.

"This is Carter, Johnny and Celia's lawyer. We're here to speak to the Eagles. I hear they've gone fishing."

"The police were here a few days ago asking the same thing."

"I brought Carter along to give Celia and Johnny some legal advice."

"I thought Stan Hewitt was their lawyer?"

"Carter is from Stan's law office. Stan is in the hospital and I don't think he'll pull through. I want to get back there as soon as I can. Before I do, we have to speak to Celia and Johnny."

"Sorry about Stan," Joseph nodded slowly. "He's helped me through a few brushes with the law. Okay, I can tell you the general area where they're at. There's a secret fishing hole, been in the family going on generations. It's on the Chilco River somewhere between Henry's Crossing and the junction with the Taseko River."

"Okay, Joseph. Don't tell anyone else."

Noah and Carter returned to the truck.

"Do you have any ideas which end of the river they're fishing?" Carter asked.

"My guess is that it's nearer to Henry's Crossing. We'll take the Tatlayoko turnoff, cut back to Henry's Crossing, park the truck and work downriver on horseback."

There was no road along the Chilco River, and not much of a trail. Noah and Carter walked their horses on the west side of the rushing water, keeping one eye watching for signs of horses passing through and the other on the water for a likely fishing spot. The Eagles would have tethered their horses away from their camp and would have some kind of canvas for protection from the weather. At dusk, it was Carter who spotted them eight miles downstream from Henry's Crossing.

Their camp was on the opposite side and they had to ride another mile downstream to find a spot to ford the river. It was dark when they rode into the Eagles' camp. Sockeye salmon, gutted and spread, were hanging on racks above a smudge drying. If Johnny and Celia were surprised, they didn't show it. It seemed they had heard the horses shod hooves on the rocks and were expecting someone.

Celia hailed them.

"Carter, we don't need no lawyer. So what the hell are you doing out here?"

"Let me get off my horse and I'll tell you."

"Sit and share some salmon with us," she offered.

They dismounted. Noah took the reins of both horses to a makeshift corral and put them in with the Eagles' horses. Remembering, he took the opportunity to check their horses' hooves. The pinto had a misshapen right front horseshoe, confirming that the Eagles were camped at Larson's turnoff on the night of Johanna's drowning.

Noah joined Carter and the Eagles, sitting by the smudge.

After a meal of barbecued salmon, bannock, tea and a bit of chit-chat, Noah became serious.

"Stan Hewitt suffered a stroke yesterday and is in a coma at the hospital. He was your lawyer. I thought you would like to know."

"Sorry to hear, Noah. He is like an elder to us."

"Yes, I could see he was respected by the Natives." His tone of voice changed. "In July, after the stampede and your custody case for Jewel, you rode back to your home and camped at the turnoff to Larson Lake. We figure you may have seen something or someone on Larson Road that could help in our investigation of Johanna Kent's death."

Johnny and Celia were sitting on the ground next to each other.

"She the judge's wife?" Celia asked.

"That's right," Carter answered.

"He was pretty good to us about Jewel."

Carter didn't correct her by telling her it was the wrong judge—to some clients, all judges seem the same.

"You know that frog pendant you found, Celia?"

"Yeah, I sure hated to give it up."

"You remember that you told Mary that you and Johnny found it near where you camped that night. Can you tell me again exactly where?"

"We was there, Johnny and me and Jewel, just the one afternoon and night," Celia recalled. "Yeah, we camped there at the Larson Road turnoff by the stream—good grass for the horses. Next day, pretty early in the morning, we rode through the property to the west. Paul Laboucher is building a big house. We notice a blond guy drove up. He was pretty upset." Celia thought for a bit and then added, "We come through on the trail a ways before the house and Johnny, he finds the necklace and frog there just on the trail near the ridge, on the Larson Lake side. Johnny's pretty good at finding things. We was going to show it to the blond guy 'til he shouted at us and chased us off. So we didn't."

"Did you notice the vehicle the guy was driving?"

"Yeah. It was a red foreign sportscar."

"Did you see that vehicle when you were camped at the turnoff?"

"Yeah, come to think of it."

Noah's pulse quickened, but he didn't show it.

"When was that?" he asked.

"It was in the afternoon. I saw it drive out 'bout a couple of hours after lunch, just when we was setting up camp."

"Did you see it again late that night?"

Noah was already pretty sure that Vladimir was connected to Johanna's death.

"No, I saw *you* drive in and out. And later, a black Cadillac."

"That would have been the judge's car," Carter said.

"It left 'bout dinner time."

"Did you see a vehicle come after the judge left?" Carter asked.

"Yeah, I heard one come 'bout ten."

"Could you describe it?"

"I was feeding Jewel at the time."

"Did you see this other vehicle leave?"

"No, I was sleeping."

Noah turned to Johnny, who had said nothing to this point.

"Do you agree with Celia about what happened on Larson's property that night?"

"Yep." He nodded his head.

"Can you add anything or did you see anything?"

"Nope." He shook his head.

Noah and Carter looked at each other in resignation. They got up, preparing to go. There was no moon. The overcast sky blocked the starlight. Celia left the men to tend to Jewel and to put some more wood on the curing fire.

"It's late," Johnny told them. "You don't see nothing. You camp here tonight and have breakfast with us."

Tired from her all-night reading of *The Diviners*, Mary slept in on Wednesday. The experience of reading her mother's innermost thoughts on the margins of the book made her think of her mother at Larson Lake. She decided to drive out there with a packed lunch to be with her mother's spirit. She went to the office and told Sandra, the receptionist, that she was going for a drive and wouldn't be back until two-thirty. Carter had left with Noah Tuesday afternoon to hunt for the Eagles, Stan was in a coma at the hospital and Bates was in court. Sandra called out as she was leaving.

"There's a man on the phone for you. He won't give his full name. He says, 'Tell her it's Charlie.'"

"I'll phone him when I get back."

As she was leaving, Mary overheard Sandra on the phone.

"She'll phone you mid afternoon . . . no I don't know where she's going."

Lars was looking out the picture window of his office at Cam driving the forklift. Lars had brought him into the office to learn the business side of the company. There was no need for Cam to be doing a labouring job. Irritated, he opened the back door and yelled at his son.

"I want to talk to you."

Cam sauntered into the office.

"I thought your job was to look after our accounts," Lars shouted angrily.

"Yeah, the forklift operator called in sick. Somebody had to load that flatbed. We need the money."

"Sit down," Lars sighed. "I want to tell you about that. I

haven't been able to raise any money from the banks for the winter logging season."

"We're already overdrawn, and I figure we've got a month's operating credit left. I thought you were going to speak to Volk about a loan?"

"I asked Volk for a loan a few days ago. He's agreed to lend us six hundred thousand dollars at one percent below bank interest for five years. I'm going to the cabin this morning with the papers for him to sign."

Lars waved the papers in his hand.

"Why would he agree to those terms? You've always referred to him as a money-sucking son of a bitch."

"Let's just say I was able to persuade him."

"How?"

"I can link him to Johanna's drowning."

"Lars, you're dealing with fire."

Cam had never before spoken to his father using his first name, nor questioned his father's judgement. Lars was stunned.

"Look, you little bugger, I'm doing this for you. You'll be running this show soon."

"When you're dead or in jail, you mean."

"Don't talk to me like that!"

"Lars, I don't want any part of Vladimir Volk. It's wrong to use Johanna's death to get money for the company. If you have anything on Volk, go to the police. Now I have to load that lumber."

Cam slammed the door on his father.

Lars remained seated at his desk, questioning himself about his meeting with Vladimir at the lake. In his need for money and his hatred and jealousy of Vladimir, he had lost his judgment by failing to see that by telling Vladimir what he had seen, he may have implicated himself. *But Vladimir surely wouldn't call my bluff. If he did, it would be Vladimir's word against mine and I'm from the Cariboo-Chilcotin. On the other hand, I may have to correct my mistake.*

Celia was breast-feeding Jewel cradled in one arm and tending the fire with her free hand. Johnny was fishing with a dip net. Noah and Carter had nothing new to report to the inspector besides the confirmation of the hoof marks that the Eagles had been camped at Larson's turnoff on the night of the murder. The urgency now was to get back to Stan's bedside. They led their saddled horses to the fire.

"Have a coffee and bannock before you ride," Celia said.

She set Jewel down on a blanket spread out on the ground. The girl seemed satisfied. Celia handed pieces of bannock to Noah and Carter.

They stood eating as they watched Johnny dip his net into a pool of deep water and haul up a Chinook. Celia poured coffee. Johnny came over and set the salmon down in front of Jewel. She screamed with delight at the flopping fish. Johnny saw that the visitors were readying their horses to ride out. He set down his dip net and motioned to Carter.

"Ya got a minute?"

Carter walked over to him while Celia and Noah sipped coffee by the fire.

"Yeah? What is it?"

"You know I saw that truck leave the night we were camped there."

"You did! Why didn't you tell us that last night? Tell me who was it."

"You're my lawyer, right? If I tell you, then you can't tell anyone?"

"Yeah, that's right. Unless you allow me to."

"Okay, then. The truck was a yellow Larson's pick-up.

Will I get into trouble if I tell Noah?"

"What sort of trouble are you thinking about?"

"You know. Larson's a big man in the Chilcotin. He's my employer. He's not going to hire me if I tell Noah that he was at the lake on that night," Johnny shrugged. "You know I gotta feed my family."

Carter knew out of textbooks what a lawyer's conflict of interest was. Now he was face-to-face with it.

Mary's life is at risk. Larson, who may be her mother's murderer, was on the loose. There was no telling what Larson would do. Legal ethics required him to say that Johnny probably wouldn't be hired by Larson. Johnny, his client, could instruct him to remain silent. And if he stayed silent, Mary could be harmed. He thought, *There must be a way out of this jam.*

"Johnny, if you don't tell Noah, you will be putting Mary's life in danger. Larson is on the loose and there is no telling what he might do."

Johnny took his time answering. He looked at the rushing waters of the Chilco River, full of fish, and the gutted fish drying on the racks.

"Carter, is you sweet on Mary?" he finally asked.

"Yes. I guess I am."

"Well, the hell with my job. I'll tell Noah."

Noah, on hearing the news, emptied his coffee cup on the ground and mounted up. Carter was right behind him. Noah looked over his shoulder as they trotted out of the clearing.

"Thanks, Johnny," he shouted.

Shortly before noon, Mary made the turn off the highway onto Larson Road. Just a few months ago when making the same turn, she had a mother and one father and her life was unfolding in a linear course as she had planned. Then, everything had changed.

She walked up onto the porch and sat down, listening to the hush of solitude broken by the peaceful sounds of the sparrows in the bushes nearby. She was thinking of how much her mother had meant to her, from giving birth to her to nurturing her, to protecting her and preparing her for life. She wasn't going to let her mother down.

The sparrows were disturbed by something and flew off. Vladimir emerged from the bush. She felt as timid as the disturbed sparrows when she saw him approach. He walked slowly across the lawn, stopping ten feet from the porch.

"Thank you for coming."

Battling her fear, she sat up, strong and determined as she could look.

"Oh, Vlad, I didn't know you were here. Inspector Donaldson is looking for you. I expect him any minute."

"Please, Mary, just listen to me," Vlad pleaded. "I loved your mother. We were high-school sweethearts. I gave her the jade frog last year at our high school reunion. And I bought the ranch and was building a house to be near to her. You're the only one who knows this. I thought that my feelings for Johanna were mutual until Sunday, on the night she drowned. That evening at about eleven, I was sitting in front of a fire by my trailer near the house when Johanna stepped out of the darkness. We spoke about old times. She said that, had I told her that I loved her after graduation, we may have married, but now it was too late. She respects her husband, your father, and wouldn't leave him although their relationship was strained. She told me that her main interest in life was you. She was going to get her doctorate in English and her dissertation would be on Margaret Laurence. I told her, 'I am here for you should you ever need me.'"

"She rose to go and tried to return the necklace that I had given her at the reunion—the one you had admired and mentioned in your words of remembrance. I persuaded her to keep it. I was heartbroken and, if you knew me before I met your mother at the reunion, you would know that up to then I had little feelings of attachment to anyone. I escorted her to the fence line. It was a full moon and the path to the lake was clear. She insisted that I leave her there. I wish I hadn't. I wish I had seen her back to the cabin. She walked away with the necklace in her hand. I now know who was on that trail that night. That person is your mother's killer."

"You should be telling all this to the inspector."

"Inspector Donaldson believes that I am the murderer. He wants to pick me up for further questioning. You should be the first to know what I know."

"You said that you had an idea who mother's killer might be."

"Last Saturday, after seeing your mother's frog pendant at the mock trial, I was in shock. I've explained to you why it has affected me so deeply. When I returned last Sunday from Wells, I met Larson here at his request. He wanted to borrow a large sum of money from me. I wasn't interested and offered him terms that I thought would dissuade him. He then said he would accept a loan at one percent interest below bank interest, repayable in five years. I refused. He then tried to blackmail me."

"In what way?"

"He said that he had witnessed Johanna and myself arguing at my campfire on the night she drowned, and that she had returned the necklace. I have told you what happened—we didn't argue and she left with the necklace in her hand."

"You said that you believed you knew who the murderer was?"

"Larson has admitted to me that he was there on the night of Johanna's death and saw me and your mother together. I didn't kill your mother. He is the murderer."

"Again, Vlad, you must tell the inspector."

"It was important to me to tell you first. Will you drive me to the police station? Since the RCMP are on the lookout for me, it would be safer for me to give myself up in your presence; then you won't be accused of harbouring a fugitive."

"All right. I'll drive you to Williams Lake."

She wasn't sure this was the safest thing to do as Vlad's story had yet to be tested, but he had shown some kindness towards her and tenderness for her mother.

Mary walked off the porch and moved towards her car. Vlad opened the passenger door but before he got in, Mary noticed that he put his hand inside his jacket above his heart and then removed it.

"What have you got there?" she asked.

"A pistol." He took it out and showed it to her. "It's for my protection. If it frightens you, I'll give it to you."

"I don't want to touch it. Put it in the glove compartment."

How could I believe him? He had lied to the inspector about the jade frog and about seeing Johanna late Sunday. He was as likely a suspect as Lars Larson. And what about the clue Mother left about Chas? But she had made her choice. She started the car and slowly drove back up the road towards the highway. They passed the end of the pond and were climbing a rise in the road when a yellow Larson Forestry truck came over the rise and blocked the way. Mary braked to a stop. Lars opened his truck's door and stepped out onto the road holding a rifle.

Noah and Carter arrived at their truck before ten that morning. They unhitched the trailer and put the horses out to pasture. They drove to Chilcotin Lodge and Noah phoned the inspector about Johnny Eagle's information.

"I'm leaving the office now to pick up Larson for questioning," the inspector replied tersely.

Carter phoned his office to speak to Mary.

"Mary left the office a while ago," the receptionist told him. "On the way out, she refused a phone call from a man named Charlie."

Carter knew who Charlie was. Mary had told him after she had read *The Diviners*.

"Did Mary say where she was going?'

"No, but wherever it was, it would take about four and half hours there and back."

Carter got back into the truck and as they pulled out, he told Noah the story.

"I think she's going to Larson Lake."

It was an hour and a half drive to Larson Lake. They would get there before the police, but would they get there before Mary?

44

"Vlad," Lars yelled, "step out of the car with your hands above your head where I can see them."

Vlad reached into the glove compartment, grabbed his pistol and turned to Mary.

"This is dangerous. Be calm and stay in the car," he said.

Mary was exhausted. The combination of her lack of sleep, the emotional confession from Vlad of his love for her mother and now this armed confrontation had temporarily stunned her. *Should she side with Lars or Vlad in this showdown?* She didn't know. The wrong decision could cost her her life. That thought brought her to her senses.

"No," she told Vlad. "You stay here."

She opened the driver door and got out of the car.

"Mr. Larson," she screamed, "why are you threatening us with a gun?"

"I know what's happening, Mary," he shouted back. "You're being kidnapped by Volk, the man who murdered your mother."

"That's not true. I am taking Mr. Volk to the police."

"Mary, he has threatened you," Lars yelled. "If you leave with him, we will never see you alive. Quick, run to me. I have you covered."

Vlad opened the passenger door and used it as a shield as he stepped out of the car, gun in hand.

"Larson, you killed Johanna."

Lars didn't hesitate. He brought his rifle to his hip and fired three rounds.

Two bullets pierced the door, one struck Vlad in the shoulder, the other tore into his hip.

He fell to the ground face-down in the dry dirt. Mary rushed to him, sinking to her knees beside him, touching his head with her hand. He was alive.

"Look out for yourself," he muttered. "Remember I loved your mother."

He lapsed into unconsciousness.

Lars stood over them, rifle in hand.

"I guess I saved your life," he told Mary. "He was going to kidnap you."

She beat the ground with her fist and sobbed.

"You killed him as if he was an animal. I was taking him to the inspector."

"What was he going to tell the inspector?"

Mary's survival instinct kicked in.

"He didn't say. But I am sure Vladimir didn't kill my mother."

"You're not very grateful. I saved your life."

"My life wasn't in danger."

"That's not the way I saw it. Vladimir is a killer. He killed your mother. She tore out the pages of *The Diviners* with Chas' name on them. You're coming with me. I'm going to phone the police and tell them what happened here."

"No, you go. I'm staying with Vladimir."

Lars reached down to her keening body, wrapped an arm around her and dragged her to his truck with one arm, his rifle in the other. She resisted.

"What are you doing?"

"Making sure you don't get away. You were helping a murderer to escape."

He shoved her onto the bench seat on the driver's side and got into the driver's seat beside her. Holding her by the wrist, he drove to his cabin. The digital clock on the dash read twelve noon.

At the cabin, he didn't get out of the truck. Mary stopped protesting. She went limp. He would have to drag her from the truck. He shut off the engine and stared at the lake—his lake, the lake he had made out of a pond.

Mary now knew who had caused the death of her mother. Lars gave himself away when he said that the page with Chas' name on it had been torn from *The Diviners*. No one knew that except the inspector and Mary. Mary sensed Lars' hesitation. It seemed to her that he was starting to think about what he had done and what he might do. She decided to speak quietly, conversationally, so as not to threaten or alarm him.

"Whatever happened here last July with Mum must have been an accident."

Mary's calm questioning voice, sounding like his conscience, seemed to sober him. He remained seated behind the wheel, rocking back and forth, making animal sounds and breathing hard. Then in a querulous voice, it all came out in a rush.

"All I wanted was a little kiss. She knew how I felt about her, and when I saw her with Vladimir at his place and she called him 'Charlie', I knew she had given him a kiss. When I met her on the trail and asked her for a kiss, she ran from me down to the lake. Why did she run? We were friends. I ran after her. She got into the rowboat and pushed off. I ran into the lake to stop her. I lost my footing and grabbed the boat and the boat tipped over. The clouds had covered the moon. It was dark, I couldn't see. I had been drinking. In my condition, it was all I could do to save myself. It was an accident."

Noah and Carter arrived at Larson's turnoff at twelve-twenty. A few minutes on the gravel road, they came to Mary's car with both driver and passenger doors open. Driving around her vehicle, they came upon Vladimir's body lying face-down in the dirt where Larson had left him. They stopped to check his vital signs. He was alive.

"You take the truck and drive to the cabin," he ordered Carter. "Mary must be there with Larson. I'll stay here and tend to Volk."

Carter didn't hesitate. He was desperate to get to the cabin to find Mary.

All the time Mary had known him, Lars had never talked much. Mary didn't want to rush him now, but she thought he had said all he was going to say.

"Yes," she said, "I knew it had to have been an accident. I'm sure that when you tell the inspector, he will think so too. Will you let me go inside and phone the inspector and then check on Vladimir?"

Lars wasn't finished talking. He held on to her wrist.

"I went crazy when I saw Vladimir with you. It was as if it had happened all over again just like when I saw him with her."

"I understand, Lars. You will have to let go of my wrist so I can go inside."

He relaxed his grip. It wasn't a willful act. It was as if he was reliving that night and had forgotten the present. He slumped behind the wheel. She opened the passenger door and with her feet on the ground, she stopped.

"How did the book fall into the lake?"

"When I came back the next morning, the book was lying on the dock. I tore out the page in the book where Chas assaults Morag and threw the book into the lake. I thought it would be a way of framing Vladimir."

As Mary mounted the steps to the cabin, Carter drove up behind Lars' truck. Ignoring Larson slumped behind the wheel, Carter ran to Mary standing on the porch. She couldn't move. He put his arms around her.

"Are you all right?" he asked gently.

Donaldson and Melnick arrived in a police cruiser, siren off. They had gone to Larson's mill and were told by his son that he was meeting Vlad at the cabin on Larson Lake. They came upon Noah tending Vlad's wounds. Noah had stopped the bleeding and had made Vlad comfortable. Melnick saw the wounded man and remained in the cruiser to radio for the ambulance stationed at Tatla Lake. The inspector got out of the car and approached Noah.

"What happened here?"

"Carter and I arrived five minutes ago. I believe that Volk was shot by Larson and that Larson has taken Mary to the cabin."

"Why do you think Mary is here?"

"This is her car. Carter has gone on to look after Mary."

The policemen drove cautiously towards Larson's cabin. Before the cabin came into view, they parked the cruiser and went on foot. Donaldson saw two vehicles parked by the cabin, Larson's yellow truck, Lars behind the wheel, and behind that, Noah's truck. There was no sign of Mary and Carter.

Donaldson motioned Melnick forward and, guns drawn, they both ran towards Larson's truck. Larson didn't move when they opened the driver and passenger side doors. Donaldson could see he was looking at a defeated man.

"All right, Lars, get out," he urged. "You're under arrest for the attempted murder of Vladimir Volk."

Larson turned to look at the inspector as if he'd woken up from a sleep.

"You mean that bastard isn't dead?"

The ambulance arrived from Tatla Lake. After Vlad was loaded on board, they drove to the Williams Lake hospital. Thanks to Noah, who had stopped the bleeding, there was a chance he would live.

Donaldson and Melnick took Larson to the detachment offices to be charged.

Back in Williams Lake, the Hanlons and Carter and Mary stopped in at the hospital to see Stan. Justine, Bates, the judge and Belle were there in Stan's room. Belle met them at the door.

"Stan died a few minutes ago," she announced, sadly. "We are mourning his loss and talking about his great spirit."

In the late afternoon, after Mary had given her statement to the inspector, she, Carter, Justine and Noah met Donaldson for a debriefing at his offices.

"I want to tell you that we are charging Larson with murder in Johanna's death. You have all played a part in solving this crime. Thank you for your help."

No one said anything. The inspector took this as a cue to continue.

"You also all took unacceptable risks in this investigation, which could have cost you and your loved ones their lives."

"Thank you for your help, Inspector," Noah spoke for them all.

The four of them walked out of the detachment offices together. They weren't about to accept the inspector's praise or censure for playing their part in solving the crime. Between them, there was a shared sense of satisfaction in knowing how Johanna died, so that they could be with her in their thoughts to the end. They said their goodbyes at the corner of 3rd and Oliver St.

The older couple, side-by-side, watched the lovely couple walk hand-in-hand down Oliver Street towards the law office of Hewitt and Bates and their future. Noah put his arm around Justine's shoulder; she placed her arm around Noah's waist, turned to him and caught his eye.

"Wawant'x," she smiled. "Now is the time for you to begin painting our Chilcotin creation story."

Supreme Court ruling on Chilcotin land title

In the 1990s, the Chilcotin nation sued the province of British Columbia for the recognition of their right to ownership of their lands. After a three-year trial in the Supreme Court of BC, Mr. Justice David Vickers found that the Chilcotin people's continual use of the land from time immemorial and their cultural ties to the land, including their creation story, entitled them to ownership. The province appealed this finding and won in the BC Court of Appeal. The Chilcotin nation then appealed this decision and took it to the Supreme Court of Canada.

In June 2014, the Supreme Court of Canada's decision in *Roger William v. Her Majesty the Queen* established the right of aboriginal title to their lands, which included Potato Mountain and the Brittany Triangle.

"In what legal observers called *the most important Supreme Court ruling on aboriginal rights in Canadian history*—a culmination of all previous rulings—the court determined that native Canadians still own their ancestral lands, unless they signed away their ownership in treaties with the Government."

—*The Globe and Mail*
June 26, 2014

Bruce Fraser's first novel in the Chilcotin Trilogy
On Potato Mountain
won a silver medal in the 2011 eLit Awards and a
movie is in pre-production by Really Real films.

In the untamed Chilcotin, rancher Bordy Hanlon is gunned down in his living room. His adopted son, Noah, is charged with his murder. Stan Hewitt, an alcoholic lawyer from Williams Lake, defends the young man before a white jury and later before a Native circle of elders. *On Potato Mountain* is not only a tale of love and mystery, but is also a story of a remarkable land and its people.

"If the reader wishes to begin to understand the deep magic of the Chilcotin, then this book is a gift. It reveals shadows of great historical natives like Klatsassine and Chiwid, people and events, alive once again and protected by spiritual mountains—Potato and Ts'ylos. Dramatic elements like true love, young and old, a mysterious murder, shamans and a lawyer move through the entire story—as a light for clarity and truth."

—Lorne Dufour, author of Jacob's Prayer
shortlisted for the Roderick Haig-Brown Regional Book Prize

"While fiction, this book is very relevant today, as it gives us an understanding of how deeply attached the Chilcotin people are to their land. I hope they enjoy this book as much as I did."

—Senator Nancy Greene Raine
Director of Skiing, Sun Peaks Resort

On Potato Mountain
A Chilcotin Mystery
ISBN: 978-1-894694-82-7 (pbk)
CDN/US $19.95
ISBN: 978-1-8946948-7-2 (epub)
CDN/US $7.99